Children of the Lost Gods

Oscar K. Reyes

ISBN: 978-1-7358272-0-9

Dedicated to my mother, Alma Hernandez.

CONTENTS

THE WINGS OF ICARUS

In the distance, the Sun rose from the ocean's depths. It was a rosy-fingered dawn that crept over the waters. A young boy watched the beautiful sight in the eastern sky with his arms folded beneath his chin as he leaned on the windowsill of his chamber. The window faced south toward the Ionian Sea and was the only opening in the dreary circular room. The stone chamber sat atop the tallest level of the Tower of Wind.

A flock of seagulls flew across the sky, which the boy viewed as a good omen. At only twelve years old, Icarus was tall for his age but had a lean frame and a boyishly handsome face. His brown hair matched his honey colored eyes, which complemented his thin lips, sharp nose, and dimpled cheeks. On trial days, he always wore his lucky leather sandals and blue tunic, and today he would need all the good fortune the gods could spare. He turned and walked toward a man sleeping on the opposite side of the room.

A black beaked, gray and white feathered parrot squawked in its birdcage at the center of the chamber. This was Benu, an African gray parrot that Icarus' father received as a gift from a grateful king long ago. Icarus leaned down and tapped the birdcage.

"If our creation works, we will fly just like you, Benu," Icarus proclaimed.

"You will die," Benu stated mockingly. The parrot swayed from side to side with a titter. Benu was an intelligent bird that could mimic any word he heard with annoying repetition.

"Do you always have to speak?" retorted Icarus, displeased. The bird whistled enthusiastically.

The cold, dark chamber contained a few scant personal items from a previous life. Pottery that Icarus' mother made when he was younger, two serving bowls with wooden ladles, and a toy figurine the boy had outgrown. Colorful drawings lined the walls, created from the imagination of a child with too much time on his hands. There were no bars on the window, but what greeted the inhabitants of the chamber beyond the walls was a steep drop that ended in the rocky shores below.

Icarus kneeled at his father's bedside and shook the sleeping man's shoulder. "Father, it's morning. Today's the day we finally escape this prison," said Icarus excitedly.

Daedalus groggily turned his head to face his son. Still half-asleep, his eyes adjusted to the boy's face. "Is today the day? I'd forgotten. You've only mentioned it every morning for many moons," grumbled Daedalus with his eyes half shut.

Daedalus looked older than he was, but years of forced imprisonment and hard labor seemed to have aged him. He was lanky and balding, with a long black and a gray beard that hung down several inches from his face. Using his thin arms to push himself off the bed, he sat up and knuckled his eyelids. "We have to wait for the right moment, Icarus," said Daedalus.

"We've waited long enough. It's time," responded Icarus. The boy had good reason to doubt his father's willingness to escape. They had come close to fleeing several times only to have Daedalus delay at the last moment. If the craftsman noticed a strange occurrence or felt a bad omen, that was enough to postpone. Hours turned to days, and days turned into seasons, but the boy continued to wait.

Daedalus had good reason to fear their escape; he did not have the opportunity to test their invention. There would be no trial runs, only one chance to flee or perish. The flying machines required a strong wind to carry them off the tall tower to the fields below. As much as the inventor prepared, there were still too many risks that put his son's life in peril.

The craftsman stood tall and stretched his thin body to the ceiling. He wore the same stained tunic from his workshop since it was the only garb he possessed. Daedalus was known as the world's greatest craftsman. He could delight children with a music box or topple an empire with an innovative weapon. That was why King Minos locked him and his son in the tower years ago and forced the brilliant inventor to build weaponry for his

3

army.

Daedalus placed a hand on Icarus' head and tousled the boy's hair. "It depends on the winds," Daedalus said as he stepped toward Benu's cage. He kneeled down and picked up a feather lying on the ground. Benu ate seeds from his feeder absentmindedly. Daedalus held the feather to Icarus. "You do the honors," he said.

The boy took the feather in his hand and held it close to his chest. "The gods and strong winds are with us today," he whispered to the feather. He walked to the window and released the quill into the wind. It fell and disappeared from view. Disappointed, the boy's shoulders slumped as he turned to his father. "I prayed for good winds, but the gods must have better things to do."

Daedalus looked out the window and saw the feather float up in an updraft. "Look," urged Daedalus excitedly. Icarus turned and saw the feather float up as if held by a playful spirit. This was something that had not happened for quite some time. *Finally, strong winds*, thought Icarus eagerly.

"Will die," repeated Benu.

"Quiet you," responded Daedalus coldly.

Outside the door, footsteps were heard sprinting up the stairs. Benu squawked in alarm. Daedalus looked to his son and pressed a finger to his lips. "Tonight," he whispered. He bent down to lace his sandals, as the latch outside of the chamber was removed. The door swung open, and two soldiers stood on the other side with their hands on the hilts of their swords. Their ragged uniforms

4

consisted of sandals, grieves, a breastplate, and a leather skirt. The armed men stepped inside and examined the small chamber.

"It's time for the morning inspection," said the gruff soldier. Of the two men, Daedalus only feared the gray-haired soldier with the old scar across his milky white eye. Even the other guards detested their insufferable commander. His name was Magus, and he was tasked with protecting the estate and guarding the captives by order of the King. He considered the responsibility bestowed onto him to be a great honor.

The younger soldier searched the room for any suspicious contraband. Meanwhile, Magus scowled at them all from the entrance. After a few tense moments, the soldier relented. "Nothing here, sir," said the young man.

Magus eyed Daedalus suspiciously with his blind eye. "I know you're up to something, craftsman. When I find out what it is, Zeus won't be able to protect you from my wrath," he growled.

Daedalus regarded the commander and considered his words. "I only wish to serve our King."

The commander stepped toward Daedalus but then turned to look down at his son. "And what of you, boy?"

Icarus met Magus' gaze with contempt. "I hold no secrets, but if I do, may the gods strike you down for it," stated the boy.

"What did you say?" bellowed Magus.

Daedalus stepped in front of his son to prevent any retribution from the commander. "He meant to say,

5

strike 'me' down," pleaded Daedalus nervously.

The commander eyed Daedalus with his healthy eye. Icarus stuck his tongue out at the commander behind his father's back, knowing full well that Magus could not see his face. The young soldier noticed the disrespectful act and snorted. The commander turned to face his subordinate, but the young soldier quickly placed a hand over his mouth and cleared his throat.

Magus glowered as he turned back to face Daedalus. "Time for you two to get back to your work."

The soldiers led the prisoners down the spiral staircase to the lower levels. Icarus carried Benu in his birdcage, and the bird swayed with every step the boy took. When they reached the ground floor, the young soldier opened the wooden doors that led to the underground chamber. "Go on," said the young soldier, as he stood brashly. They made their way down the last few steps, and then the soldiers shut the doors, leaving the prisoners in darkness.

Two flint rocks were struck together, and sparks flew in every direction until the torch was ignited. The orange light illuminated Icarus' face, who held the torch's wooden handle. Daedalus tossed the stones on the ground, while Icarus proceeded to light several candles throughout the square room. The large cellar held all of the craftsman's plans and inventions. Hundreds of papyrus scrolls filled the wooden racks that lined the walls of the workshop. Broken, unfinished, and completed inventions of all shapes and sizes were scattered throughout. The myriad of contraptions included the carpenter level, a wedge, a wimble, and even a miniature design for a watermill.

Daedalus removed a scroll from a hidden compartment beneath his workbench. He unfurled it on the table, and the parchment revealed a crude design for a backpack with mechanical wings attached to its flanks. The plans contained diagrams, written instructions, and sketches for a flying machine.

The invention of a device capable of giving man the ability to fly would be impressive for most inventors, but Daedalus was the most celebrated craftsman in all of Greece. He helped several Greek city-states become prominent nations on the world's stage by continuously advancing human knowledge. That was what eventually made him a target to powerful Kings.

The brilliant inventor was held in such high regard that the tower was chosen specifically to prevent him from escaping. Soldiers trained in the courtyard, while armed guards patrolled the twenty-foot-high rock wall surrounding the tower. Although they weren't called prisoners by name, the guards treated them as such. Imprisonment was terrible, but it was a form of living in Daedalus' mind. For Icarus, however, this was no life at all.

In the beginning, Icarus enjoyed assisting his father in the workshop, but eventually, the boy grew weary of the tedious routine. Nothing they ever created was good enough for the King or his army. As the boy got older, he realized that they could never leave. He could never play with the children that lived beyond the surrounding walls, nor see the world like the heroes in his father's tales. Icarus knew that this was no way to live and that they had to escape, no matter the cost.

Icarus only had a vague memory of how the inspiration for the flying machine came to him. The boy sat outside in the middle of the courtyard during his brief daily recess. With Benu on his shoulder, Icarus tried to think of a means of escape. He kept hitting his head as if trying to rattle an idea out of his mind, an act that he learned from his father. That's when the top of his hair was struck by a gooey substance. He touched it with his hand and inspected the strange green and white matter. On closer inspection, it appeared to be bird droppings. His disgusted face gave way to amazement as he looked up at the sky and observed a colony of gulls flying overhead. The seedling of the idea had been planted and began to sprout.

The boy closed his eyes and slowly willed a vision out of his mind. He looked at the birds flapping and then moved his arms up and down. Benu scratched his head in confusion. "I've got it!" said Icarus as he pointed his dirty finger toward the heavens.

He ran up to his father and whispered his idea under his breath. At first, Daedalus laughed at the notion of human flight. "Let's leave the flying to birds and the gods, son," he said. Icarus felt defeated and tried to think of another means of escape.

After many nights, Daedalus eventually considered the possibility of a flying machine. The craftsman worked on the design for the device and dedicated every waking moment to its development. He sketched the wings to resemble that of a bird but quickly abandoned the idea of using feathers in favor of a light fabric.

Icarus and Daedalus would take turns stealing material they needed from around the tower and sneaking it up to their chamber. Whenever a soldier's back was turned, they'd grab a piece of metal, wood, or cloth needed to build the flying machine. They spent a year secretly constructing the contraptions piece by piece until they were finally completed.

Below the tower, Daedalus brought out a flight helmet made from cowhide and stuffed bird feathers. Two yellow lightning bolts were stitched to the flanks of the headgear as a tribute to Zeus, the King of the gods. The craftsman tied the strap under Icarus' chin to secure it. "I invented this as a substitute to the heavy bronze helmet the soldiers wear in battle, but it proved to be ineffective against a sword," he said with a cringe. "I didn't think I would ever find another use for it, but this should protect our skulls from harsh impacts. At least, I pray it will."

Daedalus looked at Icarus as he stroked his white beard. "Something's missing," he said. "I've got it." He grabbed an extra pair of his workman spectacles from a table and fixed them around Icarus' head. The craftsman used the specs to protect his eyes when he forged heated metal with his smiting hammer. Handcrafted wood made up the rims, flat reading stones covered the eyeholes, and a horsetail rope secured them around the boy's head. "This should prevent the wind from bothering your eyes," said Daedalus as he placed the specs around the boy's eyes.

With magnified eyes from the thick glass, Icarus looked like a night owl when he blinked. "They make my head hurt," said the boy.

Daedalus placed the goggles on his son's forehead. "Only wear them when you're in flight," he said.

The boy turned to a polished bronze shield leaned against the wall. He picked it up and viewed his reflection closely.

Benu squawked and said, "Birds fly, boy will die."

"What do you know," Icarus retorted, and then rattled the parrot's cage. Benu fluttered his wings, molting a few feathers in the process.

The door at the top of the stairs opened, startling them. Heavy footsteps were heard coming down the stairs swiftly. Daedalus and Icarus rushed to hide the helmets and spectacles within their tunics. Magus and the young soldier found the craftsman and his son at their workbench.

"Night has fallen, you two are done for the day," said Magus.

"It felt like we just started," responded Daedalus with feigned surprise.

"You can keep working if you prefer, Craftsman," said the irritable Magus.

"No, that's enough for today," said Daedalus with a yawn.

They made their way past the two soldiers and up the stairs. Icarus acted solemn as he always did on the surface, but he could barely contain his excitement.

*
**

At the walls beyond the tower, the gates were opened,

and two soldiers on horseback rode into the courtyard. Unlike the sentries on the walls, the riders wore uniforms made of the finest material. Bronze helmets complete with horsehair crest concealed their faces. Long swords with gold-plated handles were holstered to their belts. They reached the tower and dismounted their steeds near the entrance. After yoking the horses to the wooden post, they made their way to the door.

Inside the tower, Daedalus, Icarus, and their two captors reached the ground floor. There was a loud knock on the door that startled them. Magus signaled to his subordinate to check the entrance. The young soldier removed his sword and opened the door slowly.

"What is the meaning of this?" Magus asked. One of the stone-faced soldiers extended his arm and presented a scroll with the King's seal. The commander took the papyrus in hand and eyed the men suspiciously. He broke the waxed stamp and unfurled the message. Impatiently, his good and bad eyes darted back and forth as he read the declaration.

When Magus finished reading, he was stunned. He looked at the Royal Guards with newfound respect, while they stood there like scowling statues.

"What does it say?" asked Daedalus timidly. "Are we free?"

Magus laughed and said, "As free as your caged bird." He shoved the parchment into the craftsman's hands. Daedalus unfurled the scroll and read it:

By Royal Decree from the Great King Minos
Daedalus and his son are summoned by your ruler.

They must return with the Royal Guards at once or face a fate worse than death. The soldiers stationed to defend him are also summoned to assist in a mission of the utmost importance, or they will be deemed an enemy of the city-state and punished accordingly. The craftsman's unique talents are needed for the insurmountable task ahead. Our mission is to save the world.
- King Minos

Daedalus' face was awestruck. "I need to gather some supplies for the journey," he said. He pretended to be feeble and fearful to the Royal Guards. The armed men exchanged silent glances and then nodded. "Come on, son," said Daedalus.

Magus grabbed the craftsman's arm and squeezed. "Be quick about it," he growled. Daedalus looked down at the floor and nodded. Icarus' shoved Magus off of his father. The commander stumbled backward until he hit the stone wall. Stunned by the insolence, he quickly unsheathed his long sword. The Royal Guards bared their blades at the commander. Daedalus and Icarus put their palms up and retreated several paces.

The silent Royal Guards had been given strict orders to take the craftsman by force if necessary. They held their swords against Magus' throat, who yielded and slowly sheathed his sword. The Royal Guards holstered their weapons. As the dust settled, Daedalus and Icarus walked toward the spiral staircase.

"Keep an eye on this one," said Icarus as they made their way up. Magus' face reddened with fury.

Father and son rushed up the stairs and sealed the door. They pushed Daedalus' cot to one side. They dug their fingers into a crevice, and then lifted a thin slab of rock from the floor. Two packs were stacked within the hidden compartment. They pulled the backpacks out and set them on the small round table in the center of the room.

Daedalus helped Icarus put on his pack first. Straps were harnessed around the child's shoulders and torso. The backpack had a cord dangling from its side, which the craftsman promptly pulled. Spring-loaded wings were released that extended from the flanks of the pack. The boy wavered until he regained his balance in the middle of the room. Daedalus inspected the flying machine.

"Do you have to do this now?" asked Icarus as he strapped the helm to his head. The boy had to adjust his helmet several times as it kept sliding forward and covering his eyes.

"The risk is too great to toss caution to the wind," countered Daedalus. Icarus rolled his eyes but understood. Two long retractable metal rods made up the top of each wing's arm and were covered with sewed cloth. The boy looked smaller at the center, but the wings were only slightly longer than his outstretched arms.

Daedalus sighed and said, "May the gods of Olympus protect us as we try to reach them in the skies."

"I'm ready," said Icarus fearlessly. The boy retracted his wings and then set the goggles on his forehead.

"If we gather enough wind-speed, we should be able to fly a great distance before they even realize we're gone," said Daedalus, as he put on his pack.

*
**

It didn't take long for the Royal Guards to grow
impatient. They made their way up the spiral stairs with
the Magus and the young soldier in tow. They reached
the door to the top of the staircase but could not push it
open. Realizing that something was amiss, the Royal
Guards began to slam the door with their shoulders.

"Step aside," ordered Magus with sword in hand.
The guards stepped back, and the commander started to
hack at the wood. Magus created an opening and reached
through the broken door to remove the furniture stacked
on the other side. They kicked the door open and
desperately searched for the captives, but the chamber
was empty.

"Wait," said Magus, entering the room. "Heed."
The guards halted and listened. Their eyes drifted
toward the ceiling when they heard footfalls coming
from above. The young soldier stuck his head out the
window and saw Daedalus' foot swing over the edge and
climb onto the roof.

"They're above us," said the young soldier.
Icarus held onto the pole at the center of the roof.
Benu landed on the weathervane in the shape of a triton
next to the boy. Fearing that the wind would blow him
off the tower, Daedalus crawled toward his son slowly. A
long sword broke through the wooden surface near the
craftsman's hand. The next one missed his torso slightly,
forcing him to roll out of the way. The next sword thrust
cut through Daedalus' pack but missed his body. He
found his footing and scrambled up the conical roof.

"Are you hurt?" asked Icarus as his father reached him.

Daedalus struggled to catch his breath but eventually shook his head. "Are you prepared?" asked Daedalus.

Icarus nodded timidly until the helmet slid over his eyes, forcing him to push the helm back onto his head. He released his wings, and the air became a solid thing that elevated the boy off his feet. He gripped the weathervane and settled himself back on the rooftop.

The royal guards climbed out the window and up the side of the tower. Magus' hand gripped the edge of the roof as he pulled himself onto the rooftop. "Craftsman! There's nowhere to go!" he bellowed.

"Hurry, father," urged Icarus. Daedalus pulled the cord on his pack and released his wings, but only felt the slightest push from the strong winds. The fabric was torn from sword thrust, and the breeze blew through the craftsman's wings. Daedalus' eyes widened as he came to the realization that he was trapped. "No," whimpered Icarus.

The soldiers surrounded them and advanced up the coned roof from four corners. They were nearly upon them.

Daedalus sighed, accepting his fate, but not the one for his son. "You have to go, Icarus," said Daedalus.

"Not without you," pleaded the boy, tears welling up in his eyes.

"The gods will protect you."

A powerful gust of wind inflated the wings like the sails on a ship. Icarus lost his grip on the pole and was lifted off the tower. He looked like a bird caught in an updraft as he was blown up into the night's sky.

The soldiers watched in disbelief as the boy flew on the breath of the wind. Magus' mouth dropped as he looked on in disbelief. "What sorcery is this?"

Benu soared off the roof in pursuit of the boy. He squawked until they disappeared in the dark clouds above.

"Help me, father!" were the last words that Daedalus heard his son say before he vanished in the darkness.

2

CY THE LITTLE CYCLOPS

Lightning cracked the dark sky, revealing an island in the middle of the ocean. The strong winds pushed the rolling waves further onto the sandy shores, while rain soaked the forest made of pine, cypress, and olive trees. Thunder could be heard in the distance, an indication of Zeus' anger. The spectacle served as a demonstration of the God of Thunder's immense power.

Beyond the entrance of a cave, the night's darkness was kept at bay by an orange and yellow glow. A small campfire at the center of the large cavern radiated light over dozens of crude cave drawings. The images depicted animals, humans, and mythical creatures living below the gods. The sway of the flames brought the paintings to life as a giant creature bellowed, "You dare trespass on my island?"

Brontes was a gigantic cyclops that could reach the top of a mountain with only a few strides. He wore a long waistcloth fashioned out of an old ship's sail. His legs were as thick as two tree trunks, while his arms were long enough to wrap around a full-grown whale. The drawings portrayed him to be an athletic and muscular cyclops, but that was no longer an accurate depiction of his physique if it ever was one. He had put on a lot of mass over the seasons, but he vowed to shed the fat every day. His single eye was as big as a steer's head, and it was fixated on the small child that sat on the floor before him. "Who goes there?" asked the giant as he leaned down toward the boy.

The child had olive-colored skin and sun drenched brown hair atop his scalp. The little one wore a waistcloth fashioned out of a pirate ship's sail. The boy's legs were as stubby as his arms, and he still had a lot of his baby fat. As the menacing behemoth approached, the child covered his mouth with his hands to stifle a giggle.

The giant Brontes was taken aback by the child's interruption. "Why do you laugh, Cy?"

"I'm sorry, Papa, but I can't imagine being afraid of you," said Cy with a sheepish smile. His eye was as big as a chicken egg, but whenever he listened to his father's tales, it grew to be twice as large, revealing its amber color.

"I'm certain the humans were afraid of you on that day," added the child. Cy was ten years old and no taller than the average human boy his age, which made him short for a cyclops. Fortunately for the little one, cyclopes did not stop growing when they reached adulthood. They grew until they became old and wrinkly, which was why his father was so colossal.

Brontes stood up and placed his hands on his broad hips. Cy looked up to his father, both figuratively and literally. The elder cyclops contemplated for a moment, and then said, "Very well." He cleared his throat and continued. "There were more human soldiers than there currently are bats in this cave, son." Cy hung on his father's words with a sense of awe and wonder.

Cy heard this tale countless times before but never grew tired of it. From the plethora of stories at his father's disposal, this one was his favorite. It always started the same way; Cy was a baby being coddled in this very cave after eating a feast. Cyclops' infants were known for their mighty appetite. Unlike the man-made tales, however, cyclopes did not eat humans. Their diet was mostly plant-based with the occasional seafood or cooked animal. Brontes preferred to let humans think that he would eat them and pick his teeth with their bones; it made it easier to frighten them off his island.

On that fateful day, from the edge of the cave, Brontes saw several ships make landfall. Humans began to disembark in short-order. The baby cyclops had just fallen asleep in his father's arms, so Brontes put Cy down on the makeshift crib made of rocks and sand. He grabbed his club and prepared to run down to the beach but halted when Cy awoke and began to wail. He picked up his son and put him back to sleep but, as soon as he put him down, the infant would wake up and start crying again. Brontes struggled to make most decisions, so he did the only thing that he could think of. "I ran down to the beach with my trusty club in one hand and you in the other," he said gruffly.

As part of the reenactment, he held a club in one hand and a baby-sized boulder wrapped in a cloth in the other. The rock had a baby cyclops' face drawn on it. Cy gasped every time he got to this part of the tale. Brontes ran around the cave, which added urgency to the story. "It was just the two of us against an army," he said with dread.

"What did you do, Papa?" asked Cy nervously.

Brontes relaxed, "I did the only thing I could do. I charged at them waving my club in the air like a mad cyclops." He pointed the club to the drawing on the wall depicting the events of the glorious day. It portrayed humans running from a giant cyclops with a baby in its arm.

"When I roared at the invaders, you shrieked along with me," he said. The giant let out a hearty laugh, while Cy began to giggle. Brontes always grabbed his big belly when he got to this part of the story. "The humans saw us coming and wanted no part," he said, as he wiped a joyful tear from his eye.

"Where did they go, Papa?" Cy asked.

"Back to the human world across the shivering sea. Some of them were so terrified that they swam back." Brontes let out another roar of laughter that echoed deep into the cave. Several bats flew out from the darkness and into the moonlit night.

"I can't wait until I'm big enough to protect the island," said Cy with a gentle demeanor.

The child couldn't hurt a fly, thought Brontes. This worried him more than any human threat. He couldn't protect his son forever. Cy needed to understand the cruelty of man, but the elder cyclops struggled to find the right approach to train his innocent boy.

In the Age of the Gods, when the world was young, and the immortals walked the land, cyclopes lived in peace and harmony. The giants worshipped and prayed to the beings that called themselves the Olympians. The gods, in turn, taught them their language and how to be civilized. The powerful deities vanished one day and never returned. Then the cyclopes began to encounter an increasing number of small, two-eyed creatures known as humans. The men spoke the tongue of the gods, but their words were always false. Humans frequently broke the pacts they made with the cyclops clan, which inevitably led to war.

A lone human could not hope to defeat even a small cyclops in single combat, but those cunning creatures had the greater numbers. Their true power came from the weaponry they created and wielded. Everything they crafted was built with wicked intent. They could raise armies and arm every soldier with a deadly weapon to attack a clan of cyclopes, which Brontes had firsthand experience with.

"Let me hear your battle cry," said Brontes.

Cy stood up and then roared, but it sounded more like a kitten's whimper. Brontes slapped his knee and chuckled. "I'm sure you can do better. You aren't going to scare a mouse with that whine." Cy let out an even louder growl that left him red in the face, but it still wasn't enough. "That's better, but try my technique."

Brontes put his hands on his knees and took a deep breath before he let out an ear-splitting roar. Cy rolled back several paces, while the campfire was almost extinguished. When he finished roaring, there was silence across the island. The rain even stopped as the clouds parted, revealing the moons silvery light. Suddenly, the flaps of hundreds of wings could be heard coming from deep within the cave. Bats flew out from the cavern and into the night's sky.

The cave fell silent once again. "Wow! That was great!" yelled Cy as he dug a finger into his ear. "I wish I could do that!"

"You will, son. It takes training."

"I need to get bigger, like you."

"Size has nothing to do with it. It's what's in here that matters," said Brontes, as he pointed to Cy's heart. His face tightened as he added somberly, "We may be the last of our kind." He looked at the drawing of his cyclops clan long gone.

"Don't worry, I'll protect you when the time comes," said Cy.

Brontes smiled, revealing his crooked and stained teeth. "Give me your word that you'll stay away from humans until you're big enough to scare them off."

"I give you my word."

"Now, get some sleep. We have a long day tomorrow. I'm going to check on the sheep one last time."

Brontes blew out the fire with one quick breath. Only a few embers remained. Cy lied down, closed his eye, and fell fast asleep on his mound of dirt. The elder cyclops looked at his peaceful son before he stepped out and made his way down the path to the beaches below.

Cy snored noisily until the early morning sunlight shined into the cave and found his face. He stirred and blinked as he sat up. Rubbing the drowsiness from his eye, his vision adjusted to the light. Brontes was nowhere to be found, which meant that he must have already started his day. The boy dusted himself off and exited the cave.

The young cyclops made his way down to a meadow further inland. He found his father keeping a watchful eye over their flock of grazing sheep. The makeshift fence circled the large clearing and was made of broken pieces of tree wood. Holding a club in hand, Brontes guarded his cherished sheep as they bleated and baud.

"Good morning, Papa," greeted Cy.

Brontes didn't break his focus from the flock as he responded, "Good morning, son." The giant's stomach let out a mighty grumble. The sheep halted their grazing to search for a potential predator. Embarrassed, Brontes looked down at his son and grinned sheepishly. "I haven't broken my fast today."

"I can find us some food," said Cy enthusiastically.

Brontes' stomach gurgled as if voicing its approval. "The figs should be ripe for the picking," he responded, although it could have been his belly that spoke. Cy nodded and made his way into the forest.

The young cyclops rummaged through the island when he spotted the fig trees clustered together. The figs hung rich on the limbs. The cyclops grabbed a fallen branch and tried to strike the fruit down. Cyclopes have trouble judging distances, so Cy swung and missed several times until he realized that he was too small to reach. What he would give to be taller.

He finally decided to climb the tree. Slowly but surely, he got past the midpoint and continued upward. Hugging the tree trunk with one arm, he stretched his opposing arm and grasped a fig. That's when he witnessed something he would never have believed had he not seen it with his own eye. He saw a giant bird flying erratically while making a screaming sound. Whatever the creature was, it crash-landed a short distance away.

Cy lost his hold on the tree trunk and clutched the ripe fig. He shut his eye tightly as he swung back and forth, his feet dangling quite a distance off the ground. Cautiously opening his eye, a feeling of relief poured over him, until the stalk snapped. He plummeted to the ground with the single fruit.

He hit the dirt with a thud and groaned after landing firmly on his backside. The fig he grabbed was crushed in his hands. Several figs fell from the branch and hit the top of his head. He wiped the muck off his face. Rubbing his scalp, he ran in the direction of the flying creature.

Cy reached a pond near the center of the island. He hid behind a bush as the bird-like creature swam out of the water and staggered onto the shore. That's when the cyclops first laid his eye on the soaked two-eyed winged human. At first, Cy didn't believe what he was witnessing, which prompted him to knuckle at his eye.

His vision blurred and refocused on the small boy panting and twisting his tunic dry on the muddy shore.

The human retracted its wings and removed the extra pair of eyes over its face. Horrified, Cy observed the human put the extra set of eyes on its forehead. *Humans have four eyes?* he thought, feeling disgusted. A gray bird landed on a tree branch above the boy and squawked.

"Alive," the bird exclaimed. Cy was astonished that he understood the words of the feathered creature.

"Just barely," the boy retorted, as he groaned and cracked his spine. "I'm glad you followed me, Benu." The bird didn't respond as it preened its feathers. "Any idea where we are?" the human asked.

"Land," the bird snapped back, as he swiveled its head around. Cy was just as amazed by the talking animal as he was by the flying four-eyed human. He had never seen anything like them before.

"Come on. Let's explore the island. Maybe some natives can offer us some hospitality," the boy said. The bird flew down and landed on the human's retracted wing as they made their way through the forest.

Cy tried to follow them discreetly, moving within the shadows of the trees. However, the young cyclops was as inconspicuous as his father lumbering through the forest. It wasn't long before the visitors got the feeling that they were being followed.

The boy whispered into the gray bird's earhole, and then the parrot flew up into the trees. Cy looked up and then back down, which was when he lost sight of the boy. Panicked, the cyclops searched in every direction.

The parrot dove down toward the panicked cyclops and screeched, frightening Cy away. Disoriented and running at full sprint, Cy collided with the boy. They both fell backward onto the ground. After the shock wore off, they looked at the person before them.

"Awww... you're a cyclops!"

"Awww... you're a human!"

Just as quickly as they met, they both ran from each other and hid within the nearest bush.

"Are you going to eat me?" Cy asked, panicked.

The boy was astonished by the cyclops' ability to speak and even more so by the words that came out of its mouth. "Why would anyone eat a cyclops?" asked the human.

"I don't know."

"I thought cyclopes ate humans?"

"I've never even seen a human."

"Who told you that humans eat cyclopes?"

"My Papa."

"Well, your father is mistaken," the human said sharply.

Cy and the boy cautiously crawled out of their hiding places. "I guess we were both wrong," said Cy, as they guardedly approached each other. The parrot watched them, perched on a tree limb, and yawned.

"I'm Icarus, son of Daedalus, the greatest craftsman in all of Greece. That makes me the second greatest craftsman, but I wish to be the best someday," he said. "What's your name?"

"I'm Cy, son—of—Brontes," he said while twiddling his fingers.

"Hello, Cy, son of Brontes," greeted the boy. Icarus extended his hand to shake, but the cyclops stared at it blankly. Unsure, Cy took the human's hand and placed it on his head.

"No, like this," Icarus said, as he grabbed Cy's hand and shook it. The cyclops was hesitant at first, but then smiled and shook back. "Now we're friends," Icarus said with excitement.

"What's a friend?" asked Cy, his head tilted to one side.

Icarus placed a finger on his chin, pondering a way to explain the idea of friendship. "It's someone who you can trust and who looks out for your well-being," said the boy.

"Like my Papa?"

"Almost. A friend usually isn't a relative."

"Oh," the cyclops considered, "I've never had a friend."

"Neither have I. Maybe we can be best friends?"

"Best friends?"

"It's like being friends, but greater."

Benu flew down from the tree branch and landed on Icarus' shoulder. "What am I?" asked the parrot.

"You're my pet," said Icarus. "This is Benu, son of cow dung," the boy quipped.

The parrot squawked angrily and pecked Icarus on the side of the head. "My pet," responded the parrot, annoyed.

"He's a little beast, don't listen to him." The boy leaned forward to examine the cyclops' eye closely. "How do you see with one eye?" Icarus asked bluntly.

He took Cy's head in his hands and used his thumbs to pry the cyclops' eyelid wider.

"I don't know. I just do. How do you see with four eyes?" Cy retorted as he jerked his head back.

"I only have two." Icarus pondered for a moment. "Oh, you mean my spectacles. They just help me see when I fly." He removed the eyewear from his head and handed it to Cy.

The cyclops took the goggles in hand and inspected them curiously. "How do you see with two eyes?" Cy questioned, as he handed the strange eyewear back to the young lad.

Icarus covered an eye with one hand and observed his surroundings. "I suppose we only need one. He removed his helmet and stuffed it into his flying machine's pack along with the eyewear. Brushing a hand through his scalp made his hair stand wildly. "What do you have to eat on this island? We're famished." The parrot whistled agreeably.

Cy thought for a moment. "Follow me," said the cyclops excitedly, as he scampered away. The boy and bird followed closely behind.

They reached the fig trees, and all grabbed several fallen fruits and ate them ravenously. Icarus opened a fig and fed a small piece to Benu. With his mouth full of food, Icarus mumbled, "Thes figss ar belicious." He swallowed and continued, "What do you call this land?"

"My Papa calls it Cyclops Island. I've lived here my entire life."

"Father," Icarus paused soberly. "I need to rescue my father."

"Rescue?" asked Cy.

"Never mind. Do you know how I can get off your island?

"How did you get here?" queried Cy. Icarus pulled the dangling cord from his backpack to extend his wings, which caused Benu to fly off of them. The cyclops was awestruck as he inspected the device. "What is it?"

"They're wings."

Benu landed on Cy's shoulder. "Bird," said the bird while extending his wings.

"Can you fly?" asked Cy.

"Not quite. That is why I landed here. Do you have any ships?"

"My Papa said there are a few that were left behind the last time humans came to our land. Come on, I'll introduce you to him."

"Your father sounds honorable."

"He's the greatest. Follow me," said Cy as they made their way through the forest.

3

BRONTES THE TERRIBLE

Brontes kept a sleepy eye over his flock of sheep while sitting beneath the shade. A short trek through the trees on the other end of the meadow was the beach where he defended his island from the humans back when Cy was an infant. Most of the island's shores were made up of rugged cliff walls with jagged rocks jutting out of the sea. It made bringing a ship to shore dreadful. For that reason, the cyclops regarded the nearby beach as a landing spot for any ship looking to make landfall. If any humans were daring enough to step onto his island, he'd quickly know about it.

The giant cyclops dug his bare feet into the hard-packed earth and yawned. He quickly shook his head, trying to fight the fatigue, and then gripped the massive club in hand before he scratched his back with it. He leaned on the tree as he observed the sheep continuing to graze. Brontes would count his sheep to make sure that one didn't wander off through the fence, but this had the adverse effect of putting him to sleep. No matter how hard he tried to concentrate, his mind drifted in and out of consciousness. Soon, the sound of the wind gently rustling the leaves soothed him into a slumber.

A young Brontes ran around the enormous legs of dozens of giant cyclopes. The cyclops clan resided within a massive cave, far grander than the one on the island. Although he was about the size of an adult human, the youthful Brontes looked up toward the diverse group of cyclopes that lumbered around. They varied in heights, weights, and ages, but the tribe conversed and laughed like a family.

As Brontes looked around for his mother, he saw the gray-haired elders speaking at the back of the cave; they made up the leadership of the tribe. He continued walking and saw the other children playing games in the middle of the cavern. The other children would tease Brontes over how big he was, and the cyclops would turn bright red and look down at his large feet. He was bigger than most full-grown humans by the time he was seven years old. Beyond the cruel younglings, he saw the mightiest cyclopes laughing as they stood guard at the entrance of the cave. Brontes wanted to grow up to be a warrior, but he was still too young to start training. He prayed to the gods every night for a chance to prove himself.

Haaarrroooohhhhh! A strange sound came from outside their dwelling. The cyclops warriors grabbed their clubs and were the first out of the cave. The children were told to stay inside where it was safe, but Brontes could see what was out in the open field far beyond. A human army was positioned just within the tree line of the forest. Soldiers sat on horses, stood in chariots, or held varying weaponry and shields of war.

"Lead the younglings out of here," ordered a female cyclops warrior. The elders called out to the children, who rushed to the back of the cave. Brontes stayed behind and continued looking out toward the army. The non-fighters disappeared into the darkness of the cave. "Brontes, get out of here," said the female cyclops.

"I want to fight with you," responded Brontes.

"You're not a fighter, run away, or I'll..."

A lone human rider in heavy armor advanced beyond the front lines. He took out a bull's horn and pressed it against his lips. Haaarrroooohhh! The soldiers screamed and charged at the cyclops clan. Brontes retreated in terror as the floor began to tremble.

The cyclopes fighters roared as they ran out to meet the army in the field. Large boulders were launched from beyond the tree line and fell from the sky. The entrance of the cave was struck, causing rock and earth to fall around them.

Brontes was pulled by the arm and followed closely behind the women and children as they made their way deep into the cave. They reached the shadows, but the echoes of the battle continued to reach their ears.

⁎

Cy, Icarus, and Benu approached Brontes from behind. "Papa, I met someone today," Cy told his father cheerily.

32

The massive cyclops awoke from his slumber and pretended that he had not been asleep.

He sat up and stiffened. "I was resting my eye," he said groggily. Brontes didn't break his focus from the sheep. "Where did you meet this someone?" Brontes asked while yawning. Cy excitedly retold the events that led to his chance encounter with Icarus, which included how the boy fell from the sky. Brontes laughed at what he perceived to be his son's imagination.

"Pleased to meet you, Brontes. I am Icarus, son of Daedalus," the boy said politely.

Brontes' eye widened as he slowly turned his neck to stare at the human. He sprang to his feet and then roared at the child. Benu was blown off the boy's shoulder and fluttered away in a panic. Icarus turned on his heels and sprinted away in terror. The giant picked up his massive club overhead and swung it down at the dirt in a fury. The frightened boy covered the back of his head as a plume of soil exploded all around. Dust blew into Brontes' eye, blinding him temporarily. The cyclops dropped the club to wipe at his face. "The human blinded me!" he cried in agony.

Cy stood in front of his enraged father with outstretched arms to block his path. "He's my friend. He isn't dangerous," the young cyclops pleaded, trying to get his father to listen to reason.

"That's what he wants you to think," Brontes hissed. He regained his vision as the human reached the tree line and scurried into the forest. Brontes lumbered forward and stepped over his son to give chase.

Icarus hid in some thick bushes and tried to catch

his breath. Benu landed on a tree limb above the boy's head. "Fly. Fly," the parrot cried out. Icarus attempted to shush the bird, but Benu continued squawking, potentially alerting any one-eyed giant to his location. Frustrated, the child tossed pebbles at the parrot, and the bird flapped away.

Brontes pushed several tightly packed trees aside and searched through the forest. The leaves on the branches shuttered, and the wood creaked as his robust frame lumbered past the boy and continued deeper inland. Icarus put his sweaty palms on his knees and let out a sigh of relief.

Cy ran into the forest frantically searching for his friend. "Icarus, where are you?" called the young cyclops.

"I'm over here," Icarus whisper-shouted nervously from his hiding place.

Cy turned around and looked everywhere for his friend but could not find him. "Where?" shouted Cy.

"Here," whispered Icarus. His fear was mounting with every bated breath.

"I don't see you," responded the young cyclops.

Annoyed, Icarus rubbed his face in frustration. He grabbed a few pebbles and started tossing them in the direction of the young cyclops.

Cy saw a rock fly overhead and turned in that direction only to be hit in the face with a pebble. "Ow!" said Cy, rubbing his forehead. He saw Icarus in the bushes and rushed to him. "I'm going to talk to Papa." Icarus reached out and put his hand over the cyclops' mouth to quiet him down, but Cy continued mumbling.

"Hush," said the boy, "or he'll hear you." Cy fell

silent, and Icarus removed his hand.

"I will talk to my Papa when he calms down. I've never seen him this angry," whispered Cy.

"You didn't tell me that he hates humans. I'm human."

"No, you're not, well not like the ones he described in stories. They usually have armor, shields, and sharp weapons."

"But I'm still a human!" snapped Icarus before he covered his mouth. He searched the area for the giant. "Where are the boats? I have to get off this island." They heard the sound of heavy footsteps and trees being pushed aside. "He's coming back."

"I'll talk to him," said Cy as he sprinted toward his father. Icarus turned in the opposite direction and ran.

Icarus reached the clearing to find the sheep continuing to graze without a care. The boy could hear the giant approaching through the trees, and quickly put his helmet and goggles on. He released his wings and sprinted through the center of the meadow. "Fly, please fly," said the boy, jumping into the air. The sheep lifted their heads to look at the distressed human momentarily but then continued grazing. There was no wind, so the wings were useless. A woolly sheep ambled into his path, and the boy collided with it. Down they went. The animal baud as they rolled over each other.

Icarus retracted his wings and stood up, his head still spinning. The sheep's four legs were pointing up at the sky as it continued to cry out. The boy looked up to find Brontes pushing through the trees and stumbling into the clearing.

The giant stood tall and turned his head slowly but did not see the boy among his flock. He noticed the overturned sheep regain its footing and frolic away, but the giant did not think much of it. He plodded ahead.

Cy sprinted out of the forest and caught up to his father. "Papa, he's not like other humans, he's my friend," pleaded Cy.

"That's just what he wants you to think, son," responded the giant, as he bent down in search of the boy. "They're all tricksters." Brontes moved through his herd like a bloodhound, sniffing the air after smelling an unusual scent.

The giant began to crawl on all fours in search of the boy. Icarus desperately clung to the bottom of a woolly sheep. Hunting the boy, Brontes lifted his sheep and searched underneath.

"What if he revealed himself, Papa? Would you allow him to leave peacefully?" asked Cy. Brontes turned to his son as he lifted the sheep that Icarus hid beneath. The boy shut his eyes, expecting to be discovered, but the giant considered his son's words and did not notice the human.

Brontes placed the sheep and the human back down. "If he shows himself, then you have my word that I will not hurt the boy," said Brontes with a sigh.

Cy jumped excitedly and yelled, "Icarus, did you hear? He promised not to kill you if you revealed yourself!"

Icarus fell from the bottom of the sheep with a soft thud. The animals cleared the area, leaving the boy vulnerable. He smiled sheepishly, which angered the giant. Brontes lurched forward as Icarus got up and ran away. The giant was upon the small child with only a few strides. The boy cried out in terror as the large dirty hands reached for him.

Brontes lifted Icarus up off the ground in one hand and held him in front of his scowling face. "I want you off my island, and never to return. Do you understand me, boy?" he said with a level of authority that would strike fear into any man.

Icarus covered his mouth and nose, not out of fear but to shield himself from the giant's foul breath. "Yes," replied Icarus' with a muffled voice through cupped hands. The boy did not break his wide-eyed gaze from the cyclops' single eye, partially out of terror but also due to his curiosity. Icarus scrutinized the giant's eye and realized that it was bigger than his head. Clutching the boy's lower half in hand, Brontes turned and made his way out of the clearing. Benu followed discreetly from high above.

Cy sprinted to keep up with his father's long strides. "Papa, does he have to leave now? Couldn't we feed him and then send him home?"

"I'm sorry, son, but I do not trust him. He may look weak and pathetic..."

"I curse you," interjected Icarus, feeling insulted. The elder cyclops shot him an annoyed glance, and the boy looked away fearfully.

Brontes continued, "But this human may grow up to be a warrior someday. We cannot risk it."

"I'm no warrior. I want to be a craftsman just like

my father," Icarus retorted.

"Silence! Or I'll toss you into the Sun," Brontes said, glowering at the lad. Icarus folded his arms over his chest and frowned.

4

ACHILLES THE WARRIOR

Apollo's chariot drew the Sun through the eastern horizon. Across the open sea, three Greek warships sailed the choppy waters on a strong wind. Below the decks, the rowers pushed their long oars in and out of the water. At the head of the narrow footpath, a man struck his drum with large wooden mallets monotonously. Sweat beaded on everyone's brow as moisture dripped off the wooden walls of the trireme. On the main deck, the soldiers sharpened their weapons on flint rocks or polished their shields as they prepared for battle.

An overgrown warrior made his way across the bridge toward the head of the ship. This fighter towered over the other men, who moved out of his way swiftly and avoided his intense gaze. This was Ajax, son of Telamon, the strongest of the Achaeans.

Ajax had a square jaw that suited his massive height, muscular build, and broad shoulders. He had dark skin and tightly coiled black hair that made him look more like an Egyptian, but he was one of the most feared fighters in all of Greece. Some argued that he was second only to one other warrior.

"How much further? The men are getting anxious," said Ajax as he approached the young warrior standing at the bow of the ship.

"We'll see how brave these men are when they see the giant. I pray they don't swim out to sea. Poseidon doesn't care for cowards," retorted Achilles as he turned to face his second in command.

Achilles, son of the great Peleus, was the most naturally gifted fighter that had ever lived. Although barely sixteen, the young lad had earned his place as commander by always leading the charge into battle. Despite his inability to grow a beard, the men respected his experience, strength, and agility. His bronze armor and helmet were polished to a sheen, and he wore a black tunic and red cape that added to his aura. Girls swooned over his piercing blue eyes, sharp chin, and flowing blond locks, but the young man only had a love for combat.

"I'll make sure they hold the line. They don't want to end up like the soldiers that ran from the Nemean Lion," said Ajax.

"The lion was child's play compared to the cyclops. There's a reason sailors avoid the island at all cost," said Achilles.

"The one-eyed beast won't know what to do when we arrive. We've prepared for him."

Achilles gazed out to the water ahead of them and set eyes on the island in the distance. "I pray to all the gods that you're right."

Achilles was the son of the great Peleus, a general that fought in the Peloponnesian War. After successfully defending the Greek nation from the Persians, the General retired to a simpler life in the countryside with his wife. Achilles was born on a farm a few years later as their only child. His parents intended to keep him as far away from warfare as possible. Still, the boy was physically gifted and begged his father to train him in the arts of combat. Even from a young age, the boy dreamed of war.

Peleus finally relented on the child's eighth birthday, and so the training began. The General would wake up his son before dawn by shouting and striking the bottom of a pot with a wooden ladle. Jumping out of his bed in a panic, Achilles ran outside to start his physical conditioning. Rain or shine, from sunrise to noon, he would work in the fields by digging, plowing, or lifting heavy stones and removing them from the plantation. Noon to sunset was hand-to-hand combat and weapons training against his skilled father. At night it was military strategizing by candlelight. This was the boy's least favorite training routine since it required mental fortitude and not physical prowess. His body and mind were exhausted by nightfall, so he'd fall asleep to his father's disappointment. Achilles did not care to learn about military tactics with painted pebbles over sheepskin maps. He was a warrior destined for the battlefield.

The villagers took notice of Achilles' physical

gifts and skills with a sword, and soon the word spread. The boy was urged by all the great city-states to join their ranks, but Peleus refused on his behalf. Feeling that his son was not ready, he hid the royal offers from Achilles. At thirteen, however, the boy discovered the parchments while searching for a sword in his father's chamber. Furious for holding him back from his destiny, Achilles confronted his father. Peleus forbade his son from accepting any bids to join the military until he could grow a full beard. Afterward, the boy trained in the practice yard with an animalistic rage for several moons.

On his fourteenth year, under cover of darkness, Achilles snuck out of his home and ran away to join the nearest military. The armed forces in Thebes weren't formidable by any stretch of the imagination, but they were led by the great King Lycaster. Peleus had told his son about the honorable leader that fought alongside him during the great war. "If there was anyone Peleus would raise a sword for again, it would be King Lycaster," his father would say. Unfortunately, following the Lycaster's untimely demise, he was succeeded by his only heir, King Minos.

Achilles pushed himself to be the strongest and fiercest warrior in the Theban army. Chronicles spread about his invulnerability, unmatched speed, and remarkable agility. People thought that he was a god in the presence of mere mortals or, at the very least, a demigod. His athleticism and coolness under pressure made the legends believable to all. He was a fearless man of action, which constantly put him at the forefront of danger.

***

The crews dropped jagged stone anchors over the stern of the warships. Below the shallow water, the hulls of the ships ripped the coral reef apart until they came to an abrupt stop. Several soldiers disembarked to set up a protective perimeter while the rowers secured the boats to the beach.

Achilles jumped off the port bow of the ship and splashed into the shallow water. At his age, he was considered a man grown, yet walked with a determination of someone beyond his years. Like a sword that's been hammered by a gifted metalsmith to its sharpest point, training had aged the young man proper.

Achilles strolled onto shore with his bronze sword holstered in its sheepskin sheath and harnessed to his leather belt. He joined the soldiers on the beach and patted them on the shoulders.

"Let's hope that the legends are true," Achilles grumbled as he glowered at the trees beyond the beach. The sailors that navigated these open waters had warned them of a horrible cyclops that inhabited the island. According to them, the giant creature ate any trespassers that stepped foot on his isle. Every man in the nearby coastal towns told them to avoid this landmass at all costs.

"Best to bypass Cyclops Island, boy. The monsters there will eat you alive and pick their teeth with your bones," said one of the local fishermen. It was the same story that had much of the infantry unit fretfully searching the forest for any signs of the dreadful creatures.

"Relax, men. Some of you may die, but that's a sacrifice I'm willing to make," said Achilles indifferently.

"I just hope that this monster puts up a better fight than the centaur did," commented Ajax. The tall warrior swung his long sword several times in preparation for the upcoming battle.

Ajax's size threatened every man he came across, except Achilles. The young warrior feared no man but had much respect for his second-in-command. "You can't use your sword, Ajax. He's no good to us dead or injured," said Achilles.

"Oh, right," acknowledged Ajax, as he sheathed his sword. The tall brute quickly grabbed a large piece of petrified wood lying on the beach. "This should do it."

No animal sounds were coming from the trees, which created an unnerving stillness to the island. *It's quiet, too quiet*, thought Achilles.

"Remember, we need him alive," bellowed Achilles to his men.

That's when a gray parrot appeared on the ship's prow. The men turned to stare at the strange-looking creature. "Danger," said the bird.

"What did it say?" a soldier asked.

"*Squawk*, danger." The bird flew off.

5

THE BATTLE ON CYCLOPS ISLAND

Hidden from view, Brontes was surprised by how quickly the soldiers disembarked from the ships and secured the beach. He knelt down to get a better look at the infantry and dropped Icarus down on the ground. The boy landed on his rear-end and grimaced. Quickly realizing that this was an opportunity to escape, Icarus began to crawl away.

Brontes noticed the boy attempting to sneak away and grasped his ankle. The giant lifted the boy upside down and dangled him in front of his angry face. "You brought them here," grumbled Brontes.

Panic-stricken, Icarus pleaded, "No, I fell from the sky."

"You expect me to believe that? You humans. Your words are always false," spat Brontes.

"It's true, Papa. I saw him fall with my own eye," Cy said, as he tugged on his father's waistcloth.

"I don't know why they're here. Let me speak to them," the boy responded sincerely.

"You humans think you're so clever. You must think I'm a fool. If I allow you to speak to them, then you'll tell them where we're hiding," growled Brontes. He grabbed Icarus by his backpack and hung him on a tall tree limb. The boy kicked and swung his arms but could not get free. He eventually settled down with his head and shoulders slumped. "I'll deal with you last," said the elder cyclops.

Brontes hunkered down next to his son and said, "Keep an eye on the human, and no matter what happens, do not come out of hiding."

"What are you going to do?"

"What I do best," he said with a smirk. Brontes pushed through the trees to meet the soldiers on the beach. Each powerful stride shook the earth, but the sand quieted the sound of his heavy footfalls. Before the soldiers could react, he grasped the nearest human in one hand.

The troops gawked at the giant's sheer size and balked. The men retreated in terror back to the ships.

The cyclops flung the man in his hand out to sea. The soldier splashed into the ocean and eventually came up for air, keeping his head above water.

Only two soldiers held their ground and tried to rally their men. "We need him alive!" barked one. Brontes remembered that humans liked to follow a leader and recognized that the one shouting orders must be him. The giant lunged at the bold commander, but he dodged the giant's large swooping hands. Brontes tried to kick and stomp the young warrior, but this foe proved to be more agile than any human he had ever faced.

The tallest man among them crept up on the giant from behind with a large piece of wood. The tall warrior swung the lumber and broke it on the back of the cyclops' leg. Brontes turned his attention to the man with the broken timber in his arms. With a single flick from the giant's overgrown finger, the tall warrior was sent flying into the shallow waves.

"Help your brother," cried out their leader. "We cannot leave without the monster!"

The soldiers on the boat gawked at their brave commander singlehandedly engaging the giant on the beach. The men stared at each other with disdain. Finally, they grunted and found their courage. "Come on men, do you want to live forever like cowards?" cried out a soldier. The fighters grabbed their bronze shields and weapons before disembarking from the boats once again. The infantry made loud battle cries as they stormed the beach and surrounded the cyclops.

Brontes stood at the center, baffled as the human's surrounded him. For the first time since he was a child, he felt real fear. The squadron set up two separate blockades. There was a beauty to their methodical offensive. They smacked their shields with the shafts of their spears or the sides of their swords as they slowly constricted the blockade encircling the giant. Brontes realized that they no longer feared his size. As long as they worked together, they had the numbers and held the advantage.

Brontes turned around, desperately searching for

an escape, but he was surrounded. The soldiers angled their polished bronze shields up and used the reflected sunlight's glare to blind the cyclops. The giant used his hands to shield his eye from the blinding beams but lost track of the men below. He shut his eye and stomped the ground to keep them at bay, but they dodged his attacks and regrouped.

A spear with a rope tied to the end of it went flying over Brontes' head. "You missed," said the giant with a snicker. More spears were thrown overhead, confusing him further. The weapons landed in the sand, where men took hold of them. While the cyclops was distracted, two soldiers ran around his legs in opposite directions with a thick rope.

"Now," ordered their commander. Several soldiers grabbed onto the loose rope around his ankles and pulled the line with all their might. The ropes thrown over the giant's shoulders were also tightened. The lines stiffened, and before Brontes could react, the cord around his legs caused him to stumble and fall. He was able to grab and pull a few ropes off his body and flung several soldiers holding on to them, but more lines were tossed over his arms as the trap was fortified.

Brontes twisted and turned on the ground, but this bound him further. He was like a fly caught on a spider's web. "Let me go!" the giant bellowed.

The soldiers used mallets to drive wooden spikes into the dirt to secure the ropes. When the cyclops was fully restrained and exhausted all of his strength, the men cheered in ecstatic victory. They smacked their shields with their weapons, grunted in triumph, or hit each other in celebration.

Cy watched in anguish as his father, whom he believed was invincible, had just been defeated by a band of overjoyed humans. "No," he said helplessly. Icarus watched from his vantage point on the tree limb. Although terrified of the giant, the boy did not want to see any harm come to the father of his new friend. He felt sympathy for the young cyclops. No one should suffer the injustice of watching a loved one slain.

The soldiers fell silent as their commander and his second-in-command moved through the crowd and approached the restrained giant. The cyclops breathed heavily as large beads of sweat dripped from his forehead. The young warrior kneeled before the giant and looked him in the eye. "I am Achilles, son of Peleus, the best of the Greeks. It was an honor to meet you in the field of battle."

"Get on with it, human," spat Brontes. "Strike your killing blow. Claim your legend."

"We aren't here to slay you. We're civilized men," said Achilles with a devious grin. The soldiers let out a few laughs and hoots before settling once again. "I do hope that you put up a better fight next time," he said.

"If you're so fearless, then why don't you fight me alone? Man to cyclops."

"All in due time, monster." Achilles stood and looked down at the giant. "Are there any more of you?"

Brontes gave Achilles a stern look and then said, "I'm the last of my kind."

"That's a shame. We could have used more of you."

"What for?"

"You can come with us willingly, or we can set fire to this island and destroy any chance of you ever returning home," said Achilles. A soldier sprinted past them and reached the edge of the forest with a flaming torch in hand. Brontes turned his head and looked at the tree line in the distance. He found Cy's frightened face hidden among the leaves.

"What chance do I have of ever returning?" Brontes asked.

"Help us on our mission, and I give you my word that you'll return someday," Achilles put his right hand over his heart.

"What mission?"

"Saving the world," said the young warrior.

A soldier stood next to a tree with the torch, prepared to set the forest ablaze. The giant's eye was fixated on the flames and then refocused on his son. Brontes looked at Achilles and reluctantly nodded in agreement.

The soldiers bound the giant's wrist and ankles before they cut the ropes that secured him to the ground. Archers aimed their arrows at Brontes as they slowly transported him off the beach. Soldiers cautiously placed several rounded logs beneath the cyclops' large frame and gradually rolled him out to the water. They pushed Brontes onto a large wooden raft. Eventually, they cuffed his wrist and ankles to the vessel with enormous metal shackles.

A soldier told Achilles that they were ready to launch. Achilles gave Brontes a stern look, and then turned to several of his men and said, "Search the area for more cyclopes."

6

TO THE HUMAN WORLD

Icarus witnessed the entire battle while hanging from the tree limb. He never expected the soldiers to be victorious over such a terrifying giant. Yet, there they were, securing the overwhelmed cyclops to a raft.

The boy found the soldiers' method for transferring the restrained giant from the beach to the water vessel ingenious. However, he did not understand why they wanted him alive. *They must need his unique abilities for a specific reason*, he thought, but what that reason could possibly be made his head spin. Who would require the services of a terrifying giant?

Benu landed on the tree limb and preened his feathers. "Can you help me down?" asked Icarus as he continued to flail his arms and legs. Benu hopped over to his flying machine and tried to pull it off the branch with his beak.

Icarus could see Cy becoming increasingly

agitated below. Cy was about to charge out of the forest when Icarus called out, "Wait." The cyclops halted and looked up. The boy kept trying to get loose when he finally realized that he could release the harnesses that secured him to the pack. He untied himself and plummeted straight down. Icarus hit several branches on his way down before landing on a large bush that broke his fall.

Cy approached him. "Are you alive?"

Icarus gingerly poked his head out of the shrubbery. With a groan, he muttered, "I'll live." The noise of breaking branches made them look up when the flying machine came crashing down on the boy's head. The cyclops and parrot cringed as Icarus disappeared into the bush once more.

Cy reached into the shrubbery and gave his friend a helping hand. With his head throbbing, Icarus slowly strapped the flying machine onto his back. "You can't go out there. They'll take you as well. Your father must have agreed to go with them to protect you and keep you on this island." The young cyclops looked out at his father and wondered how anything would ever be the same after today.

Even though it would give him a headache, Icarus placed the goggles over his eyes and looked out toward the ships. His vision was magnified tenfold, and he got a closer look at the soldiers continuing to celebrate on the beach. "The soldiers are boarding their ship and preparing to cast off. They must be taking your father to the mainland." Brontes began tugging at his restraints on the raft as if trying to escape.

"We have to stop them," pleaded Cy.

Icarus noticed several soldiers running toward them. "We have to hide." He placed the goggles back on his forehead and pulled on Cy's arm as they hid behind the nearest bush. The soldiers walked into the woods and halted less than ten paces from where the children were concealed.

"Get out," bellowed Benu, from above the trees. The soldiers panicked as they created a protective phalanx to defend themselves.

"Who said that? Show yourself," said a panic-stricken soldier. Except for a few birdcalls, there was silence. Icarus and Cy covered their mouths to keep quiet.

"You think there are more cyclopes on the island? Capturing one was difficult enough," said a worried soldier.

"This place is called Cyclopes Island. Meaning more than one," muttered his bearded companion.

"What if there's an army of them?" said the other anxious soldier.

"Army," hissed Benu.

"One bigger than the one we captured?" asked another soldier as he listened to the forest.

"Bigger, bigger, bigger," repeated the parrot.

Panic swept through the once bold soldiers. The leader of the unit searched the trees. The forest was so dense that they lost visibility the deeper they journeyed into the island, which made them vulnerable to an attack.

The leader of the unit turned to his men. "We could report to Achilles that we didn't find anything."

"In truth, we have searched," responded the bearded soldier.

"Let's head back to the ships and get out of this accursed land," ordered their leader. They scurried back to the beach swiftly.

Icarus and Cy peeked their heads out of the bush. "They're gone," said Icarus. They made their way back to the tree line.

"Why didn't you go with them?" asked Cy. "You're human, they mean you no harm."

Considering that he had been imprisoned for most of his life, Icarus didn't think this was true. The soldiers' uniforms even reminded him of the guards at the tower. Still, Icarus didn't know how to explain his situation to someone that had never been in contact with humans before.

"Not all humans are kindhearted," admitted Icarus somberly.

The cyclops looked out to the beach as the sailors heaved the stone anchors back onto the deck. The ships were helped back out to sea by dozens of soldiers pushing from the shallow waters. Once the boats were afloat, the men climbed aboard the vessels. The oarsmen took to their benches in the lower deck. Long oars extended out from the portholes and onto the saltwater. The sailors rowed until there was a strong gust of wind at their backs. Men seized the rigging and unfurled the sail from the tall mast. The largest ship towed the floating raft transporting Brontes.

Cy stumbled out onto the beach and sprinted toward the water with tears streaming down in his face.

The ships had put some distance between them and the island, but that didn't stop Icarus from worrying. "Cy, get back here!"

Brontes fought back the tears when he saw Cy running onto the shore. The anguish of not calling out to his son was excruciating, but he did not want to alert the humans. A grim expression came over his face.

A soldier ran up to Achilles and Ajax at the ship's bow. "Sir, a small cyclops appeared on the beach," the man reported.

The three men made their way to the stern. They observed the young cyclops in the shallow water. "Should we go back for it?" asked Ajax.

"No, he's too small. Best to just leave him behind," responded Achilles.

The ships vanished over the horizon. Cy was left sulking in the water until an enormous wave washed over him. He was pummeled and spit back out onto the shore. Icarus approached his friend, who was lying face down in the muddy sand. "I'm sorry," he muttered.

Cy wiped the wet sand from his face as he got up. "Are you going to leave me, too?" asked Cy nervously.

"No, I can't abandon you on the island. We're friends, remember?" said Icarus. "Friends stick together through thick and thin." A smile stretched across the boy's face.

"Thank you," said Cy, wiping the tears and wet sand from his face.

Icarus hunkered down to look his friend in the eye. "We're going to get him back. We just have to find a way off this island."

Cy sniffled as he got to his feet. "My Papa said there are a few ships in a cove not far from here." The cyclops plodded along with his shoulders and head slumped. "Follow me," he mumbled glumly.

Benu landed on Cy's shoulder and nuzzled his cheek to cheer him up. The bird's feathers tickled the young cyclops' face and lifted his spirits. Icarus put an arm over his friend's shoulder. "The gods will protect your father," he said earnestly. Cy cracked a feeble smirk. They made their way down the shoreline.

Night had fallen as they continued their trek down the beach. Lit by a bright moon and thousands of stars, they reached the cove. Dozens of ships inhabited the pond with a waterfall cascading down a high cliff. Benu flew around the striking environment to get a better view. Icarus was in awe of the water that seemed to glow in the dark. "How did all these ships get here?"

"My Papa has been protecting this island since before I arrived. He never hurt any humans, only frightened them away. Some would swim back to the human world," said Cy as he jumped onto a small skiff.

"That means we aren't that far from the mainland. We have to choose the best ship," said Icarus. He tried to jump onto a boat but missed and splashed into the pond. The boy kept his head above water as he swam to the nearest vessel.

"What about this one?" Cy climbed aboard a sailboat, but it quickly sank to the bottom of the pond. The cyclops garbled in the water.

Icarus boarded another craft and stomped on the

wood to gauge its strength. "I think this one will do. The haul looks promising, but it's missing its sail." Benu landed atop the mast of the vessel and spread his wings. The boy observed the parrot curiously. "I have an idea," he said excitedly.

It took some time, but Icarus modified the boat by placing his flying machine on top of the ship's mast. He pulled the cord, and the expanded wings created a makeshift sail. The funneled winds within the cove pushed them toward the exit. "Here we go," said Icarus. The boy angled the wings with some spare ropes they found. "Move those boats out of the way," said the boy. Cy rushed to the bow and pushed the other vessels out of the way with his hands.

Slowly, they reached the open waters and headed back to the human world. Icarus steered the boat by maneuvering its tiller and used the stars to navigate. Those were skills his father taught him while they were locked in the tower. With Benu on his shoulder, Icarus looked like seasoned sailor. "We'll reach the mainland in no time."

"I've never been off the island," Cy admitted nervously. Reaching over the side of the boat, he brushed the top of the water with his hand.

"I haven't seen much of the mainland myself," said Icarus. "We'll discover the new land together." The dread on Cy's face slowly vanished, and he began to smile at the idea of seeing the human world.

"You think we can save my Papa?"

Icarus looked at the vast ocean. "There's something I have to tell you," he said soberly. Cy sat down and turned to face his friend. The boy proceeded to tell his companion of the forced imprisonment he suffered with his father, their plan to fly off the tower, and his lone escape. Icarus had trouble recanting the moment that he flew away because his father had stayed behind. When it was all said and done, Icarus rubbed at his eyes to hide his tears.

"You see, I share your dilemma. My father is also a prisoner," said Icarus.

Cy didn't understand everything that his friend told him, but the cyclops understood the most important details. Icarus' father had been taken, like his own, and they were going to attempt to rescue them both. "How are we going to free our fathers?"

"I don't know, but I'm sure I'll think of something," said Icarus with half-grin.

Cy and Icarus both looked at all the stars in the night's sky in awe. They wondered why the gods decided to put those lights up there in the first place. Just then, a group of dolphins swam and jumped out of the water alongside their boat. They both viewed this as a good omen. *Poseidon has given us safe passage*, thought Icarus.

*
**

They saw land within a few hours. Recognizing that they sailed farther north than expected, Icarus followed the shoreline back south.

When they finally reached the rocky shores near the tower, both Icarus and Cy struggled to pull their boat out of the water. They eventually drew the ship onto the rocks, while Benu watched them from his perch atop the mast. Icarus pulled his flying machine off the boat, and they were off.

They hid in the shadows near the entrance of the surrounding wall. Icarus observed the area for a time. He noticed that no torches had been lit, and there were no soldiers stationed at the gates. The tower was dark, quiet, and seemingly abandoned.

"Benu, go find father," said the boy. Perched on Icarus' pack, the parrot whistled and took flight.

Benu flew above the surrounding walls to ensure they were empty and then made his way up the side of the tower. He entered through the chamber's window and landed on the floor. There was no one to be found in the ruined room. Benu let out a sorrowful whistle.

Icarus cautiously entered through the doors of the tower, holding a large rock above his head. Cy followed with Benu on his shoulder. The cyclops had never seen a human habitat before and wondered how they built such a structure. Since meeting Icarus, Cy became fascinated by humans and their ability to create objects that helped them fly and travel over open water. The tower was an improvement over the cavern that he and his father inhabited.

Icarus tossed the rock aside and grabbed a beeswax candle near the door. After lighting the string, the boy used the candlelight to search throughout the tower for his father.

They reached the cellar and found that Daedalus' workshop had been destroyed. Hundreds of scrolls were scattered throughout the floor. Most of the craftsman's inventions were smashed to bits.

Cy timidly walked down the steps and made his way through the workshop. He looked at all the different inventions hanging from the ceiling.

Cy was about to touch an odd device with sprockets and coils around it when he heard Benu squawk angrily. The parrot eyed him while perched on a broken table. Defiantly, the cyclops put one finger on the device, and the parrot screeched until he retracted his hand. Rather than face the bird's wrath, Cy walked away.

Icarus sat down at his father's workbench. He tried to piece together what had conspired while he was gone. It wasn't difficult to recognize that his father was in peril.

7

DAEDALUS THE CRAFTSMAN

Daedalus regained consciousness at nightfall but wasn't sure how much time had passed. A sharp pain radiated from the swollen lump at the back of his head as he sat up wearily. Hay lined the floor of the large wooden box he found himself within. It rocked back and forth, causing him to stumble as he got to his feet. He staggered to the only door in the room and tried to push it open, but it wouldn't budge. Desperately searching for a means of escape, he reached a small barred window on the opposite end. He looked outside and realized that he was imprisoned in a transport that was being hauled by two horses.

Outside, a soldier on horseback held a rope that was leashed to a bound centaur with a bronze collar around its neck. Daedalus had heard tales of creatures with the upper body of a human and lower half of a horse but never witnessed one in the flesh. The horseman had an expressionless face until he noticed Daedalus gawking at him from the window. "What are you staring at?" spat the four-legged centaur. The craftsman looked away as the creature trotted ahead with a snort.

Daedalus looked at a cell that was advancing alongside his transport. It was three times larger than his box, but instead of wood, metal bars enclosed the creature within. It was too dark to see what was being contained, but he heard a strange clicking sound. Two large white orbs came into view within the darkness. They looked like eyes floating mid-air. The craftsman became transfixed until the monster jumped out of the shadows and crashed into the barrier. Daedalus recoiled and fell back when the giant crab snapped its pincers within the metal bars. The wild creature rocked its transport, causing the horses towing the cart to whinny. The driver seated on top of the cell pulled on the reins to settle the steeds. The crustacean gradually calmed down, but never took its eyes off the craftsman as it observed him from the shadows.

When the terror subsided, Daedalus rubbed the back of his head as the pain returned. He rubbed the swollen lump. That's when he realized this wasn't a terrible nightmare, but his reality.

It took Daedalus a moment, but he recognized the road they were on. It was known as the King's Road because it connected most of the city-states within Greece. It was the only path of its kind. They were about half a day's ride from the tower, which meant that he had been on the dirt road with this large convoy since he was knocked unconscious. They were trudging at a slower pace than if he had been taken alone on horseback, so he assumed that the task the King required of him was somehow tied to these creatures.

Whatever he was involved in now was stranger than anything he had ever dealt with before. Daedalus had been so preoccupied with the bizarre creatures that he failed to consider where they were going. He looked up the road and saw a seemingly endless line of soldiers, wagons, cages, and chariots. Several sentries walked back and forth along the side of the caravan with lit torches, assuring that no creature tried to escape.

"Where am I?" yelled Daedalus, "Where are you taking me?" The roars of several creatures in cages could be heard down the line.

"Don't bother the monsters, Craftsman!" warned Magus as he appeared alongside the carriage. "Unless you want us to feed you to them."

"Where's my son, Magus?"

"Don't you remember, Craftsman?"

Daedalus shut his eyes and rubbed the back of his head, trying to recall the moment. Images of Icarus being taken away by strong winds flashed across his mind. His eyes opened in shock.

"You remember now, don't you? You killed your boy," reveled Magus.

"No, he - he escaped," said Daedalus, uncertain.

"We tackled you to the ground, so you did not see. Your son fell and crashed into the rocky shores. I saw it with my own eye," he said, enjoying the anguish in the craftsman's face.

Daedalus' closed his eyes and leaned his head on

the bars. "It's not true."

"Believe it or not, it makes no difference to me," said Magus.

"I want to see for myself. Let me go," pleaded Daedalus.

"Oh, of course. Let me just grab the key." Magus unhooked a ring of keys from his belt and shook them cruelly in front of the craftsman. "You'll keep quiet if you know what's good for you," Magus growled, hooking the keys back onto his belt.

"Where are you taking me?"

"I don't want to spoil the surprise, Craftsman. You'll know soon enough," said Magus with a devious grin.

Someone at the head of the long convoy called out to halt the line. Every rider and driver pulled on the reigns of their horse until everything came to a screeching halt. Soldiers continued to yell the same order down the convoy until there was silence. An uneasy calm and stillness took hold.

Daedalus heard rough ocean waves crashing onto the nearby shore. Magus joined several guards running past as they headed out onto the sandy beach. The craftsman could distinguish several wooden ships offshore. Torches illuminated a flat wooden raft that was being hauled out of the saltwater by dozens of horses and oxen tethered to it with ropes. The animals stepped wearily and bellowed as they dug their hooves deep into the sands, while soldiers berated and whipped them. The raft gradually emerged from the sea and revealed four wheels attached to its sides. It was not a raft but a sizeable flat cart.

A massive creature was secured to the top of the transport. As the wagon approached, Daedalus could distinguish the creature's features clearly. Initially, he thought it was a whale until he noticed its large humanlike body.

"Let me go!" bellowed the giant. "I will destroy all of you."

Daedalus was surprised that he understood its tongue as it yelled at its captors. It was massive and more terrifying than anything Daedalus had ever seen. He finally noticed its single eye and knew that it was a cyclops. The inventor had never seen any of these frightening creatures before, but the one-eyed giant gave him a chill that radiated down his spine.

The behemoth thrashed at its chains and roared as his cart joined the rest of the caravan. The other monsters fell silent when the cyclops joined their ranks. Once the giant was added to the long line, the soldiers were ordered to continue onward. The convoy lurched forward once again. *What was the meaning of all this?* Daedalus wondered. He had to find a way to escape this transport of horrors and find the truth of his son's fate.

8

LAELAPS THE TRACKER

Icarus groggily lifted his head off his father's workbench.
Sleep was no longer an option after a pesky mosquito
kept buzzing around his ear in the early morning. The
boy did not remember falling asleep, but the tender spot
on his forehead implied that he passed out on the table.
He massaged his head as he walked out of the room.

Still half asleep, he assumed that his adventure
from the day before was just a terrible nightmare.
Rubbing the sleep from his eyes, he chuckled at the
absurdity of it all. *Inventing the flying machine, crash-
landing on an island, befriending a little cyclops, and finding
the tower abandoned were all parts of a silly dream,* he
thought.

It was one of those delusions that seemed real at
the time, but you laugh about it when you wake up.
Suddenly, Icarus tripped over something soft and round.
He instinctively stretched out his hands to break his fall.

A grunt emanated from both the boy and the person he stumbled over. He turned around to find a frightened little cyclops getting up off the floor. "You're real?" Icarus called out.

"What?" Cy retorted, massaging the back of his head.

"That means my father is missing," Icarus admitted gloomily.

Benu clicked his beak, while perched on a worktable.

Cy stretched and yawned, which caused the boy to do the same. He looked to Icarus for a plan, but the boy had none.

"We have to find our parents, but I don't know where to begin," the boy admitted.

"Don't you have some clever creation that can find them?" Cy asked as he inspected the crafts lying around. Icarus pondered, while Cy surveyed the remarkable objects in the room with the curiosity of a newborn. The cyclops wanted to learn more about their purpose.

The boy finally had a brilliant thought and immediately smacked his bruised forehead. "Ouch," he winced. "Of course!"

"What is it?" Cy asked excitedly.

"Not a creation but a dog."

"Great! What's a dog?"

"A dog is an animal that walks on four legs. I'm not just talking about any dog, but the world's finest tracker. My father feared that we would be separated by a great distance when we flew off the tower. There was no telling where the winds would take us, so he devised a plan to find each other. Laelaps is a hound that can find anyone in the world, and I know just where to find him."

The tower was near a village where the locals spoke of an animal blessed by the gods. The story went that Laelaps had the unique ability to track any person or item on the planet.

Although Daedalus was doubtful of the dog's divine ability, he felt that Laelaps could prove a useful tracker if they were separated during their escape. The young boy felt that if they could find Laelaps, they would have a guide that could lead them to their fathers.

Icarus raided the tower's abandoned food stores and packed all the essential supplies they could carry for their journey. He wrapped bread, fruits, and cheeses into sheepskins to preserve them. He gathered all the necessary items and packed them into a leather pack. The boy worried that the supplies would prove too heavy for the small cyclops to carry, but Cy was surprisingly sturdy.

Icarus strapped his flying machine on as they exited the tower. They filled their water skin pouches at the well in the courtyard and then secured them to their packs. They walked past the gates of the outer wall and did not look back.

The Teumessian fox casually strolled out from behind several bushes and made its way to a stream. The critter had orange and white colored fur with a furry tail. His ears perked up, and he began to search the area for any movement that signified danger. Laelaps watched the fox hidden beneath a mound of dead leaves. The brown hunting dog focused its beady eyes on its target and growled softly. It was waiting for the right moment to strike his greatest adversary.

No one was certain of Laelaps' origin, but the locals believed that he was abandoned in the woods as a puppy. Left to fend for himself, he began to starve as predators waited for him to weaken. Alone and afraid, Laelaps whimpered for several rainy days, curled up within a tree hollow. That's when a god heard his whines and took pity on the scrawny animal. That night, Laelaps was blessed with a divine ability to hunt and track food. From that moment forward, survival for the hound was simple. When local villagers came upon the fully-grown Laelaps in the woods, it didn't take long for them to comprehend his unique ability.

It was a close-knit community that resided in the surrounding areas of Laelaps' forest. A hound that could track anything in the world could be used for good or evil, depending on the person who wielded him. He could be forced into captive servitude for the rest of his life if he fell into the wrong hands, so no one ever spoke of him to soldiers. Most people alleged that the dog was merely a gifted tracker, but the locals who had been aided by Laelaps understood that he was a gift from the gods.

When Laelaps wasn't recruited for a hunting expedition, he spent all of his time tracking the Teumessian fox, who was the only creature that could evade him. The fox had a divine gift of his own, the ability to never be captured. It created an enigma that would give Zeus a headache, but that didn't deter Laelaps from trying.

Sensing a presence, the fox craned its neck in search of a potential predator. Eventually, it dipped its head toward the water and sipped.

Laelaps burst out of the pile of dead leaves and ferociously charged after its foe. He opened his slobbering mouth and prepared to bite down on the fox. The hound snapped his jaw shut and bit the wind. His teeth chattering, he skidded to a halt and turned.

The fox jumped over the dog and landed with a smirk. The hound locked eyes with his adversary before sprinting away. The dog gave chase until he was a stone's throw from the fox's furry tail. Still, each time Laelaps was about to catch his prey, the critter pulled away. They bounced from tree to tree, until the fox crawled down a wide rabbit hole.

Laelaps yelped and ferociously dug into the dirt frantically, believing that he had finally trapped his nemesis. The fox climbed out from another opening and sat behind the distracted canine mockingly. The trickster was always one step ahead of Laelaps, which infuriated the hound to no end.

Icarus, Cy, and Benu trekked aimlessly through the forest. The Sun was directly above them now, yet they were no closer to finding Laelaps than they were at dawn. They reached a clearing in the woods and heard frantic barking in the distance. Benu perked up on Icarus' shoulder, while the boy searched for the source of the uproar.

"What's that noise?" Cy asked, as he nervously hid behind Icarus.

"That's our guide."

The fox reached the clearing with the canine snapping at its tail. They ran around Cy and Icarus several times. Finally, the fox jumped and climbed up to Cy's head, while Laelaps continued circling the children. He realized that he lost track of his foe and desperately sniffed the ground to regain its scent. Laelaps found the snickering fox perched on top of the cyclops' scalp.

The hound tackled the cyclops to the ground and bared his teeth. Petrified, Cy looked up at the snapping rabid dog, but then looked past the hound to the fox standing on a tree limb directly above them. Laelaps craned his neck upward and saw his adversary casually jumping from tree branch to tree branch as it disappeared into the leaves. The dog leaped up and barked, but the fox had evaded him once again. Icarus tried to calm the hound down. "He's gone, boy. Relax." He petted the dog's head, which eventually calmed him down.

"What was that?" Cy called out.

"That was the Teumessian fox," said Icarus. The hound growled at the mere mention of the name. The boy smiled sheepishly before continuing, "My father said orange critter is a creature that can never be captured."

Within a few moments, the dog fell silent and began to wag his tail. The canine sniffed Cy, Icarus, and Benu. "Cy, this is Laelaps, the world's finest hunting dog."

"How can he be the best if he can't even catch that fox?"

Laelaps tackled Cy once more and pinned down the cyclops' shoulders with his front paws. "Easy boy, he didn't mean it," Icarus pleaded, as the dog growled. The hound slowly backed off and took a seat to scratch the back of his ear. "I wouldn't mention the you-know-what anymore."

"The fox!"

Laelaps barked at the cyclops again, who put his hands up in confusion. "I didn't say anything," pleaded Cy. Benu laughed fiendishly from the tree limb above.

"Quiet, Benu," snapped Icarus. He approached the dog again. "Laelaps, we need your help to find our missing fathers. We aren't sure where they are or why they were taken." Disinterested, the dog yawned and lied down.

"We're wasting our time. He's not going to help us," grumbled Cy.

Icarus snapped his fingers with a clever plan. "Laelaps, if you aid us on our quest, then we'll help you capture the Teumessian fox." The hound's ears perked up as he sat on his hindquarters. He swayed his head from side to side, considering the proposition. The dog finally nodded and presented his right paw. The boy took the leg in hand, and they shook on the pact. Icarus removed his father's spectacles from his pack and presented it to the hound.

Laelaps sniffed the item, and his eyes went milky white as he sat still in an unblinking trance. The children leaned in curiously. "What's he doing?" asked Cy.

"I think he's searching for my father," said Icarus. A moment later, the dog blinked, and the color in his eyes returned. The hound's tongue rolled out the side of his mouth. "Do you know where my father is?" asked the boy. The canine barked and nodded assuredly. "Cy, do you have anything that he can smell that belonged to your father?"

"I don't have anything of my Papa," Cy said solemnly. The dog bounded up to the cyclops. "What's he doing?" asked Cy nervously, as the canine sniffed him over. Laelaps gagged at the odor, and his vision was transported away from where they stood. As if shot from a catapult, his foresight traveled at breakneck speed. Through a forest, over a mountain, and finally to the road where Daedalus and Brontes were being transported. He could see each of them constrained to their transports.

His mental image eventually reverted back to the clearing with the others, as the dog came out of his reverie. He was connected to the scent of their fathers.

"Did you find Cy's father?" asked Icarus as he studied the hound. Laelaps barked and wagged his tail. "Excellent, we'll rescue whoever is closer..."

The dog whined and stood on his back legs. The children looked at the hound with confused expressions. Laelaps rolled on the dirt and then got up to chase his tail. "Together," Benu said, and the hound barked as if relieved that someone could decipher his meaning.

The children looked to Benu, and then back to Laelaps. "Our fathers are being transported together?" asked Icarus curiously.

The dog barked and nodded. Laelaps immediately got up and led the way out of the clearing.

"Do we follow him?" questioned Cy. He was skeptical of the dog but trusted Icarus' judgment.

"I've never done this before, but I believe so," Icarus said. They sprinted after Laelaps.

9

WRATH OF THE KARKINO

Caged creatures and soldiers trudged down the broad
path that cut through a dense forest. An enormous
tortoise was being transported on a large flat cart. Chains
were crisscrossed over its hardened shell, restraining the
creature to the transport. Slowly moving its head back
and forth, the tortoise observed the serene scenery.

"Psst... you, turtle, why don't we help each other
escape?" whisper-shouted Brontes, as he was pulled
alongside the creature. The tortoise looked in the giant's
direction momentarily, and then slowly retracted its
head into its massive shell.

The cyclops looked at the diverse group of
creatures around him. "Can any of you worthless
monsters speak?"

"Who are you calling worthless, monster?" said a
deep voice. Brontes turned his head and eyed the centaur
suspiciously. The four-legged creature had his wrists

bound and wore a bronze collar with a cowbell securely fastened to his neck. The bell rang with every step. Several paces ahead, the guard on horseback continued to lead the centaur by a rope tethered to the collar. The rider yanked the leash out of habit every few paces to assert his dominance over the horseman. Although not as tall as Brontes, the centaur's muscular physique and battle scars made an intimidating impression.

"We have to help each other escape," implored Brontes, as he tugged at his restraints.

"Unless the gods intervene, there's no escaping this fate. It's in their hands." The centaur's tail swatted at flies involuntarily.

"Just surrender and wait for them to slaughter us? I make my own fate."

Inspired by the cyclops' determination, the centaur stated proudly, "My name is Rhath of the Ixion tribe." He pounded his chest with his bound fist, a declaration of tribal unity among his people. "What is your plan..." Rhath leaned in inquisitively.

"I'm Brontes."

"What is your plan, Brontes?"

The cyclops fidgeted in his shackles. "I was hopeful that someone else would have a scheme in mind."

"You have no plan?"

Brontes' lips thinned as he shook his head. The centaur sighed and looked up at the sky in disappointment. "May the gods have mercy on us."

"Hurry it up, freak," said the rider pulling Rhath. The guard jerked the centaur's leash to hasten their pace.

In a fit of rage, the four-legged warrior quickly grabbed the rope and pulled the soldier off his steed. The man came crashing down to the dirt floor with a loud thud. The rider stumbled to his feet and unsheathed his sword as several other soldiers surrounded Rhath. "I'll break you like my horse, freak."

Rhath whinnied as he stood on his hind legs and kicked with his front legs to keep the soldiers at bay. The men hesitated, but their hostility rose as they drew their weapons. No one advanced as the centaur kicked and turned unpredictably.

Achilles cried out, "Stand down!" The young warrior arrived on his warhorse. "What is the meaning of this?"

The frustrated rider advanced on Achilles. "We should be killing all these monsters, not taking them for a leisurely stroll," he demanded.

"Then you would be disobeying a direct order from your commanding officer and the king, which is an offense punishable by death," Achilles irately retorted. "I expect disobedience from these beasts, but not from my men."

"We wouldn't even have to capture these monsters if Achilles was brave enough to enter the Labyrinth," whispered Magus to another soldier within the gathered crowd.

"Who said that?" Achilles narrowed his eyes at the half-helmed faces, but no one exposed the disrespectful soldier. "If you don't like taking my orders, then you're welcome to challenge me for command," declared Achilles with authority.

The soldiers shuffled their feet and avoided eye contact with the warrior. "You should expect these monsters to defy you. These beasts are hungry, and I don't mind feeding them rebellious soldiers. Now, get back to your post." The men reluctantly lumbered back to their stations. The angry rider got back on his steed and took hold of the rope tethered to Rhath. The centaur nodded at the cyclops before trotting ahead.

"I accept your challenge for command, warrior," said Brontes. "If you aren't a coward."

Annoyed, Achilles jumped on top of the flat cart and unsheathed his polished sword. The point was a hair's length away from the cyclops' eye. Brontes turned his head away from the blade instinctively. "I win, monster," said Achilles, as he flashed a winning smile.

"You need me. I don't know what you have planned for all of us, but this pitiful group of creatures won't help you. I'm the only one worth the trouble."

Achilles holstered his weapon. "Don't press your luck, cyclops. There are plenty of monsters in the sea."

"It doesn't matter what this is for, I'm not serving you," Brontes spat.

"You'll fight, or you'll perish, it's that simple." Achilles jumped back onto his warhorse and rode off. Brontes hit the back of his head on the cart in frustration.

"I couldn't help but overhear your proposal," said a man standing in the shadows of a wooden transport. Daedalus stepped into the sunlight and looked out of his bared window. His wagon was being hauled next to Brontes'.

"You aren't one of us, human."

"I'm a prisoner, same as you."

"Imprisonment doesn't make us allies."

"I have the knowledge you seek. A plan of escape."

"Then why haven't you broken out already?"

"I don't have the brawn or swiftness of feet needed to outrun the soldiers. Their trackers would be upon me before I got far."

"I won't fall for your trick, human. Besides, I finally have a plan to escape."

"You should wait until nightfall, friend," cautioned Daedalus.

Brontes ignored the man, as he spotted several horses hauling a large cell approaching. He roared at the steeds and frightened them into a gallop. The driver on the perch of the carriage desperately tried to regain control of the animals. The panicked horses maneuvered themselves around soldiers, carts, and chariots until the wagon reached a ditch on the side of the road and tipped over. The driver was flung off and hit the dirt awkwardly. He rolled for several paces until he came to a complete stop. The horses broke free from their harnesses and trotted away down the line. The transport crashed on its side and slid down a trench until it hit a tree.

The entire caravan came to a screeching halt, as several armed guards rushed toward the commotion and surrounded the cell. There was an eerie silence.

"Maybe the beast perished," said a worried soldier. Officers trembled in their armor as the spears and swords wavered in their hands. Suddenly, a giant pincer punched a hole through the side of the damaged cell. The monstrous crab crushed several bars and ripped them away. It created a gap big enough for it to climb.

Achilles tried to reach the site of the crash, but dozens of fleeing soldiers blocked his warhorse's path. The Karkino landed on the ground with a loud *thump*. Its pincers snapped at several guards that evaded its attack. Archers shot arrows at the beast, but its crustacean shell proved impenetrable. Realizing that it was outnumbered, the King crab quickly scuttled into the dense forest to escape.

Achilles and Ajax dismounted from their steeds and sprinted to the site. Achilles yelled, "You six, come with us. The rest of you will continue onward. We'll catch up after we recapture the beast." Achilles, Ajax, and the six soldiers ran into the dark forest with their weapons drawn.

10

THE HOODED HERO

Icarus and Cy followed Laelaps as he sniffed the ground like a bloodhound. Benu was perched on Icarus' flying machine, fast asleep. Laelaps followed his nose, only pausing briefly to mark a tree or scratch fleas off his body. They were already on the same road that the large caravan was traversing. The Teumessian fox sneakily followed the foursome hidden within the dark forest that flanked the road.

Icarus closely observed the military tracks left in the dirt. *There are a lot more soldiers than there were on the island,* he considered. "Rescuing our fathers is going to be difficult, Cy."

"You'll come up with a scheme, won't you?"

Icarus let out a half-hearted smile. He appreciated the confidence the cyclops had in him, but if only he felt the same way. If a giant terrifying cyclops and his brilliant father couldn't avoid capture, what chance did they have?

If only the flying machine worked, he thought, *then he could provide a distraction long enough for their fathers to escape.* Icarus' mind thankfully drifted to a different matter, something that he had wondered ever since he met the young cyclops. "Cy, were you and your father the only two cyclopes on the island?" Cy nodded. "Where is the rest of your kind? Where is your mother?"

"What's a mother?" Cy asked.

"You don't have a mother?" Icarus asked, bewildered. He knew next to nothing about the parentage of cyclopes, but he was certain that most creatures required a mother and a father. "How did you come to be?" Icarus pressed.

"My father said that Poseidon answered his prayers and spat me out of the ocean."

"Poseidon is your mother?"

"I still don't know what a mother is."

Icarus mused over a manner in which to explain the idea of a nurturing female cyclops to someone that had never seen one. "A mom is someone that loves and takes care of you when you're a baby and raises you when you're a child."

"Is my Papa, my mother?"

"No, he's your father. A mama usually has long hair and other features that I can't describe to you," Icarus said, clearing his throat nervously.

"I think I'm starting to understand. Where's your mother?" Cy countered curiously.

Icarus had a somber expression take over his face as the image of his mother flashed in his mind. Her name was Lysandra, and the memories of her weren't ones Icarus intentionally suppressed. Nevertheless, he focused on his present and future rather than on his past for that reason. His eyes welled up as he tried to control his emotions. The boy looked away as the faded memories flickered in and out of his consciousness like the flames on a candle.

*
**

Before he was locked in the tower, he remembered Lysandra being sick in bed for most of his young life. At the tender age of five, Icarus would run into his parents' chamber and hug his ill mother. He would talk excessively of the latest marvel his father was building.

The boy understood that his mother was unwell but did not understand what that meant. The idea of death was a foreign concept at his age. He would always take Lysandra by the hand and try to lead her out of the room, believing that all she needed was to see Apollo's golden chariot in the sky. He felt crossed at her refusal to stand and leave her room. He would pray to all the gods to make her better, but they never did.

"My beautiful, Icarus," Lysandra would say with a smile. "Someday, you are going to change the world." She would hold his little cheeks in the palms of her trembling hands and sing to him. He'd forget about going outside and lie in bed next to her for hours. Her sweet lullabies would put him to sleep instantly.

The day finally arrived when his father prevented him from entering their chamber. Lysandra had fallen asleep and never awoke. Daedalus solemnly uttered the words, "She's with the gods." The boy tried to run past his father, but he was held at the entrance of the room. Icarus caught a glimpse of her motionless body wrapped in a blanket. He's missed his mother ever since.

Icarus tried to wipe away the tears rolling down his cheeks discreetly. Several drops escaped before he was finally able to take control of his sorrow. He turned to Cy and said, "She's no longer alive, but she's in here." Icarus pointed to his heart. "And here." He put a finger to his temple. Cy nodded and instinctively put a hand on his friend's shoulder.

"Do you think I have a mother?"

Icarus was finally able to show the trace of a smile. "I'm sure you do. You just need to ask your father about her. It might not be something you want to hear."

"I think it's better to know who your mama was than to believe you never had one," Cy admitted sorrowfully.

Laelaps stopped sniffing the ground and turned to growl at the dark forest to the right of them. He could sense something amiss just beyond the trees and began to bark. Benu awoke abruptly, squawking as he flapped his wings. There was a strange clicking sound coming from the woods. A sea salt aroma emanated from the trees when a gust of wind pushed past the weary travelers. The fallen leaves glided over them as if encouraging them to flee. "What's wrong, boy?" asked Icarus.

Suddenly, a monstrosity jumped out of the forest and landed on the road a few paces from where they stood. The giant crab snapped both pincers menacingly, while the children and dog stepped backward. It gargled saliva bubbles in its mouth before it screeched. Each of the king crab's six legs advanced on them chaotically. Icarus finally collected his thoughts and yelled, "Run!"

Icarus, Cy, and Laelaps fled from the Karkino's ravenous mandibles. Benu took flight, while the rest of them dashed to the woods on the opposite side of the road. It felt like an eternity before they reached the dark forest and put some distance between themselves and the crustacean. The beast struggled to maneuver its wide shell between a dense cluster of trees and lost sight of its prey.

The children and hound hugged each other behind a large tree as the beast lurked toward their hiding place. "Stop," said a voice. The crab spun in search of the man.

"Halt," crowed Benu, while safely hidden within a tree hollow. The crabs extended eyes darted in search of the speaker but saw no one. Aggravated, the monster pulled a huge boulder out of the dirt and threw it viciously. It struck a cluster of trees sending chunks of wood, leaves, and splinters flying in every direction.

After the debris hit the ground, there was silence, until someone yelled, "You missed!"

The Karkino ignored the smart mouth and refocused its attention on the children it was stalking. He grabbed the tree trunk and ripped it out from the roots, but its prey was nowhere to be found. Fuming, the crab tossed the tree behind its body. "Lost them?" quipped Benu as he flew to another tree.

Several paces away, Icarus peered around a different tree and saw the crustacean frantically searching for them. He huddled back with Cy and

Laelaps, and whispered, "We have to flee before it..."
Suddenly, the tree was crushed in half by giant pincers.

The crunch of the thick trunk was deafening.
Splinters flew far and wide. The top half of the timber
toppled to one side, fortunately away from the children.
The trio hugged each other and shrieked, as the Karkino
approached menacingly. It put a pincer around each
child's body and prepared to snap them shut when a
hooded figure appeared. The stranger ran up the crab's
back and used a staff to smack its extended eyes. The
beast recoiled in pain and bucked the attacker off its
shell.

The children looked up at their savior flying
through the air valiantly. The cowl concealing the
person's identity fell back, revealing a girl with dirty
blonde hair. She landed on a tree limb with the grace of a
cat. The crab reached up to grasp the nuisance, but she
somersaulted down to the ground. She goaded the beast
away from the trio to give them a chance to escape.
Unfortunately, the children stood gawking at her battle
the crustacean.

"What are you fools waiting for? Get out of
here!" she yelled. The girl dodged and used the staff to
block the crab's attacks. She poked and prodded the beast
to keep its attention with the hope that they would have
more time to flee.

Laelaps barked at the two boys to get their
attention. Icarus and Cy broke out of their stupor and
followed the sprinting dog deep into the forest. They
reached a safe distance before Icarus stopped running. Cy
and Laelaps skidded to a halt and looked back.

"What's wrong?" asked Cy.

"I have to go back for her. Carry on without me. We'll catch up." Icarus ran back the way they came.

The girl continued dodging the monster's attack, but her breaths became short and fast. She tried to flee, but the beast blocked her path. Finally, she saw an opening and ran straight toward the creature's mandibles as it widened its frothing mouth. Before the shellfish could take a bite out of her, she slid beneath its body. The crab slammed its rigid shell down on the ground to crush her, but she reached the other side. While she continued to slide, the girl planted one end of her staff into the dirt and used the momentum to carry her up. Without a stumble, she got to her feet and sprinted in the direction of the others.

She looked over her shoulder and saw the ugly creature turn its enormous shell and give chase. Distracted, she crashed into Icarus, and they both tumbled down a hillside. Sliding and rolling chaotically, they managed to dodge passing rocks and trees. The Karkino vaulted into the air as it retracted its arms and legs. Landing on its belly, it slid down the slope smashing through everything in its path.

Benu was tracking the children from high above when he noticed a row of trees collapsing beneath him. The two children hit the ground at the base of the hill, their minds spinning. They stumbled to their feet when they realized the monster was careening down toward them. In a daze, the girl grabbed Icarus' wrist and pulled him forward just as the crustacean skidded past them. The Karkino crashed into several trees until it came to a brutal stop. It extended its legs and dizzily continued its pursuit.

"What were you thinking?" the girl yelled at Icarus as she released his arm.

"I came back to save you," he responded with a scowl.

"I didn't ask for help!"

The crab was nearly upon them and ready to strike when a spear hit the back of its shell. The soldiers led by Achilles and Ajax had finally caught up to the escaped monstrosity. The crab was distracted long enough for the children to sprint away. The Karkino tore another tree from its roots and tossed it at the soldiers. The men took cover just in time to evade the projectile. The crab turned around and continued to chase after its smaller prey.

Laelaps led Cy to a river and they followed it downstream until they came across a boat tethered to a rock. Without giving it a second thought, Cy untied the rope, while Laelaps jumped aboard.

Icarus and the girl ran out of the woods in search of the others. Laelaps barked to get their attention. "Over here!" called out Cy, as he pushed the boat out to the deep end of the river and jumped inside.

Icarus and the girl splashed in the water as they climbed aboard. "Where did you get this boat?" asked Icarus.

"Laelaps found it," said Cy.

A fisherman came rushing down the river with a fishing net. "What are you doing?" he yelled. "You thieves, get off my boat!"

The Karkino rushed out of the woods and blocked the fisherman's path. The creature hit the fisherman with the backside of its pincer, launching the poor soul into the water.

"Sorry," Cy called out, as the fisherman swam to the riverbank on the other side.

The Karkino jumped into the water, and the boat rode the ensuing wave. The children put some distance between them and the crab, but the crustacean was now in its element and moved swiftly in the water.

The soldiers rushed out of the woods and noticed the creature pursuing the boat. Achilles looked closely and realized that the same small cyclops he saw on the island a day earlier was now in the skiff. He was caught off guard and wondered how the little monster could have made it off the island.

"Achilles, are you all right?" asked Ajax, as the other soldiers dashed ahead.

"I'm fine, keep moving," he ordered.

The Karkino maneuvered its massive shell advantageously in the river and would soon be upon the ship.

"Start paddling!" ordered the girl as she pressed oars into the chests of the two boys. Icarus did as he was told. Cy tried to imitate his friend's rowing technique but he held the oar upside down, which was of little help. Laelaps used his front paws to paddle over the bow of the ship in an attempt to move them along hastily.

"Keep us steady," said the girl as she stood at the back of the boat with her staff in hand. The Karkino snapped at her, but she swung her stick to keep its jagged pincers at bay. She jabbed at the crab's mandibles to prevent it from grabbing onto the ship.

The frustrated Karkino punched the stern and sent the craft spinning out of control. The boat finally stopped whirling and righted itself, but the children were left in a daze. Cy put his head over the port-bow and started heaving. The crustacean grasped the rear of the skiff and brought them to a halt. The second pincer sprang out of the water like a cobra preparing to strike.

"Ka-kaw," a bird screeched from high above. It startled the crab as it searched for the source of the sound. The Karkino saw the parrot diving toward it at breakneck speed. Benu clawed at its left eye with his talons, blinding it temporarily. The parrot flew away as the crab snapped at his attacker. In all the confusion, the crustacean released the boat and stumbled backward. Laelaps barked, and the children shouted in excitement. The beast staggered momentarily before it regained its forward momentum. The water picked up speed as the river transformed into a roaring rapid.

Achilles and the other soldiers tried to keep up on land, but they quickly lost sight of the monster and children. The men halted to catch their breath, but Achilles kept running, determined to capture the beast.

Cy and Icarus tried to maneuver the boat as the perilous waters doused them. The Karkino kept pace at every turn, but violently bounced off rocks and boulders. With a single eye, the crustacean saw something in the distance that terrified it. The beast screeched and grabbed onto the first tree limb that it could reach. It halted midstream as the children cheered. The crab pulled itself out of the water and onto the rocky shore. "Victory!" proclaimed Icarus.

Laelaps was the first to turn and notice why the monster ended its pursuit. He barked and yelped, trying to get everyone's attention. They each turned and saw the river's end and it was over a steep cliff.

"Why have the gods cursed us?" murmured Icarus.

They frantically tried to paddle the boat to shore, but the stream was too powerful. Icarus picked Laelaps up in his arms and stood in the middle of the ship. "Hold onto me!"

Cy and the girl each wrapped their arms around the boy's torso. He pulled the cord and released his wings just as they went over the edge of the waterfall. They glided briefly before plummeting to the water below.

THE CITY OF THEBES

"Why would you free the crab and not the rest of us?" asked Rhath in a hushed tone. With several guards within earshot, the centaur kept his voice to a low growl as he marched near Brontes. He tried intimidating the giant, but it was difficult to make threats in restraints.

Brontes responded in an annoyed whisper, "I wanted to know what the guards would do if we escaped. The cowards run and hide once we break free."

"The soldiers will be prepared for it next time," interjected Daedalus, who was eavesdropping on their conversation.

"Quiet, human," Brontes retorted.

Rhath clip-clopped his way to Daedalus' transport. He narrowed his eyes at the man behind the barred window. "What do you mean?"

"They assumed a creature couldn't escape, so they were caught off guard when it did happen. They'll be ready next time."

"Your words are wise, but why should we trust you?" asked Rhath.

"I've been captured like the rest of you. What reason have I given not to be trusted?" said Daedalus.

"Humans are deceitful, none of you can be trusted," responded Brontes with a scowl. Daedalus met his intense gaze and sighed.

"Enough, the both of you. We must consider all options," stated Rhath.

Their section of the convoy reached the top of a hill. In the distance, they could see a vast sprawling city-state made up of close quarter housing, a massive stadium, theaters, and an immense palace at its core. Even from his low vantage point, Brontes caught glimpses of the manmade structures. He had never seen anything like this fast-paced overgrown village. There were more humans—to Brontes' disappointment—then he ever imagined existed.

"What is that?" Brontes marveled.

"It's the City of Thebes," stated Daedalus begrudgingly. It had been years since Daedalus stepped foot in the place he once called home.

The craftsman was born and raised in the City of Thebes. His father Metion and mother Alcippe were grain merchants that worked on the outskirts of town. Metion was a brawny bearded man that held deep-rooted traditional values. He never understood Daedalus' fondness for staying indoors with his mother to build useless things. "Your toys are a waste of time. You

94

should be out playing in the field with the other boys," Metion often grumbled.

Alcippe was a bright-eyed and curly haired woman that loved her son. Despite her husband's disapproval, she encouraged her son to continue creating his unique crafts. "I believe your creations will change the world for the better," Alcippe would tell her son.

When he became a man grown, Daedalus opened a small shop in the heart of the city where he sold his crafts to both young and old patrons. The local children were delighted by the clever puzzles and toys, while the older customers purchased his innovative farming equipment.

That's where he met Lysandra, the eldest of three sisters that frequented the shop to view his latest music boxes. Daedalus struggled to speak to most girls, let alone someone he was enamored with. Not only was Lysandra lovely, but she was his equal in age and intellect. She wanted to learn how he came up with such remarkable inventions, but Daedalus struggled to find the words. Eventually, he divulged that they came from his mind, but that she inspired him.

One day, Daedalus offered Lysandra an apprenticeship in his shop, which she promptly accepted. They happily worked together for years and became inseparable. Daedalus taught her how to build unique creations, and she taught him how to talk to patrons.

Despite their fondness for each other, Lysandra knew that he would never court her, so she eventually offered her hand in marriage. They were wed during the winter months to honor Hera, the goddess of matrimony. Their marital bliss was short-lived, however, when the King of Thebes arrived at Daedalus' shop.

∗
∗∗

The convoy approached the outskirts of Thebes, and the captives would soon be among its people. Daedalus no longer recognized most of his hometown. New structures and shanty homes were sprawling out of the edges of the city like weeds in a garden.

"We won't be able to escape now, we're too close to the city," cautioned Daedalus. "We need to wait."

"I will escape when I please, human," spat Brontes.

"You'll never make it out of Thebes with that many people surrounding you, and I don't want innocent people to be injured. Believe me, we should wait."

With his head lowered, the centaur trotted between them deep in thought. Rhath turned to Brontes and said, "I trust the human. We should delay."

Brontes grumbled as he dropped his head on the cart. "Why would I ever trust a human?"

"You're the giant cyclops, I'm too cowardly to betray you. I don't have a choice but to trust you. I must learn of my son's fate, and the longer I'm here, the less likely I will ever know what became of him."

Brontes sighed and said, "Once the soldiers are asleep, we escape."

12

AJAX & THE CENTAUR

At the waterfall, Achilles and Ajax stood near the edge of
the cliff and stared straight down. The six soldiers
approached them from behind.

"No sign of the Karkino, sir. We searched the
woods until we reached a beach. It must have made its
way back to the sea," said one of the men.

"What about the cyclops?" asked Ajax.

"No sign of it. There's little chance the beast
could have survived that fall," added another soldier.

Achilles couldn't break his gaze from the long
drop before he turned to address his men. "Ajax and I
will climb down the cliff and search for the one-eyed
monster. You six will rendezvous with the army and
continue transporting those creatures. Don't allow
another one to escape. Tell the King what happened here.
We'll catch up to you in a day."

"Yes, sir," answered the six soldiers

simultaneously. They sprinted away and disappeared into the forest.

"Why are we searching for this cyclops?" questioned Ajax.

"This monster was the same one from the island. Somehow, it reached the mainland. It must be trying to rescue the adult we captured," said Achilles.

"We beat the giant, so this puny monster shouldn't pose a threat," stated Ajax confidently.

As a true warrior, Achilles feared no monsters, but he was only as strong as the man standing next to him. After defeating the giant cyclops on the island, his men had found their bravery on the beach. What concerned him now was the brashness. This little cyclops didn't seem dangerous, but an adversary needs to be respected, no matter the size.

"Never underestimate a foe. No matter how big or small they are," he said. Achilles needed to teach his second-in-command what it took to be a true warrior. Although he knew that Ajax aspired to be a greater warrior than even him, he could not fail to train his men. His thoughts drifted to when he met Ajax after a battle.

The unit was several weeks into their current campaign. They finally came across the tribe of centaurs they were tracking through the Foloi woods. Achilles knew that a group of centaur warriors known as the Ixion tribe inhabited the forest. Their unit was tasked with capturing several fighters alive on direct orders from their King.

The clan proved to be formidable opponents. The

scouts were amazed by the centaur's organizational skills
and fighting prowess. The four-legged creatures used the
land to their advantage and handled bows like skilled
archers. In the end, the humans won the battle by
utilizing their superior numbers and employing the
military strategy of flanking the tribe. Most of the clan
retreated back into dark woods, but the humans were
able to corner a single centaur. Achilles gave the order to
halt his troop's advancement into the dark woods, fearing
a trap.

Several soldiers surrounded the lone centaur as it
bucked its legs and whinnied at any soldier that took
steps toward him. "Stand down, or we will be forced to
kill you," warned Achilles.

Turning to face the young warrior, the centaur
retorted, "I will not surrender unless I am defeated in
battle. I'll yield if a man can beat me in one-on-one
combat." The intimidating four-legged creature advanced
on Achilles, "Are you brave enough to fight me?"

Achilles smirked and prepared for a fight.
"Wait!" a tall warrior called out from the crowd. He
pushed through the ranks and then ran to kneel before
Achilles. "I am Ajax, son of Telamon. Please allow me
the honor to fight the horseman in your stead." He was
the first and only soldier to step forward. Achilles
nodded, and the bulky warrior threw down his weapon
and armor. He stepped into the circle opposite the hoofed
beast.

The centaur towered over every man in that
forest, especially when it stood on its hind legs. His long
dark hair was wrapped in a ponytail that hung down to

the black coat of his horse half. The creature's muscular torso and arms made Ajax look like a scrawny child in comparison.

"My name is Rhath, if you care to learn the name of the centaur that fights you," grumbled the centaur.

"Ajax, I am honored to be the one that defeats you," said the tall warrior with a smirk.

Ajax wasn't as imposing as the creature, but he still stood boldly. Still, it was unlikely that Ajax even weighed half as much as the centaur, but what he lacked in strength he would make up for with speed and agility.

"Get him, Ajax, breaker of stones!" a voice hollered from the crowd of enthralled onlookers. Ajax and the centaur stood in the center of the gathering and stared at each other. This would be what the centaurs called Pankration, a form of unarmed combat where you wrestled, kicked, punched, or strangled your opponent into submission or until they were unconscious.

Rhath made the first move as he charged at full trot. Ajax quickly rolled out of the way and sprang up. He put his arms around the centaur's barrel to try and tip him over. Rhath bucked around, trying to shake the man off of his flank, but Ajax quickly climbed onto its back and wrapped his arms below the centaur's head. The human warrior's biceps bulged as he applied intense pressure to his opponent's neck. The horseman's face reddened until he leaned forward, causing the rider to tumble over his head and down to the ground.

Ajax was stunned momentarily until he saw the bottom of Rhath's hooves coming down toward him. He rolled over, narrowly dodging the attack, and got back to his feet. They grasped each other's hands at the center of the circle and tried to overpower one another with brute force. Achilles watched and shook his head, knowing full well that Ajax had just conceded his only advantage: speed. Rhath was surprised by the strength of his opponent, but he knew that when it came to might, no human was his equal.

The centaur stepped forward, putting all his weight on the body of his challenger. The tall warrior came close to kneeling on the ground. Knowing that he would be unable to overpower his opponent, Ajax looked to his commander for guidance. Achilles, noticing the panic in the warrior's eyes, pointed to his forehead with the implication that he needed to use his mind to win. Ajax, however, interpreted that gesture to mean *use your head.* Ajax pulled Rhath's arms down and head-butted the creature in the face. Disoriented, the horseman staggered backward. Ajax seized the opportunity to grab the centaur's front legs with both arms and forced him to the ground.

Once a centaur was on its side, it struggled to stand. There was nothing Rhath could do. Ajax took advantage of his position and put the creature in another headlock until the centaur tapped the warrior's flexing arm and yielded. Ajax claimed his captured prize and bound the wrists of the four-legged warrior. He led him out of the Foloi forest to the cheers of the other soldiers.

Despite the celebration, the captured centaur proved little more than a morale boost for Achilles' men. The pitiful creature was nothing without its tribe, and having only seized a lone centaur, it wasn't enough to achieve the King's lofty goals. Achilles allowed the soldiers to rejoice this minor victory with the hope that it would give them the mental fortitude to clash with their next terrifying opponent, the cyclops.

⋆⋆⋆

"Achilles, what is your command?" asked Ajax.

The young warrior snapped out of his stupor and looked down the waterfall. "We can use this small cyclops as leverage to force the giant to fight for us." The young warrior cracked his knuckles.

"That's a brilliant plan, commander," responded Ajax with excitement. "Let's hunt down the little beast."

13

HARMONY THE BRAVE

Laelaps pulled on Icarus' tunic with his teeth and dragged him out of the river water. He set him on the muddy banks next to Cy. The girl that fought the beast laid with her face to one side a stone's throw away from the two boys. The children were breathing yet unconscious. The dog bounded back into the water and swam away.

Benu flew down and landed in the muck. He pecked Icarus' head several times until he awoke. The boy looked up and noticed the parrot swaying back and forth, excited to see him alive. "Hello," said the parrot as he leaned into his master's face.

Icarus rubbed his head and then nudged Cy, who awoke in a panic. "Are we dead?"

"Unfortunately, no," said Icarus. He noticed the blonde heroine asleep near them. He hadn't realized it when they were running for their lives, but she was quite stunning even with all the dirt on her face. The boy's heartbeat quickened, but he didn't understand why as he gazed at the sleeping maiden. It had been years since Icarus laid eyes on a girl, especially one his own age.

The girl awoke abruptly and looked all around. She searched their surroundings. "Where's Laelaps? Where's my dog?" she demanded. They found the hound swimming downstream with the maiden's walking stick in his mouth. "Laelaps, come here," she commanded.

The dog's head bobbed as he swam toward the children. He ran out of the water and spat out the staff at the girl's feet. "Why did you leave without telling me?" she asked angrily.

Laelaps answered with several barks followed by a whine and a grumble for good measure.

"How many times have I told you not to talk to strange travelers?" Icarus, Cy, and Benu watched the two of them, perplexed.

Laelaps sat down and dropped his head below his shoulders as if he understood her scolding. "Stop it. You're acting like a child." Laelaps dragged his rear-end in the dirt to reach her hand and licked it. "Get off. Bad dog." She smiled as she rubbed the hound's head.

"Who are you?" asked Icarus. She took the staff in hand, ignoring the boy. "I'm talking to you!" the boy demanded. Icarus and Cy stood as they wiped the mud from their clothing. The dog shook his body and dirtied everyone nearby.

"We have a long journey home," she told Laelaps. He grumbled and barked at her.

"We need him for our quest," interjected Icarus.

"What quest?" She turned to them, confused. Laelaps laid down and rolled back onto the mud. His legs were folded into his body as he looked up. "Get up. We don't have time for this." She grabbed his legs and dragged him several paces, but the hound refused to stand. "Don't make me carry you home," she said, annoyed. He turned his head away and barked. "What do you mean you shook on it?" she questioned the dog.

"Laelaps made a pact with us, and he can't break that pledge," said Icarus.

"He's a dog! You can't expect him to understand what was asked of him." She crossed her arms and scowled. "What was the agreement?"

The next few moments were a jumbled mess of incoherent words out of Icarus and Cy's mouths. They tried to explain their ordeal simultaneously.

"I had been imprisoned in a tower with my father for years. I was the only one that managed to escape thanks to my flying machine, but I was blown to a remote island ..."

"I was picking figs from a tree when I noticed a giant creature fall out of the sky. It turned out to be Icarus falling from the ..."

"I met this little cyclops, and we became friends, but then his terrifying father tried to kill me ..."

"These three warships full of soldiers arrived and captured my Papa to take him..."

"We left the island on an old ship and..."

"Sailed to the mainland to find Icarus' father, but he was taken by the same soldiers that captured ..."

"My father told me to find Laelaps if we got

separated. We found him in the woods, and he agreed to help us if we helped him catch the Teumessian ..."

"Your dog led us down the same path that the army took, and that's when the giant crab ..."

"Silence!" she shouted. Icarus and Cy shut their mouths. She paused to collect her thoughts. "It sounds like you're going on an adventure." Icarus, Cy, Laelaps, and Benu exchanged silent glances and then nodded in unison. "In that case, I wish to join your quest."

"No. No. No. We need Laelaps. This expedition is too dangerous for a *maiden*," Icarus countered.

"This *maiden* saved you from the crab monster," she responded with a glower. The girl may have been Icarus' age, but she was taller in stature.

She took a step toward the boy, and he took a step back. "I was about to slay the beast when you arrived and ruined my plan," he asserted.

The girl took another stride forward and replied, "Did your plan require that you be eaten by the beast? Because it nearly worked."

Icarus finally stood his ground defiantly. "I went back to save you."

The girl grabbed the boy by his tunic and lifted him up off the ground with one arm. He was amazed and frightened by her might as his feet dangled off the ground. "I think what you meant to say was, 'thank you for rescuing us.'"

Cy scuttled up to them. "We could use someone as brave as she is, Icarus."

She put Icarus back down on the dirt, gently. "It seems to me that you need a damsel like me on your quest. You seem clever, but that doesn't matter in a fight like the one we just survived."

He walked past her in a huff and hiked up the riverbed. "Fine, but I will not save you again."

The girl rolled her eyes and turned to the cyclops. "Is he always that stubborn?"

"I've only known him for two days—but yes, he seems to be. I'm Cy, he's Icarus, and the talking bird is Benu."

The bird landed on her shoulder and flapped his wings. "Hello," said the parrot with a whistle.

"I'm Harmony." They walked side by side along the riverbank.

"Harmony," Cy paused to consider. "Are you a girl?"

"Um... yes," she responded in a confused manner.

"I've never met a girl before."

"I've never met a cyclops before, so we have that in common."

"What makes you different from a boy?"

She thought about it carefully, "Well, girls are smarter than boys."

"I see," said Cy with a smile.

14

KING MINOS

In the City of Thebes, the streets were bustling with merchants, patrons, and nobles. Yet, citizens stopped to gawk at the monsters being paraded around. The creatures were being transported through a road that cut through the heart of the city. The beasts roared at the children that approached their cages to get a better look. The frightened kids scampered away to hide behind their parents.

Most citizens hid in their homes, sealing their doors and windows, while some threw trash at the restrained creatures and yelled obscenities at them. Unable to shield his face, Brontes pulled and thrashed at his chains as people pelted him with rotten food. Even Daedalus wasn't spared from the hail of putrid waste as he huddled in the corner of his box. The cyclops roared, and the Thebans stopped aggravating the riled beasts.

The giant studied all the different human faces

and could not comprehend how there could be so many of them. Even as a child, he never imagined that there were this many people in the world. *Did they multiply to these vast numbers in a short amount of time, or have they always been here?* Brontes wondered.

The city looked impressive from afar, but within the streets, one could see the buildings were old and ruined. The homes were falling apart, the roads were littered with waste, and there was a rancid aroma that stung your nostrils. This was not a cheerful place, and these were not privileged people. At long last, Brontes understood why men wanted to settle on his island. Living in any area outside of this city was better than surviving within it.

The convoy halted abruptly in front of the courtyard of the King's enormous palace. Dozens of soldiers stood guard at the base of the dwelling, ensuring that the citizens kept their distance. They eagerly waited for their leader to address the masses.

Magus approached Daedalus' transport and removed the keys holstered on his belt. He opened the door with a smirk. "Come with me, Craftsman."

"Where are we going?"

"To meet with the King. I consider it a great honor, so don't make me drag you out of this box by your beard," retorted Magus.

Daedalus exited the carriage and was led by several soldiers through the palace gates. Brontes and Rhath exchanged suspicious glances. "See, it was all a trick to learn of our escape," Brontes murmured to the centaur.

"No, he is with us, but if they decide to torture him, then the soldier will learn of our plan," said Rhath. "Either way, this doesn't bode well for us."

The prisoner and guards made their way through the palace gates and toward the entrance of the palace. At the bottom of the staircase, Daedalus noticed a marble bust of King Lycaster. The previous King's eyes were weary, the beard was trim, and the hairs on his head were receding. *The sculpture must have been completed just before his demise*, thought Daedalus, for it was the face that he remembered.

Under the rule of King Lycastus, son of Parthenius, the city of Thebes flourished. He was a virtuous leader and a champion of the people that accepted counsel not just from nobility but from commoners. Even if he was given advice that went against the interests of the powerful, he took it under advisement. He'd often weigh the will of the people against what was best for all of Thebes.

Years ago, King Lycastus entered Daedalus' shop without his guards. He wanted to obtain a gift worthy of his son, Prince Minos. That is how the King came to know a soft-spoken craftsman with a talent for building extraordinary objects. Seeing the brilliance Daedalus possessed, the King invited him to attend a Theban council meeting. The craftsman wanted to reject the offer, but one cannot deny a request from the King. Daedalus reluctantly agreed to join assembly yet planned to silently observe the proceedings.

At the meeting, the King grew tired of the usual

bickering between his council members. He ordered
Daedalus to give his opinion on matters of state. A quiet
man under most circumstances, the craftsman tried to
avoid suggesting a solution that conflicted with the
recommendations of the nobles at the table. After careful
consideration, Daedalus provided a resolution that no
one even considered. The high-ranking officials were as
impressed by the outsider's knowledge, as was the King.

Together, Lycastus and Daedalus led Thebes to
economic prosperity. Soon, the craftsman became the
King's most trusted advisor. It was the King's dream to
unite all the kingdoms of Greece into one peaceful
nation, and with Daedalus at his side it all seemed
possible. Unfortunately, the King allowed his son to sit
at council meetings, a decision that would prove to be his
undoing.

Lycastus' only flaw was that he did not discipline
his son. Prince Minos acted like a gentle soul in the
presence of his father yet became a beast when he was
away. The Prince had a talent for manipulating the King
and bending the council to his will. Realizing that Minos
would one day be King, the council members refrained
from challenging the Prince, but Daedalus did not. The
only one that did not fear the son was the craftsman. The
Prince would come to despise Daedalus for being a
commoner and holding sway over his father.

The King truly believed Thebes would be in good
hands with his heir, but those hands proved to be
corrupt. The death of Lycaster occurred swiftly and
without warning. One day, he was as strong as an ox,
and the next, he did not wake from his slumber. No one

dared sow the seeds of dissent by questioning the odd circumstances surrounding Lycaster's death. The citizens mourned their fallen King but recognized the young Minos as their new leader.

Within the first few days of inheriting the throne, King Minos seized control of Thebes by disbanding the council. His Royal Guards detained anyone he feared could usurp his reign. He started wars against neighboring nations once considered allies and pushed the city into massive debt. To pay for his extravagant lifestyle, the King taxed his people into poverty. No offering or sacrifice was ever satisfactory to satiates the King's greed. When a meager farmer presented a priceless Phoenix egg to pay for his taxes, the King tossed the man in the dungeons yet kept the majestic creature as a pet.

Daedalus would have fled the city, but he was mourning the death of his wife at the time. Under the cover of darkness, the Royal Guards detained Daedalus and his young son. The craftsman was brought into the palace's throne room to face the King's justice.

Daedalus felt that his life was forfeit, but begged King Minos to spare his innocent son. The King sat on his throne in silence, while the craftsman begged. Finally, Minos decreed that he would spare both their lives if Daedalus built weapons that served his army for the rest of his life.

With tears in his eyes, Daedalus nodded and accepted the decree. The craftsman and his son would be imprisoned in the Tower of the Wind far beyond the city to ensure that they could not escape. Daedalus and Icarus were escorted to the far reaches of the Theban realm to live out the rest of their lives in forced imprisonment.

From time to time, Daedalus would hear about an attack from a warring nation that no longer considered King Minos an ally. The City of Thebes became one of the most coveted cities in all of Greece. It had an advantageous location if you wanted to control the Gulf of Corinth, declare war on Athens, or had the ambition to conquer all the city-states in Greece. Unfortunately, its position was also vulnerable to attack from armies to the north or warships from the sea. Daedalus viewed King Minos as an entitled child that threw his father's glorious kingdom into disarray. Still, after the King's coronation, no one dared challenge his reign.

Within the grandiose master's chamber of the palace, King Minos sat in front of his luxurious gold-trimmed mirror. A servant stroked scented oils into his thick beard, while another ran a comb through his long black hair. The King's features were as rough as his personality. He had disheveled eyebrows, eyes as dark as night, a hook nose, and thin frowning lips that signified his endless displeasure. His armor was made of the finest boiled leather, polished bronze plates, and medallions. He stood, revealing his impressive height and stout frame that was equal parts girth and muscle. A servant tied a lion skin sash over his broad shoulder, but the King removed it and tossed it aside, dissatisfied with the color.

On the far end of the room, a servant brushed the coat of the King's white stallion. They were preparing the horse when there was a knock on the door. The steed whinnied, and King Minos turned to his Royal Guards. They opened the double doors, and several soldiers entered. Magus tossed Daedalus onto the floor, and the feeble craftsman rolled to a stop.

"Here's the prisoner, my Liege," said Magus with a bow.

"Did I say you could hurt him?" growled Minos.

Magus' eyes widen as he spoke nervously, "No, my..."

"Get out," bellowed Minos with a glower, "Out!" Magus and the other soldiers scurried away. The Royal Guards shut the door and blocked the exit. The servants stood with their heads bowed in silence. Minos grabbed his goblet and took a drink. "You may rise." Daedalus lifted his body off the ground. "You look skinnier than I remember," he said, observing his former rival.

Daedalus got to his feet but kept his head lowered and stared at the King's sandaled feet. "What is it that you need of me, my Liege?"

"Is that any way to greet an old friend?"

"My apologies."

"We served on my father's council together, the least you can do is look me in the eyes." King Minos shortened the distance between them.

Daedalus looked up to face King Minos. "If it pleases you."

Minos patted the craftsman's shoulder. He walked back to his mirror, swirling the drink in his goblet. "How have you been?"

"Surviving, my Liege."

"Stop calling me that. It gets tiresome," the King

said. He took another drink from his cup. "They treated you well at the tower, didn't they?"

"The accommodations were -- suitable."

"Good, as I ordered. How's that spirited boy of yours?"

Daedalus had trouble finding the words but eventually croaked them out. "He fell from the tower."

King Minos put his goblet down and lowered his head. "The gods can be cruel."

Daedalus struggled to hold back his anger but did so. "They can be."

"We shall have a great feast in your son's honor when all this is over, but it will have to wait." The King stepped toward the balcony window. "I have an important task for you." He waved the craftsman forward.

Approaching cautiously, Daedalus asked, "What is all this for?"

"Have you heard of the legend of the Labyrinth?"

"An old wives' tale. Told to children to make them behave."

"It's as real as you or I. It was discovered deep in the mountains."

"What about the Minotaur?"

"Unfortunately, the half-man half-bull abomination is also real. I've sent legions of my men into the Labyrinth to kill the Titan, but no one has made it out alive."

"Is that why you captured all those creatures?"

"Rather them then my men. I planned to rid the world of those beast one day, I merely found a way to do it with a single sword thrust." King Minos opened the curtain to get a better look at the creatures. "I'm going to release those monsters into the Labyrinth. One of them is bound to kill or at least injure the Minotaur. They're my army," the King said with a smirk. He was clearly excited to reveal his scheme to the craftsman.

"Is that how you plan to save the world? By killing the Minotaur?"

"In one way, but Pandora's box also lies within the Minotaur's lair." King Minos stepped away and approached a map of Greece with battle plans drawn over it.

"Isn't the box dangerous?"

King Minos moved several of his soldier figurines to Athens, Sparta, and Crete. "Perhaps to a mere mortal like Pandora, but not for a King. I've seen visions, Daedalus. I am wielding that precious power of the gods. I plan to use this weapon to bring peace to all of Greece. I will fulfill my father's dream of uniting all the Greek nations under my rule."

"How do I fit into your plan?"

"The weapon isn't out in the open for any man to seize. It's hidden at the center of a Labyrinth, and I need the world's greatest mind to chart a course to it. I remember that you were quite the cartographer."

"I haven't charted a map in years."

"I have confidence in you," said the King, "But do not fail me, Daedalus."

Daedalus took several steps back. "What if I can't help you?"

King Minos took a long swig from his goblet and

then smirked. "I'll throw you in the Labyrinth with those ferocious beasts. See how you fare. Once you've all been destroyed, I'll find the next best mapmaker to chart the Labyrinth. It's only a matter of time before I hold the power of the gods."

Daedalus stared down at the floor.

"We're not at the gates of the Labyrinth yet, but I'm confident you'll find a way to the weapon once we arrive." King Minos looked at the head of his Royal Guard. "Take him back to his cell."

Two guards grabbed Daedalus by the arms and dragged him out.

The door was shut after they exited the room. "Time to address the cretins," the King said softly.

A creature that resembled an overgrown vulture with red and orange feathers, sat on a perch overlooking the terrace. The animal arched its neck as it observed the crowd for any threats to its master. It flapped its lengthy wings and screeched at the masses as if warning the citizens to settle down.

King Minos appeared from behind the red curtain riding his white stallion to the crowd's delight. He brushed his exotic bird's head as he rode out onto the large balcony. The King's armor made it difficult for him to get off his high horse, so several servants rushed in to assist him. He waved them off once he dismounted.

Lumbering to the edge of the balcony, he took a moment to catch his breath. Lifting his arms, the crowd fell silent. "Citizens of Thebes! Today is a monumental day. Greater than the time when I was first crowned your King. Soon, we will rid the world of all the monsters that have terrorized the good people of Thebes for generations."

The crowd erupted into exuberant cheers and applause. The creatures were riled up in their chains and cages. "I'm going to personally see to it that we trap all these beasts in the Labyrinth and let them destroy each other," King Minos declared, as he put a fist up in triumph. "By getting rid of all these vile creatures, prosperity will finally return to the City of Thebes. We will make our city as great as Mount Olympus." The crowd went into a frenzy. The King turned and walked back to his horse. With help from his servants, he got back on his stallion and rode the steed down the side steps to the courtyard. He met and shook hands with his generals.

From its perch, the exotic bird took to the sky. It circled over the King like a hawk protecting its young. The creature looked down and noticed several soldiers carrying a thin man to a carriage.

Brontes and Rhath watched Daedalus get tossed back into his box by the guards. Magus shut the door and locked him inside. "Looks like the King didn't pardon you, Craftsman," said Magus with a grin. The soldiers dispersed, and Daedalus was left to sit alone in his transport. Brontes sighed, feeling sorry for the human that was being treated as harshly as he had been. The convoy crept forward once again.

15

THE THEBANS ATTACK

The children arrived at the end of the forest on the outskirts of the city. At the lead, Harmony halted abruptly and raised a fist. The others froze as they watched her with anxious eyes. She looked toward the outer wall and was surprised to find the edge of town deserted.

"It's silent. Too silent," Harmony whispered. "Wait here." She sprang out of the trees and rolled forward. She crept on her hands and feet like a cat until she reached a passageway through the city's wall. Leaning against the archway within the shadows, she waved them forward.

Cy and Laelaps crawled out of the forest on their bellies. Icarus rolled his eyes and stepped out of the woods with Benu on his shoulder. "There's not a soul in sight," he said, annoyed, as he walked past them. Embarrassed, the others stood and walked to the tunnel.

"I'd rather be cautious than captured," Harmony warned.

"At this rate, we'll never catch them," retorted Icarus as he moved around her.

They made their way through an alleyway and followed the loud throng of cheers. Cy paused when he noticed a papyrus scroll on a wall with a crude image depicting a monster's face with an X over it. "What does it say?"

Icarus read what was written beneath the drawing out loud. "No more monsters." Harmony ripped it down and tossed it aside.

"We have to disguise you," she said to Cy. Harmony removed her hood and tossed it over the cyclops, revealing her warrior armor underneath. She wore a leather skirt, greaves, and a bronze breastplate. The boys gawked. "What?" she asked befuddled.

Both Icarus and Cy looked away. "Nothing," they said.

"Come on, we have work to do," she groaned. Cy pulled the cowl over his head as they ran toward the crowd.

Sprinting toward a jam-packed hilltop to get a better view of the acropolis, they noticed the caravan advancing out of the city's center. "There's my Papa," yelled Cy pointing at his giant father sprawled on the large cart.

Icarus and Harmony's eyes widened; they had never seen so many mythical creatures in one place. The line of transports and soldiers stretched through most of the city. *Why had they captured all these creatures? What purpose did his father serve in all this?* Icarus pondered.

"You didn't tell me there were other creatures that had been imprisoned," said Harmony.

"We didn't know," answered Icarus.

"We can approach the transport among the crowd. Come on, let's get a closer look," said Harmony. They carefully maneuvered their way down from the hilltop through the throng of citizens.

"How are we ever going to free our fathers with all of these people around?" muttered Icarus.

Achilles and Ajax stepped on the parchment Harmony crumpled as they sprinted through the alleyway. They saw the crowd of people ahead of them.

"Are you certain we're going the right way?" asked Achilles.

"Their tracks led to this passageway. They're in here somewhere," said Ajax.

"There are too many people. We'll cover more ground if we split up. Keep a lookout for three children and a dog." They rushed into the streets in separate directions.

The Teumessian fox yawned as he watched the crowds from a safe vantage point high on a windowsill. Its head turned, following the children as they maneuvered around people.

Behind Laelaps, the children made their way through a walkway. A baby being held by its mother noticed a brown cloak bobbing past and took hold of the garb. Amused, the infant pulled the hood off Cy's head and revealed the cyclops to everyone in the vicinity. The baby giggled while his mother screeched in horror. There was a loud gasp from the crowd as they all stepped away from the little creature. Cy didn't know what the humans were gawking at until he felt his exposed scalp and realized the cowl was no longer concealing his face.

"I-it's a c-cyclops!" yelled a terrified man within the crowd. There was silence as everyone stared at the one-eyed child in the middle of the expanding circle.

"He's small," stated another citizen. The crowd exhaled in relief and then began to laugh.

"Let's kill it!"

"Yes!" cried out the mob. The throng of citizens quickly armed themselves with the first item they found. Pitchforks, torches, and clubs came out of seemingly nowhere. Cy could feel his heart beating out of his chest. Icarus, Harmony, Laelaps, and Benu could only look on in dismay as the crowd closed in on their friend. The mob of ravenous citizens gradually advanced on the young cyclops. Cy's gaze shifted between the different faces of the enraged populace surrounding him.

Icarus closed his eyes and concentrated. He tried to force a plan out of his mind at will by whispering to himself, "What would father do? What would father do?"

Through some divine intervention, he heard Daedalus' voice in his ear. "You can do it, son." *Could it be,* he wondered, *was his father standing behind him?* Startled, he opened his eyes and turned his head. Benu met the boy's gaze. "Helping," said Benu. The bird flew off the boy's shoulder to safety.

Angered by the deception, Icarus prepared to curse at the bird when a thought came to him. Hearing his father's voice jolted his mind. "I have an idea!"

Like a child possessed, he ran to Harmony. "Quickly, you have to hit me," he urged. Without a second thought, Harmony pulled back her hand and slapped the boy across the face. He riled in pain as his hands covered his nose. Blood trickled out of his nostrils as his eyes watered. "Ow, I didn't even tell you what my plan was."

"There's a plan?" Harmony said with a confused look on her face.

"Forget it!" he moaned. He took the blood in his hand and spread it over his face.

Icarus forced his way to the center of the circle where Cy stood. The crowd's eyes darted between the cyclops and the boy. They gasped once they realized the lad had suffered a blow to the head.

The boy shrieked, "He's a killer!" Lurching forward for dramatic effect, Icarus collapsed onto Cy's arms. The boy rolled his eyes to the back of his head and stuck out his tongue with a final gasp.

In utter shock, the cyclops dropped his friend and threw his palms up in surrender. Harmony rushed in and screamed, "He killed my brother!" Trying to weep on command, Harmony only managed to contort her face, frightening the onlookers further. "He's dangerous," she shrieked to the crowd, and then whispered to Cy, "Aren't you?"

Cy noticed the murderous expressions on the faces of the Thebans transformed from executioners to terrified victims. The cyclops stepped forward and could hear the nervous inhalations of the spectators. Cy announced, "Stay back, or I'll eat you all!" He pounced and hissed like a cat. A burly man at the head of the mob fainted, which created mass panic as the citizens turned and ran for their lives.

Separately, Achilles and Ajax heard the wail of the crowd. They turned and saw people running away in the distance. "There he is!" yelled Achilles. They recognized the little monster terrorizing the citizens. They sprinted toward the cyclops but were shoved back by fleeing civilians.

Delighted in the odd turn of events, Cy got carried away and continued pursuing the frightened humans. Harmony held the head of her supposedly dead sibling when Laelaps rushed in to sniff the boy's forehead. Laughing, Icarus pleaded, "Get off me. I'm alive." He wiped the blood off his face with his tunic.

They quickly got to their feet, and Harmony called out, "Cy, get back here."

Cy skidded to a halt and ran back to his friends. An old man fleeing with a walking stick looked over his shoulder and noticed the cyclops running back to the children. Realizing the injured boy was now standing, the toothless elder spat, "They've played us false!"

The crowd halted and turned around. There was a stillness in the air as the mob considered the deception. Finally, someone yelled, "Get them!"

The children saw the horde of Thebans rushing back toward them and ran away swiftly. Achilles and Ajax now sprinted alongside the crowd and tried to maneuver themselves to the lead.

Icarus, Cy, Harmony, and Laelaps reached the stairs that led down the hill. Confused people lounging on steps saw the children rush past only to be engulfed by the angry mob that followed.

"We have to split apart if we want to lose them," called out Icarus. Houses lined the left side of the steps, so the boy climbed onto a roof. Several citizens broke off from the leading group to pursue him. Icarus sprinted and ran over several rooftops, while the others continued down the stairs.

"We'll draw more of them away from you. Just stay ahead of them, and Laelaps will reunite us," said Harmony. She whistled to the hound, and he led her down an alleyway. Half the remaining mob broke off and chased after her.

"But what if they capture me?" cried Cy as he tried to keep his balance. Reaching the street below, he tumbled forward headfirst and rolled under a passing cart. He crawled out the other end and scampered down the nearest corridor.

Achilles pointed in the direction of the young girl. "Meet me at the Temple of Apollo once you seize the girl."

Ajax nodded and pursued her down the same alleyway. The big brute maneuvered himself past most of the citizens and got to the head of the mob. The alley turned into a market street where foods, drinks, and goods were sold. The warrior was a stone's throw from the girl when she began tossing obstacles in their way. She threw harvest crates, barrels of wine, and tipped a cart of caged animals over, which freed dozens of exotic pets. The people chasing her tripped or slipped as they crashed into the obstructions. Ajax avoided the traps by jumping, ducking, or maneuvering around them. Before long, only he remained.

***

Icarus hurdled across roofs until he reached the edge of the last home. He turned around to find the citizens blocking every escape route. "We have you now," said a bearded man. Icarus pulled the cord that released the wings of his flying machine. The crowd halted and gawked at the fascinating contraption.

"Who are you?" said a woman at the front.

With the deepest voice he could muster, he announced, "I'm Icarus, son of Daedalus." He dove off the roof's edge and glided away. The crowd walked forward and watched the boy fly over the streets.

Looking back at the fascinated onlookers, Icarus turned a corner and disappeared from view. Having escaped, he cried out in excitement until he noticed a building fast approaching. His eyes widened as he tried to maneuver his wings to avoid the structure, but he smacked into a glass window like a sightless bird. With his arms and legs sprawled, Icarus slid off the glass and fell back onto the top of a merchant's tent below. He stared up at the sky in silent anguish until he let out a whimper.

***

Cy tried to lose the Thebans around several street corners, but they matched his pace stride for stride. Achilles muscled his way through the other runners and reached the front of the mob. He swiped at the young cyclops with the same fury the elder cyclops used during their battle. Cy avoided every attempt from the warrior to seize him.

The street began to narrow as the row of homes on each side became compacted. Searching frantically for an escape, Cy finally saw a slender passageway in the distance between two tall structures. His lungs were burning, but he urged his legs onward by sheer strength of will. Turning his body at the last moment, he dove into the opening and squeezed his small frame inside.

Achilles reached the passageway but was too muscular to fit. He turned his body and stuck an arm into the opening. Cy managed to wriggle beyond the warrior's outstretched hand and continued through the gap.

Realizing that the cyclops was escaping, Achilles turned in search of another path, but the mob converged at the entrance of the narrow passageway and prevented the young warrior from finding another route.

"Out of my way!" he yelled, but no one listened.

"Where is he?" asked one confused Theban, while another added, "Did we lose the cyclops?"

Cy managed to wriggle his way through the narrow passageway until he squeezed out to the empty street on the other end. Panting on the floor for several moments, he eventually staggered to his feet. The people started cursing and bickering at each other. They had no idea where the cyclops went. Cy put the hood back over his head and ran to escape the city.

*
**

Harmony and Laelaps sprinted until they reached a stone wall dead-end. They tried to run back, but Ajax blocked their retreat. "It's finished, you're coming with me," he snarled.

"It's only you?" she responded with surprise.

"You're going to tell me everything you know about the cyclops." Ajax paused and stared at girl, confused. "What are you doing?"

Harmony stretched her arms and legs as if she was getting ready for a fight. Cracking her neck and knuckles, she approached the brute.

"I don't have time for games, little girl."

"Don't call me little."

"Come with me peacefully, or suffer my wrath," he asserted, pointing a finger at her face. Ajax towered over Harmony, so like most of his opponents, he did not fear her.

Standing defiantly, she countered, "I choose wrath." Sitting far behind Harmony, Laelaps covered his eyes with one paw.

"I am one of the most skilled fighters in all of Greece, trained by the great Achilles. This is your final warning," he said with a scowl. She grabbed his finger and bent it until he fell to one knee, writhing in pain. With his free hand, he tried to pry her hand off his finger but could not. "Let me go," he cried out.

"Will you let us go in peace?"

"I cannot," he responded in agony. She put more pressure on his finger. He gritted his teeth. "I will. You have my word. Just let me go."

Harmony released him, and Ajax dropped to the

ground clutching his swollen red finger. She whistled to Laelaps, who bounded up beside her. As they walked away, the warrior lunged at her.

Harmony swiftly turned around and bowed beneath his powerful arms. She countered with a mighty fist to his gut, which lifted him off his feet. Bewildered, he staggered backward, holding onto his midsection in anguish. The wind was knocked out of his body. Ajax gasped for air and crumpled to the ground. Despite enduring rigorous training his entire life, the tall brute had never felt such pain. One thing was certain, he would never tell Achilles about how he was bested by a little girl in a fight.

"I detest dishonest soldiers," Harmony spat. Shaking his head, Laelaps gave the warrior one long disappointed look. The girl and her hound turned a corner and disappeared, while the humiliated warrior lied on the ground.

16

THE SEARCH FOR CY

Benu floated down and landed on Icarus' belly. Still asleep, the bird bounced up and down to wake the unconscious child. The boy's eyelids fluttered until he stared blankly at the white clouds and blue sky. "Am I dead?"

"Alive," said Benu, as he blocked the boy's view of the heavens. Icarus heard several barks and tried to peer over the side of the merchant's tent, but his aching body made it difficult to move. After retracting the wings, he found Laelaps and Harmony waiting below.

"Did you have a nice slumber?"

"Not nearly long enough." He collapsed back onto the canvas.

"We have to find Cy."

Icarus groaned as he slowly slid off the edge of the tent and down to the ground. Harmony paid the merchant underneath the canopy for some food to

130

replenish their supplies. She handed Icarus an apple and Laelaps some bread. After he was done eating, Icarus fed the apple core to Benu, who was perched on his pack. They followed Laelaps through the corridors in search of their missing friend.

Achilles arrived at the Temple of Apollo. The massive stone pillars that covered the side of the structure were a sight to behold. Ajax sat, waiting on the steps that led up to the shrine. The tall brute held on to his abdomen as he stood gingerly.

"What happened to you?" asked Achilles.

"I fell as I came within a step of seizing the girl," responded Ajax with a grimace. "How did you fare against the cyclops?"

"He got away," Achilles snapped. "The little beast proved cleverer than I anticipated. Come on, we know where they're heading. We just have to catch them before they reach convoy." They made their way down an empty street toward the road.

Cy emerged out of an alleyway on the outskirts of Thebes. He walked past the city's outer wall. Alone for the first time, he yearned to be back on his peaceful island. The cyclops never imagined the human world to be so perilous. He missed his father, but for the first time, he felt lost without his new friends.

Tired and hungry, he sat on a rock. Resting his elbows on his knees, he held his head in his hands and pondered. There was a puddle of water underneath his muddy feet. He leaned forward and looked down at his reflection. Studying his features, he wondered why humans feared and hated his kind. He lightly pinched his bulbous nose and then stroked the side of his face. *Is a cyclops all that different from a human?* he thought. *We both have arms, hands, and feet. Is it the size of my giant Papa they fear? If that is the reason, then why are they so afraid of me? We both have hair on the tops of our heads, ears, a nose, and a mouth.* He stuck his tongue out to his reflection and uttered, "Ahhh." *Is it my single eye that terrifies people?* Cy wondered.

He felt conflicted about humans; on one hand, the soldiers on the island and the citizens of the city were what his father warned him about. Yet, his friends' compassion convinced him that not all humans were full of hate. They could co-exist in peace if humans and cyclopes spoke to one another.

Cy lost his train of thought when he heard approaching footsteps coming from the same path he took. He ran and hid behind a lone tree in the distance and peeked around the corner. The trunk wasn't wide enough to conceal his frame, so he covered his eye, anticipating capture.

Laelaps walked out of the alley first, followed by Harmony, Benu, and Icarus. "Do you think he was captured?" asked Icarus.

The hound lifted his head and barked disagreeably before returning to sniff the dirt.

"Laelaps would have sensed other people. Cy came this way alone," said Harmony.

"How far do you think he went?" asked Icarus, concerned. Laelaps halted and pointed with his snout.

Cy stepped out from behind the tree and waved at his friends. "Over here," he said excitedly. Running toward each other, they embraced midway and held the cyclops as if he'd been missing for days.

"We were worried about you," said Harmony. They separated to get a better look at him.

"How did you escape?" asked Icarus.

"There was a small path only I could fit through," Cy said.

Icarus smiled and ruffled his friend's hair. "I'm glad you're safe."

Laelaps barked and pointed his snout to a small dirt road. "The transports are beyond the city," said Harmony, rubbing her dog's head.

"We need a new plan," said Icarus. "We were almost captured trying to catch up to the convoy." Icarus thought for a moment.

"What should we do?" asked Cy.

Harmony spoke up. "We have to get ahead of them and block their path. If we can stop them from advancing, then we'll have an opportunity to set your fathers free."

Stunned by the ease by which she realized her plan, Icarus reluctantly admitted, "She's right. But we'll never get ahead of them on foot."

Harmony looked at the farmlands beyond the city. "Come on, I have a plan." They followed her to a horse farm in the distance.

The caravan was beyond the city limits and back on the open road. The King sat on his throne atop a wagon being pulled by several white stallions. Servants fed him cheese and bread, while others filled his goblet with wine. The colorful bird swooped in and landed on a wooden perch behind his seat. The servants were anxious around the exotic creature, as it peered at them with an intense gaze. The King nourished his pet with grapes and then stroked its head. "There-there, they are only my loyal subjects. They pose no threat."

The six soldiers that were with Achilles in the woods arrived to speak to the King. One of the men stepped onto the wagon and bowed on one knee. "Your Majesty. I bring word from Achilles."

The King didn't break his focus from stroking the bird's head. "I've been told that you allowed a captured monster to escape. Is that true?"

"Yes, sir," the soldier confessed.

"Add that to the growing list of failures from this miserable army. It's no wonder why the Spartans laugh at us."

The man swallowed nervously. "There's more, sir."

The King narrowed his brow at the anxious soldier. "Where is Achilles? Why are you speaking in his stead? Is he ashamed to face his King?"

"There was another cyclops in the woods," interjected the soldier. "We believe he's trying to save the one we're transporting."

The King's expression shifted to one of concern. "Another one, you say. How big is it?"

"I didn't get a good look at it. It was the reason the Karkino got away."

The King envisioned this new cyclops to be twice the size of the one they captured. Far more hideous as well. His expression softened. "You're lucky to be alive. The gods reward the bravest among us, as I do."

"Thank you, sir. Achilles and Ajax are tracking the other cyclops as we speak. They're hoping to capture or kill it."

"That's brave of them, but I'm confident that Achilles will fail. I know what to do." The King scratched the neck of his exotic bird. "Find the cyclops and destroy it, my Phoenix." The bird took flight, and with a screech, burst into blue flames. Fire engulfed its body, and it grew three-fold in size, to the amazement of everyone but the King. Although it was now aflame, the creature kept its birdlike form with two piercing red eyes. With a powerful thunderclap, it shot straight up and flew back toward the city in search of the cyclops. A streak of gray and white smoke charted its path in the sky.

17

THE PHOENIX

Night had fallen, but the full moon's silvery light lit their path. The spring aromas were in the air as the year was in the midst of a seasonal transition. Harmony looked gallant while riding a full-grown black mare. Meanwhile, Icarus and Cy jostled on the back of a short, plump, chestnut coated horse with a lazy eye. Benu circled overhead, keeping a watchful eye on the children, while Laelaps led them through the narrow dirt road.

The trail was flanked by a peaceful landscape. On one side, there were stunning mountains in the distance, while the other held a crystal-clear lake. The fields of golden wheat on each side of the road promised a bountiful harvest that was undoubtedly blessed by the gods.

"I'm weary," said Cy as his head slumped to one side.

"We should make camp for the night,"

acknowledged Icarus.

"There's a full moon lighting our way. A gift from the gods, and you want to waste it because you're worn-out?" asked Harmony.

"Yes, of course," said Icarus.

"Absolutely," added Cy.

"The army has probably stopped for the night, which gives us a golden opportunity to get ahead of them."

"As long as nothing else goes wrong, we should reach them tomorrow by midday," said Icarus.

"We wouldn't have to push ourselves if I knew where they were going. Do you have any idea where the army might be heading?" asked Harmony.

"I haven't the slightest. I've been trying to unravel that mystery ever since we left the city," responded Icarus poignantly.

"I'm certain the King wants to force them to fight each other in a gladiatorial tournament," said Harmony.

"If that were true, why would they be led out of the city and away from the bloodthirsty spectators," countered Icarus, his forehead crinkled in concentration.

They rode past several rusted bronze helmets, broken spears, and a wheel-less chariot on the side of the road. *A remnant from a battle fought long ago*, thought Harmony. "What do you think happened here?" she asked.

"A clash must have taken place, but it is impossible to know the reason or who the victor was," said Icarus.

"Nor the conquered," expressed Harmony

glumly. For a moment, they silently wondered what happened on this land.

"Maybe the King wants to use the creatures for something that men can't do," said Cy, breaking the silence.

"But what could that be?" pondered Icarus.

"My wager is on a fighting tourney. Men can be cruel when filled with bloodlust," said Harmony, while riding past a corroded sword impaling a tree.

"I hope that isn't true," said Cy solemnly.

"Not all humans are vile," said Icarus, not fully believing his own words. They rode in silence some more. Only the sounds of the horses' labored breathing and crickets chirping were heard.

Harmony cleared her throat, cutting the awkward stillness. "We must free all those creatures, not just your parents."

"No, our task is to save our fathers, and that is all."

"I cannot allow the King to carry out whatever terrible scheme he has for the others."

"We cannot take responsibility for all those captives," argued Icarus.

"They're innocent. They don't deserve whatever this King has planned for them. They're prisoners, no different from your parents," said Harmony.

"What if they only want to get home to protect their young?" asked Cy sorrowfully.

"Then you should pray to the gods for their freedom. The others are not our responsibility. We need to stay focused on our objective," insisted Icarus.

"Who made you the leader of this group? I didn't pledge fealty to you," hissed Harmony.

Icarus' lips tightened as his blood began to boil. "I don't recall making you a vital member of this campaign. You came of your own free will. That means you can either help rescue our fathers with us or save all those creatures alone. There is no in-between."

"We can do both," pleaded Harmony.

"It's too dangerous," argued Icarus.

Harmony gripped the reins of her horse but held her tongue. Yet, Icarus continued unable to hold back. "And why do you get to ride the larger horse by yourself, while we get stuck with this wheezing pony that's ready to keel over?"

"I like our steed. I named him Pegasus," interjected Cy.

"I bought the horses with my last silver coins. That only afforded us one good horse. I had to bargain with the farmer just to gift us your steed. Otherwise, you'd still be on foot."

"A gift worthy of a beggar. Where did you get the drachma to purchase a steed in the first place? I don't know anyone with that kind of wealth," Icarus inquired with a raised brow.

"My family isn't special," Harmony retorted, timidly.

"There is something you aren't telling us, Harmony. I have never met a maiden willing to risk her life to go off on an adventure with people she scarcely even knows." Icarus and Harmony glared at each other intensely.

"I'm surprised you know any girls at all," snorted Harmony. Cy's stomach grumbled, breaking the tension.

"I get hungry when I'm nervous," said Cy anxiously.

"I'll unpack some food for you. I think we'll make camp now," said Icarus as he pulled the horse's reins.

"We still have a long journey ahead," said Harmony.

"We're weary and in need of rest."

"I'm trying to help you two, remember?" said Harmony irritated.

"Why did you even want to come on this quest?" asked Icarus.

"Because I want to be a hero," she snapped. "The kind people sing songs about," she added sincerely.

"What's that?" asked Cy with a perplexed expression.

"A hero is someone that saves lives," Harmony answered.

"No, not that. The flame in the sky descending our way."

The Phoenix dove in their direction and released a ball of fire from its gullet.

"Get down," cried out Harmony. They all covered their heads as the fireball hit the ground a short distance behind them. It erupted into a fiery blast that shook the earth. Clumps of dirt and sand rained down all around them, but they were unharmed. Harmony jerked at the horse's reins and shouted, "Follow me!" Her steed galloped forward with Laelaps running by its side.

Icarus pulled on the reins of his chubby pony and

attempted to keep up. "What is it?" Cy cried out.

"I don't know, but I don't want to find out," responded Icarus.

The Phoenix circled back around and swiftly gained ground on the two horses. Benu swooped in front of the creature, cutting off its flight path. Caught off guard, the firebird flapped its ignited wings and hovered in place. Benu flew around the beast, trying to confuse and distract it long enough for his friends to escape.

The Phoenix clapped its wings together, which created a deafening thunderclap. The ensuing shockwave struck Benu with the force of a charging bull, sending the parrot crashing down to the dirt below. The fiery creature moved past the bird's wilted body and continued its aggressive pursuit of the others.

The creature spat a second fireball in the direction of the chubby horse. Icarus did everything in his power to urge Pegasus to gallop faster, but the ball of flame reached the ground near their heels. The blast sent the steed and the two riders spinning into the air. The children came crashing down with a loud *thud* and rolled on the ground for several paces. The smoke from the explosion engulfed their motionless bodies.

Harmony heard the blast and felt the heated wind reach the back of her neck. She looked over her shoulder and realized her companions were no longer riding behind her. Pulling on the horse's reins, she rushed back for them. Harmony whistled to Laelaps, who circled around to meet her.

"Find them," she pleaded, as Laelaps dashed up the road. She urged the nervous horse forward as the cloud of ash engulfed them. The black smoke concealed her from the flaming bird soaring overhead. The horse neared the charred earth.

"Where are you?" Harmony asked in a whispered yell. She coughed when she heard the clip-clopping of the chubby horse running past. Pegasus swiftly vanished into the wheat fields beyond the road. She heard barking nearby and rushed toward the sound until she found Laelaps with the others. Icarus and Cy were covered in soot as they staggered off the ground. "Come on. We have to move," she said.

Icarus picked up Laelaps and slung him over his shoulder. Harmony extended her free hand and helped the boy climb onto the saddle. Once settled, Icarus lifted an anxious Cy onto the rear of the horse. Harmony whipped the reins, and the steed galloped out of the smoke. They dashed up the road holding each other tightly while frantically searching for the firebird in every direction.

The Phoenix swooped down and flew out of the smoke-filled road like a bat out of the Underworld. It screeched like an eagle as it gained ground on its prey. Harmony did whatever she could to hasten the steed, but with three riders and a hound on its back, the colt was weighed down.

"Where is it?" shouted Harmony. The swiftness of the steed jostled Cy on its rump until he was completely turned around and facing the horse's bouncing tail. Fast approaching, the Phoenix narrowed its blazing gaze at the cyclops.

Cy cried out, "I found it! It's almost upon us!" In

desperation, he reached into the supply pack harnessed to the horse's flank and seized some of the fruits and cheeses. Cy pelted the creature's face with food until the beast lost altitude and one of its wings clipped the dirt, forcing it into the ground.

The overgrown bird screeched furiously as it slid on the topsoil, tossing dust into the air. "Take that!" yelled Cy. The children cheered triumphantly as they dashed up the road. Icarus looked over his shoulder to observe the creature carefully.

The Phoenix fluttered like a wounded bird until it staggered onto its talons. The charred dirt smothered the fire on its belly and wings. A few glowing embers shone through the cracked grime on its underbody until it shook itself to remove the filth. Enraged, the beast reignited its feathers and shined brighter than Apollo's golden chariot. It flapped its burning wings, stirring dust until it reached the night's sky.

The boy saw it take flight once more. "Curse you."

"We only need to reach the forest," Harmony cried out. "Brace yourselves." The Phoenix spun mid-air and released several fireballs in every direction. Harmony saw the rain of fire coming down from above and maneuvered the steed past the flaming orbs and ensuing explosions. Before they could rejoice at surviving the attack, a massive blazing sphere traveled overhead and up the road.

Harmony yanked on the reins, halting the colt. The fiery orb touched down on the path ahead and detonated. It was powerful enough to lift the dirt like an ocean's wave with several ensuing ripples. The horse stood on its back legs and kicked its forelegs in terror. The children clung to each other and held on to the animal. It took all of Harmony's considerable might to regain control of the frightened horse. The children were fortunate to avoid the destructive power of the glowing sphere. As the smoked cleared, they saw the massive crater the explosion left behind, preventing their escape.

"My gods," uttered Harmony. Searching the landscape for an escape, she noticed a clay hut near the lake. Whipping the horse's reins, they rode toward the shelter.

They galloped past an old catapult near the abandoned home. *Another remnant from the battle fought long ago*, thought Icarus, as he scrutinized the device. Harmony halted the steed in front of the door. They dismounted and scampered toward the entrance of the refuge.

Harmony kicked open the door, and the others rushed inside. Cy inspected the interior of their shelter, and his mouth was left agape. "This can't protect us," he said shrilly. Harmony tried to draw the panicked horse inside by its reins, but the steed jerked its head free and trotted away. The Phoenix shrieked in the distance as Harmony slammed the broken wooden door shut.

The firebird landed outside the house with a loud *thump,* and gradually advanced on their rickety sanctuary. The old clay hut could withstand some of the beast's heat, but the children did not feel confident in their chances of survival. Cy, Harmony, and Laelaps all peeked through the various holes in the walls of the dilapidated dwelling. Icarus noticed the terrifying creature ignite small patches of grass beneath its talons. A strong gust of wind forced a whirl of fire embers off the Phoenix, but the cinders extinguished before they reached the ground. Icarus observed this trait and reasoned that whatever ignited the creature came from within its body. Any flame that separated from its core would die out shortly unless it was in the form of a flaming orb.

"He's going to burn this hut to the ground," said Harmony.

"Does anyone have a plan?" asked Cy.

They all turned to look at Icarus, who was nervously pacing back and forth, trying to think of ... "I have an idea, but you aren't going to like it," said Icarus. The others looked at him with concern. "We should pray to the Olympians before we begin."

Reaching the door, the Phoenix started heaving like a cat with a hairball stuck in its throat. It was gathering a fireball in its gullet. Cy squeezed his stout body through a narrow opening in the back and sprinted toward the lake. The firebird turned its head and swallowed the orb in its neck. It took to the sky once more and gave chase to the little cyclops. The entrance to the hut was cleared when the door opened. Harmony, Icarus, and Laelaps hurried outside and rushed to the old catapult.

Icarus rapidly assessed its capability. "Help me turn the handle to pull the arm down," he said. Harmony pulled on the circular wheel that turned the rope and lowered the catapult's arm. This would be a task designated to two strong infantrymen, but Harmony was capable of doing it alone. He stood in stunned silence as he tried to estimate her might.

A latch locked the catapult in place, and the *click* snapped Icarus out of his stupor. "It's catching up to him. You better work your scheme before it's too late," she urged. The boy quickly climbed to the bucket at the end of the arm. Harmony handed him her staff. "I pray you know what you're doing."

"Keep praying," said Icarus as he put the helmet on his head and goggles over his eyes. Icarus released his wings and readied himself for launch while clutching the staff in hand.

"May the gods protect you," she said nervously. He nodded, and Harmony pulled the lever that released the arm. Icarus was flung through the air like an arrow shot from a bow. Learning from his previous flights, the boy held onto the wings to steer his course and maneuvered himself toward the beast.

Cy reached the muddy shore of the lake and had nowhere else to run. "Why did I ever agree to this?" He turned around to stare at the flaming beast. The Phoenix opened its fiery talons to grasp him. Time slowed as Cy looked past the creature's head and saw Icarus emerge above it. Sensing that something was amiss, the Phoenix craned its neck around. Before the flaming bird could evade the attack, the soaring boy brought the staff down with all his might and clubbed the beast in-between its blazing white eyes. Like a candle reaching the melted wax, the blue flames from the firebird burned out. In an instant, the bird went from terrifying sky demon to plucked chicken.

Icarus and the bird became entangled mid-air and splashed into the lake. Cy stood on the edge of the lakeshore and desperately searched for his friend. The boy reappeared from beneath the water and inhaled deeply. The Phoenix splashed and flailed to keep its head above water.

Icarus sighed and reluctantly swam back toward the drowning creature. The Phoenix sank, and the boy held his breath to retrieve the submerged foe. They both resurfaced from the lake with the young lad dragging the charred bird by its scrawny neck onto shore. Cy took the staff from Icarus and knelt down beside his friend. The boy held his exhausted body up on all fours as Cy instinctively patted him on the back. Icarus spat out water but was seemingly unharmed.

Harmony and Laelaps rushed to meet them. She put a sturdy grip around the Phoenix's throat and asked, "Who sent you?" The once-mighty creature was now terrified. He couldn't speak in the human tongue, so it gestured a crown above its head with the ends of its blackened wings. "The King knows about us?" she pressed. The bird nodded nervously.

Benu chirped from the darkness as he struggled to flap his wings. They spotted him in the moon's light. His flight path was erratic before he collapsed into Icarus' arms. "Are you all right, Benu?" The parrot passed out in his hands with labored breaths. The Phoenix grinned sheepishly when it saw the injured gray parrot.

Harmony turned toward the creature with fury in her eyes. "Give the King a message for us. Tell him that we're coming to free all the creatures he imprisoned, and he may want to flee this land before I get my hands on him. Understood?" She applied more pressure on his neck, and the Phoenix squirmed but nodded. Harmony brought her forehead down on the creature's face and knocked it unconscious. She let his limp body collapse face-first into the mud.

18

ESCAPE BY TWILIGHT

The cyclopes wearily made their way through the caverns of their ancestral home. They felt the walls and held onto each other for guidance within the darkness. At the head of the small group, the young Brontes felt shame for fleeing the battle at the entrance of the cave, but he had never known fear until he saw hundreds of charging soldiers. Still, he knew leading the elders and children to safety was just as important as the clash between his clan and the human army.

Since he was old enough to walk, Brontes had explored the deepest recesses of his clan's cave. His mother would scold him for disappearing for a day, but his curiosity would now be their saving grace.

Brontes heard the crashing waves of the ocean and urged everyone forward. "We're almost there," he said. The clan saw the light at the end of the tunnel. They walked out onto the rocky shores into a bright and sunny day. The elder cyclopes basked in the warm glow of the Sun, while the children looked out to the seemingly endless blue sea. Seeing how peaceful the land felt, you would have never known that a battle was raging on the other side of the mountain.

"Stay here. I'm going back to help the others," Brontes said. Before anyone could oppose, Brontes sprinted back toward the back entrance when an arrow flew out of the dark tunnel and over his head. The young cyclops halted when several hoplites emerged from the shadows. With shields and spears at the ready, they let out a guttural grunt and prepared for combat.

The elders and children scattered in different directions, while a few juvenile cyclopes began throwing rocks at the soldiers. Brontes' mother took his arm and led him away. Although he wanted to fight, his mother urged him to lead the few remaining cyclopes away to safety.

They moved swiftly down the shores, as soldiers on horseback hunted them. Brontes noticed a large ship just offshore and made his way into the water. The sailors saw the horde of cyclopes approaching and dove into the water rather than risk being eaten. Only a few members of the clan made it onto the boat.

From the shore, the humans ceased their assault and allowed the cyclopes to commandeer the ship. The soldiers gave out an exuberant cheer as the horses neighed.

The cyclopes drifted away into the vast ocean. No one from the Cyclops Clan had ever been on a ship before, so no one knew how to steer ship in the open waters. They floated aimlessly for what seemed like an eternity, not knowing if they would ever see land again. Their hunger reached its peak when they finally spotted an island in the distance.

*
**

Brontes awoke abruptly in the middle of the night. He often dreamed of the attack he survived as a child. Pulling the chains on his wrists, it took him a moment to remember where he was. The giant peered around to gather what had transpired while he slept.

The caravan had halted for the night. Soldiers rested within their sturdy tents. Tall torches were planted on the sides of the road to keep the slumbering beasts visible within their cages. A sentinel marched past Brontes' carriage as the giant closed his eye and pretended to sleep. The guard walked past as the cyclops cautiously raised his eyelid. He looked to Daedalus' cage to find the man sleeping soundly. "Pssst...wake up," Brontes whispered, as he kept a lookout for patrolling soldiers.

Daedalus got up briefly and then laid back down.

"Wake up, human," growled Brontes quietly.

"I'm awake," Daedalus murmured. Groggily, he acknowledged Brontes with a languid wave. The craftsman stood, and then shuffled to the door. He blinked and squinted at the keyhole, which was scarcely visible in the darkness. The craftsman stroked his long white beard and pulled out two concealed metal picks.

During his reunion with King Minos, Daedalus noticed several pieces of jewelry strewn around on a table. As the craftsman was called forth to the window, he slid his hand over the King's jewels. While the servants stared at the floor, and the King was busy explaining his grand scheme, Daedalus broke off the metal clasps that held the gold bracelet in place. He concealed the metal pieces in his beard before anyone noticed. He thanked the gods and his unkempt beard for keeping the instruments in place as the Royal Guards tossed him back in his transport.

Daedalus stuck the metal pieces through the keyhole and picked at the lock. The craftsman had created puzzles that were far more complex, but the lock still proved challenging. The longer Daedalus struggled with the door, the more Brontes anxiously stirred in his chains. The giant kept a vigilant watch for any soldiers that could find the craftsman trying to escape.

"Hurry it up, human," whispered Brontes impatiently.

An eternity went by before Daedalus finally heard a clicking noise within the keyhole. He gradually pushed the wooden door open to diminish the screeching sound created by its rusted iron hinges. Exiting the cage, he tiptoed toward the cyclops.

"Help me first," Rhath muttered.

"I'm going to free him, and then come back for you."

"The giant will make too much noise once he's freed. I can protect the two of you after my collar is removed."

Hesitant, Daedalus looked to Brontes for guidance. The cyclops sighed but gave a subtle nod. Daedalus made his way to Rhath, who kneeled and lowered his head. Upon reaching the centaur, the craftsman began to pick the lock that secured the collar around his neck. After releasing the locking mechanism, they carefully removed the bronze restraint over Rhath's head. Without ringing the attached cowbell, they placed the contraption down on the ground without making a sound.

With his wrist still bound, Rhath stood and towered over Daedalus. "Thank you," the centaur whispered. The craftsman carefully made his way to Brontes' carriage once more. He worked on the cuff around the right wrist and unlocked it. The cyclops carefully wriggled his meaty hand out of the metal restraint, but it hit the wooden carriage with a loud *thump*. They frantically searched their surroundings to ensure that they didn't alert a soldier. Daedalus took a deep breath and then made his way to the other restraints.

A short distance up the dirt road, a man crawled out of his tent. Daedalus halted like a statue as the guard stumbled into the woods with drooping eyelids. He seemed to be sleepwalking, but then they heard a trickle of water coming from the trees.

Brontes and Daedalus heard rustling leaves coming from the opposite end of the road. They turned to Rhath, but he was nowhere to be found. The centaur disappeared into the forest and abandoned them. "You should run before the soldier returns," Brontes murmured somberly.

"I'm not leaving you behind," said Daedalus. "We're escaping together."

Surprised to finally meet a decent human, the cyclops pressed his lips together. "Stubborn fool. As you wish, get me out of here."

Daedalus unlocked the restraint on his left wrist, and then quickly made his way to the giant's feet. The cyclops sat up and tried to break the chains attached to the cuffs around his ankles. Brontes became red in the face as he used all his might, but it proved futile. As if Hephaestus, the god of blacksmiths, forged the metal links on Mount Olympus, the bulky shackles were unbreakable. "Let me pick the locks," urged Daedalus.

Brontes looked over his shoulder when he heard footfalls over dead leaves. The soldier reemerged from behind a tree and lumbered back to his tent. He collapsed into his wool blankets and nearly allowed a dream to take him when his tired eyes shot open. He tripped out of the tent and then followed the centaur's chain. Crawling on his hands and knees, he found the vacant bronze collar in the dirt.

"The centaur's escaped!" yelled the soldier. He rang the cowbell to alert everyone in the vicinity.

With torches and weapons in hand, several guards converged around the soldier holding the collar. They held torch flames to the dirt and noticed hoof tracks leading into the woods. The King lurched out of his carriage and marched to the gathering. The men stood upright with their weapons at their sides. "What is the meaning of this?" Minos demanded.

"A beast escaped, Your Majesty," said a nervous guard.

"Which one?"

"The centaur, sir."

"What in the Underworld is a centaur?"

"It's a creature with the upper body of a human and the lower half of a horse."

"That abomination exists?"

"Yes, My Liege. It's like a satyr, but instead of two goat legs, it has four horse legs."

"What's a satyr?" The soldiers stood around idly, unsure of what to say. "Well, it couldn't have gone far. Set up a perimeter and recapture the beast." The soldiers quickly dispersed.

A unit organized and followed the hoofprints into the woods. Magus stayed with the King to keep watch. A twig snapped, and the old guard spun on his heels. Gripping the shaft of his spear, he crouched between the transports and cautiously made his way to the source of the sound. Reaching the cyclops' large feet, he found Daedalus hiding beneath the cart. "Well, if it isn't the Craftsman."

Putting two fingers in his mouth, Magus whistled. "I found an escaped prisoner!" Magus planted the tip of his spear in the dirt and unsheathed his dagger. Soldiers arrived with their weapons drawn. The King made his way to the gathering.

Two soldiers dragged the craftsman out from the beneath the cart and held his arms. "Did you free the horseman?" the King questioned. Daedalus looked Minos in the eyes and nodded. "What else did you free?"

Brontes sat up and bellowed, "Me." From the cart, he lunged at the King, but Minos pushed Magus toward the overgrown hand and dove out of reach. The cyclops clutched Magus in his hands while the King crawled behind several Royal Guards. A dozen hoplites surrounded the carriage with a spear or bronze sword. Archers arrived and aimed their quivering arrows at the giant.

"Stay back, or I eat this soldier by the mouthful." Magus wailed in fear as Brontes snapped his crooked teeth near his head.

The panicked King hid behind his men until he realized that the giant was not attacking. Observing the cart closely, he noticed that the cyclops' ankles were still shackled. Minos confidently stood and stepped in front of his Royal Guards to address the giant directly. "If you eat him, then they'll be nothing to stop us from killing you."

"I don't want to die, My Liege! Mercy," pleaded Magus.

"Quiet, you coward," the King said scornfully. "It looks like we're in a bit of a stalemate," he told Brontes nonchalantly.

"You must be the King. You've already sentenced me to death, so why don't I take this soldier to meet Hades with me?"

"What about your companion?" Two soldiers dragged Daedalus by the arm to the foot of the carriage. One man unsheathed his dagger from its scabbard and held it near the craftsman's throat.

"That human? I would have eaten him once he freed me."

"Very well. I'm going to count to three, and if you do not release that soldier, then you can say goodbye to the man that tried to give you your freedom."

"He means nothing to me."

"One."

"I threatened him into doing it."

"Two."

"Told him that I'd eat his family if he didn't free me."

"Three."

The soldier pressed the blade to Daedalus' throat.

"Stop!" Brontes called out as he released the soldier from his grasp. Magus fell to the dirt and then crawled away with tears in his eyes.

"Now lie back down so we can restrain you," demanded the King. Brontes reluctantly did as he was commanded. The guards hastily put the cuffs back on his wrist.

"Forgive me," said Daedalus. Brontes did not acknowledge the craftsman.

King Minos scowled as he approached the craftsman. "Since you're so fond of these beasts, I guess we'll have to toss you into the Labyrinth with them," he told Daedalus. "Get him back to his cage," ordered the King. The soldiers confiscated the metal picks and dragged Daedalus back to his cell. They tossed him back inside the cage and locked the door. A sentry was stationed between the giant and craftsman to guard them both overnight.

"Do I have to do everything for you, useless soldiers? Find that horseman," the King commanded, as he stormed back to his tent. "Let me sleep for Zeus' sake."

19

A TALE BY FIRELIGHT

The warmth of a flaming torch awoke the Phoenix. He lifted his scrawny neck from the muck to find Achilles and Ajax holding torches. They hunkered down to examine the battered bird. "What happened to you?" asked Achilles. The creature staggered to its talons and then covered one eye with a wing.

"You were defeated by the little cyclops?" asked Ajax with a laugh. Achilles was as stone-faced as ever. Trying to justify its defeat, the embarrassed creature squawked hysterically.

Achilles did not care for the bird's explanation. "You were defeated by children and their dog. You are a disgrace to the King." The Phoenix put its head down in shame. "I need you to relay a message to the King. Tell him that you failed to capture the rogue cyclops, but we will have it in chains by the morrow. Understood?"

The Phoenix nodded. Achilles grabbed the bird

and flung it high into the night's sky. It frantically flapped its muddy wings until it flew.

"The soldiers must have reached the King and told him about the cyclops," said Ajax.

"The King of Kings has never been confident in my abilities. Let's accomplish our task and prove to him that a skilled warrior is worth ten times more than his pet," said Achilles sternly.

Ajax looked up at the cloudless night sky and noticed a sliver of smoke far off in the distance. "Look," he said, pointing with his torch. "The fools must have set up camp for the night."

Achilles turned and saw the trail of gray fumes wafting out of the forest. "If the gods are good, that's them," he said, grinning. They sprinted in the direction of the smoke.

Harmony set up a ground snare within the small clearing in the forest. She covered the trap on the ground with dead leaves to conceal it from any animal that approached in the middle of the night. She used a finger to strum the tight rope that went over the tree.

Harmony made her way back to the encampment where Icarus, Cy, Benu, and Laelaps were gathered around a wood fire. The crackle of the campfire created a tranquil mood. Benu rested in a bird's nest they built with twigs and leaves. Cy laid the back of his head on Laelaps' body, who was curled up fast asleep. Icarus tried desperately to fix his flying machine but could not straighten a twisted metal arm. The right-wing could no longer expand like it did before his mid-air collision.

Icarus pushed his contraption aside in frustration. "I can't fix it. I need my father's help." Silence hung in the air for a moment.

"Thank you for saving me, Icarus. I know your flying machine meant a lot to you," said Cy.

"It was my scheme that put you in peril. I'm just glad you're safe."

"I never thought your idea would work," admitted Harmony.

"Now you tell me," said Cy.

"I defeated the beast, and no one praises me," grumbled Icarus.

"We all played a part, but it was your idea," said Harmony with a closed-lip smile.

"This must be how all heroes feel, except instead of saving a damsel, I saved a cyclops," said Icarus with a smirk. "What about you, Harmony? Have we finally earned your trust? Are you going to tell us more about yourself?"

"Not much to tell."

"Where do you come from?" asked Icarus.

"I'm from a coastal village near the forest where you found Laelaps."

"What do you do there?" asked Cy.

"I help my father with his fishing nets before he sails out to sea, and then I train while he's gone."

"Train for what?" inquired Icarus.

Harmony sighed. "My father wanted me to be a delightful maiden, so he could arrange a marriage for me someday with some Greek champion." Harmony swayed her arms around like a prim and proper girl. "I don't want to marry a hero, I want to be a hero," she asserted. "Completing this quest will prove to everyone that I'm more than a dainty damsel that needs saving."

"I'm certain you'll earn his respect," said Cy. Laelaps' tail thumped on the dirt as he barked in agreement.

"You're the bravest damsel I know, even if you are moody," said Icarus.

"That's the kindest thing you've said to me during this entire expedition." The sap within the burning wood popped, distracting them momentarily.

"Can you tell us a tale?" Cy asked Harmony.

She nodded and then thought for a moment. "Have you heard the one about the goddess that fell in love with a mortal?"

"No, tell it," said Cy as he sat up to listen. Even Icarus leaned forward to pay close attention.

"No, maybe I shouldn't tell this one," said Harmony.

"Please," begged the two boys simultaneously, the word giving way to a toothy smile.

"By the gods," she said with an eye roll. "Fine." She crossed her legs and sat up. "I'll try to recall as much as I can. My father told me the tale when I was little." The boys listened attentively.

"Years ago, Aphrodite looked down from Mount Olympus as humans celebrated at the festival in her honor. Seeing so many people worshipping at her altars and temples pleased her greatly. That's when Ares approached her."

"The God of War, Ares?" asked Icarus.

"Yes, that God of War. Love was in the air, which Ares loathed. The remedy for war is love. People do not fight in battles when they feel affection for each other. Humans fall in love when Aphrodite is in a spirited mood, so Ares wanted to put an end to her bliss. He told her, 'The reason humans fall in love depends entirely on how beautiful they are. Hideous people will die alone despite your best efforts.' Aphrodite disagreed, of course."

Benu listened with the others from his nest.

"Ares goaded Aphrodite into a wager. She would have to transform into someone that didn't—look like she did," she said, struggling to find the words.

"She was going to look like a hideous person?" Icarus asked bluntly.

"Yes," Harmony reluctantly admitted. "To win the wager, Aphrodite would have to look like a mortal and have a man of Ares' choosing to fall in love with her before the next full moon. Ares chose a man named Calisto. The goddess couldn't use any of her divine powers, however. No love spells or promising the man riches. Under cover of darkness, the goddess flew down to the small village where Calisto lived. She transformed into a—a..."

"An ugly woman," interjected Icarus.

"Yes, thank you," she acknowledged. "Ares did not make it easy on the Goddess of Love. He chose the most handsome man in all of Greece. Maidens fainted at the mere sight of his beauty. But Aphrodite was confident in her abilities to charm any man even under

162

an unpleasant disguise."

"What did Aphrodite look like—in this hideous form?" inquired Icarus.

Harmony sighed, knowing this question would eventually be asked. "She transformed into a bucktoothed, pug-nosed, and scrawny woman in tattered rags. She even walked with a limp and had an annoyingly shrill voice. Aphrodite became the complete opposite of what she normally prided herself in."

"Was Aphrodite able to make Calisto fall in love with her?" asked Cy.

"Not quite. Leading up to the full moon, she tried every day, but he was too shallow. He couldn't love anyone as much as he loved himself, and that is why Ares chose him. Even if she had transformed into the most beautiful woman in the world, he wouldn't have noticed her. The God of War had tricked Aphrodite and won the wager."

"Wait, if Aphrodite lost the gamble, then how did she fall for a mortal?" wondered Icarus.

"There was a sweet young man named Eris who befriended the goddess during her time in the village. She told him that she was in love with Calisto, so he tried to help her court him. In the process, they became close friends and developed an affection for each other."

"Awwww," said Benu. Icarus and Cy smiled absentmindedly at the romance.

"They fell in love?" asked Cy.

"Yes, the only dilemma was that Aphrodite wasn't who she said she was and needed to confess to Eris," Harmony said. "She had never been so anxious to reveal to a human that she was a beautiful goddess. In the end, she couldn't and decided to stay in her hideous form to keep the secret. They were both happy, and a few months later, she was with child."

"They lived happily ever after?" asked Cy.

"Having a baby is different for a goddess than a mortal woman. Aphrodite hide her true form during childbirth, and Eris realized that she was a goddess."

"How did he respond?" wondered Icarus somberly.

"Not well. Eris felt that their entire union was a cruel jape from the gods meant to mock him. She wasn't the woman he fell in love with. Aphrodite eventually returned to Mount Olympus, where she had to endure Ares' ridicule," Harmony said somberly. The mood around the campfire shifted. The children stared down and avoided each other's glances.

"What about the baby?" asked Cy.

"Eris raised the child on his own, and the boy grew up to be a hero."

"What's his name?" asked Icarus.

"I don't know. My father never told me that part," she said. The boys groaned, displeased with the ending. "We should try to get some rest," said Harmony, as she kicked dirt on the fire until only bits of ember and smoke remained. "We have a long journey tomorrow."

The boys reluctantly laid down and closed their eyes for the night. Harmony kept her eyes open restlessly, unable to sleep. A dream eventually seized her, and they rested after their long, challenging day.

*
**

Icarus was flying higher than any god. His father appeared, gliding beside him with golden wings. They flew among the white clouds surrounding them as the sunshine warmed their backs. From this elevation, the boy could distinguish Apollo's golden chariot through the Sun's radiance. The distant world below was made of lush green meadows, clear lakes, and tall mountains with a layer of white snow on the summits.

"Don't fly too close to the Sun, Icarus. Our wings are made with wax," Daedalus yelled to his son, but the boy was too enamored with the majestic scenery to listen.

This must be what the gods see, thought Icarus. The boy kicked clouds as he somersaulted and flew higher. He noticed his winged shadow on top of the white puffy clouds he glided past. Spinning and yelling in excitement, he failed to realize his father wasn't soaring higher. Daedalus continued to shout warnings to his son from below, but Icarus was too distant to hear.

A strong gust of wind caused the boy to lose altitude. He regained control, but the joyous expression on his face changed to one of concern. The Sun's heat was blinding now, and he observed a bonding substance melting away from his wings. He touched the white goo and realized that it was melted wax. He plummeted through dark clouds.

His idyllic vista became shadowy and gloomy. Lightning slashed the heavens around him, and the pelting rain dissolved his wings further. He fell out of the sky. Down he went until his father swooped in and clutched his wrist. "Hold on to me," urged Daedalus.

Icarus desperately clung to his father's arm. The boy did as he was told, but the rain slicked their hands, and he began to slip away.

"I'm sorry, father," he cried. They lost hold, and the boy plunged once again. Daedalus did not surrender and pursued his son once more. They continued to miss each other's fingertips as the ground advanced on them quickly. Just as all seemed lost, they were able to grasp each other. Daedalus pulled them both up before they struck the ground.

Relieved, they smiled as they regained altitude and cleared the storm. They made it through the worst of their excursion when a bolt of lightning struck Daedalus' wings, and they both fell once more. There was no saving Icarus this time as he reached the earth.

Icarus awoke in a cold sweat after his nightmare. He inhaled shaky breaths and looked at his surroundings. It was still nightfall, and his friends were fast asleep. He felt thankful to be alive and glad that he had not awoken his companions. The boy settled his head back on top of his flying machine's pack. "It was only a dream," he murmured, as he tried to fall back to sleep. He couldn't help but wonder if his dream was a vision sent by the gods. It felt like a warning to keep his feet on the ground.

20

CAPTIVES

Achilles and Ajax lost sight of the sliver of smoke wafting out of the forest during the night. The fire was extinguished before they could reach its source, but the young warrior was confident that it was the children. After wandering in the dark woods blindly for some time, they decided to rest and continue searching in the morning.

Achilles had trained himself to wake at first light and sprang up just as the Sun crept over the horizon. He nudged Ajax with his foot, and the big brute yawned as he sat up. They resumed their search and plodded through the forest aimlessly. The morning glow shined through the leaves when they heard loud snoring in the distance. They followed the sound, which led them to the young sleeping cyclops and the others.

The children continued to slumber as the two warriors concealed themselves in the shadows of the trees. Achilles made several hand gestures to Ajax to coordinate their attack, but the large brute merely stared and scratched his head. Unable to comprehend what his commander was trying to communicate, Ajax shrugged his shoulders and put his palms up in confusion. Frustrated, Achilles signaled to remain in place by pointing down, and Ajax nodded assuredly.

Achilles crept to the other side of the clearing. He softly rolled, darted, and crawled to reach the opposite side of the encampment.

Sniffing the air, Laelaps awoke and sensed something amiss. He stood with raised hackles, ears lowered, and nose wrinkled. Growling at the trees, he was primed to attack. Achilles sprang out of the woods and into the clearing with his sword drawn. "Now," he yelled. Laelaps barked at the warrior but retreated backward.

Icarus, Cy, and Benu were startled when they saw the warrior brandishing his blade. The children got to their feet and stood back-to-back, panicking. "I said, now," repeated Achilles.

Ajax jumped out and drew his sword. "Now we have you," he said. Benu took to the sky and escaped. He hovered above the trees and looked down at the clearing.

Laelaps snapped at Achilles' hand, but Ajax grabbed the hound from the back of the neck, subduing him. The children tried to flee, but Achilles put Cy in a bear hug while tripping Icarus to the ground. The boy slid to a halt and let out a wheezing cough. Before Icarus could get to his feet, Achilles placed his sandaled foot on the boy's back and held him in place.

"Let me go!" shouted Icarus.

"You're in no position to bargain, boy," growled Achilles.

Benu fluttered frantically when he realized that someone was missing from the skirmish. "Harmony," he said, as he flew in search of the girl. He soared in several directions but could not find her. Finally, he saw someone on a hilltop in the distance.

For years, Harmony had gotten up at the break of dawn to train in the woods. No military would accept a girl into their ranks, nor would a hero teach her, so she had to learn how to be a skilled warrior on her own. Knowing that her considerable strength was not enough, she'd sneak away and practice defensive and offensive attacks.

Harmony held her staff in a defensive position as she circled around an unseen opponent. An acorn fell from above, and she attacked the oak tree in front of her. With several precise strikes from her pole, she jabbed and swung at the sides of the oak as if it were a multi-armed beast. She was about to give the killing blow when Benu flapped into view. She pulled back before striking the panicked parrot, but the fright still dropped the bird to the ground.

"Benu, what are you doing?"

Turning over to regain his footing, the bird squawked, "Soldiers." Without hesitating, Harmony sprinted down the hill.

*
**

Icarus and Cy were sitting back to back and tied together with a rope. Laelaps' legs were bound together, but he continued to bark. "Would you shut it up?" said Achilles.

Ajax bound the hound's muzzle with a leather strap. Unable to bark, Laelaps growled at their captors.

"You two gave us more trouble than I would like to admit, but it was all in good fun," said Achilles. He kneeled before Icarus and asked, "Who are you?"

"I am no one," responded the boy.

Achilles unsheathed a blade holstered to his ankle and brandished it near Icarus' face. "What's your name?"

The boy's eyes were focused on the gleaming light reflected off the dagger's sharp edge. He swallowed nervously and said, "I am Icarus, from Athens."

"Why are you aiding this little cyclops?" asked Achilles as he pointed the blade at Cy.

Icarus looked to his friend, who was staring down at the ground hopelessly. "He's my companion," said the boy.

Achilles got to his feet and chuckled. Ajax stepped forward and asked, "You're a friend to a beast that can eat you? Why not befriend a lion instead?" The tall warrior laughed, while Icarus scowled at him.

Achilles kneeled before the docile cyclops. "What is the giant to you?"

Cy slowly raised his head and said, "He's my Papa."

"Are there more of you?"

"I've never seen another," Cy responded glumly.

Achilles considered and said, "I plan to reunite you two, but I have no use for the boy or the hound."

"Wait, where's the girl?" asked Ajax.

Achilles stood and turned to face his companion.

"What girl?"

Ajax's gaze shifted nervously. "The one that was with them in the city."

"You mean the one you lost?"

Ajax's massive shoulders slumped. "Yes, that one."

Achilles turned to the children. "Where's the girl?"

In an instant, Achilles heard the swift slash of the wind and the loud *thwack* of a strike. They turned to Ajax, who stood motionless before he fell forward stiffly. He hit the ground with a loud *thud* and did not move as the dust wafted around his body.

Achilles drew his long sword and stood in a defensive stance. He made his way to his companion and nudged the tall brute with his foot. Ajax's eyes were closed, but he took in steady breaths. The sound of rustling leaves turned the young warrior on his heels, but he did not see a foe.

"Who's out there? Show yourself you coward," urged Achilles.

"Leave us," bellowed an ominous voice from above. Achilles looked up, searching for the attacker but only saw a gray and white bird fly overhead.

The young warrior searched anxiously but did not see the young girl sneaking up behind him. The children sat in silence as Harmony neared Achilles. She gripped her staff and prepared to strike.

From the corner of his eye, Achilles noticed the children's eyes following someone approaching his backside. Swiftly, he placed his sword behind his head and blocked the swing of a weapon. The young warrior deflected the staff and spun around to face the assailant. Harmony staggered backward but quickly regained her footing.

"You have a mighty swing for a little girl," said Achilles, advancing on her with his sword. She stepped back carefully but held a defensive stance.

Noticing his search for an opening, she jabbed at him with the end of her staff to keep him at bay. He repelled each thrust with the flick of his sword and continued to bide his time. She swung at his legs, torso, and head. Still, he dodged the attacks effortlessly. "You're more powerful than you appear, but you're raw and untrained," he said.

Harmony lunged at Achilles, but he spun and smacked the back of her head with the flat side of his sword. "Ow," she roiled.

"I admire your bravery, but a skilled warrior with steel will always win the day. Now yield."

Harmony stood defiantly, "Never." She took a big step back over a small mound of leaves.

"Then I will have to make you surrender, little girl," he growled. He rushed with his sword in hand and stepped on the dead leaves. A twig snapped beneath his foot, which caused him to pause. In his haste to attack, the young warrior triggered the ground snare. A heavy boulder nestled in a tree limb fell. The rope bound his ankle and pulled him off his feet. His face smacked the dirt before he was lifted off the ground and dangled between a sturdy tree limb and the soil.

Harmony reacted swiftly and smacked the sword

from Achilles' fingers before he could attempt to cut the rope. Disarmed, he grimaced and clutched his pained hand. He did not see the following strike, and everything went black as a moonless night.

*
**

Achilles awoke in a daze hanging upside down. There was no telling how much time had passed, but he found Ajax hanging upside down before him with his arms bound behind his head. The young warrior tried to move his arms, but his wrists were restrained behind his back with leather bindings. Their cache of weapons lay far out of reach. Several daggers, two long swords, a bow, arrows, and a grinded ax littered the above-ground roots of the distant tree.

"Where are they taking the creatures?" asked Harmony sternly.

Achilles smirked and said, "I'll never talk."

Ajax's eyelids fluttered open as he shook his head. "Where am I? What's going on?" he asked in a panic.

"We've been taken captive, now keep your mouth shut," ordered Achilles.

"I look forward to breaking your will," said Harmony, as she cracked her knuckles. She presented a small piece of wood to Ajax. "You may want to bite down on this." Ajax stared at his commander with wide eyes.

"We've been trained to withstand tortures beyond anything you can imagine. Do your worst," urged Achilles. Ajax took the piece of wood in his mouth and bit down.

"Are you sure you want to do this?" asked Icarus,

timidly.

"I see no other option," responded Harmony.

"I'm going to be sick," said Cy, taking in hurried breaths.

Benu stood on the boy's shoulder and shook his head in protest. "I thought you wanted to be a hero," said Icarus.

"Do you want to save your loved ones or not?" retorted Harmony with contempt. Icarus, Cy, and Benu looked away, defeated. Laelaps covered his eyes with a paw. She narrowed her eyes at Ajax. "This is your last chance to tell me what I want to know." He shook his head.

"Stay strong, brother. The gods honor the bravest warriors in the afterlife," vowed Achilles.

Harmony rolled her eyes and crept behind Ajax. "I didn't want it to come to this." Ajax squealed nervously, as she reached between his armor and started to ferociously tickle his sides. He tried to hold his breath, but within a few moments, he began to laugh hysterically. The tall brute swung away and wriggled upside down, but there was no escaping Harmony's fingers. "This pains me more than you," she said with an evil smirk.

With tears rolling up his overturned face, he spat out the piece of wood and cackled. He cried out, "I'll speak the truth. Just stop. Please."

"Swear to the gods," she said.

"By the gods, I swear!" Ajax shouted. Harmony stopped tormenting the unfortunate warrior.

"You couldn't last longer?" asked Achilles

disappointedly.

"You know the gods cursed me with this one weakness. You would have talked too if she merely touched your heel," Ajax said. Achilles glowered at the big brute, who promptly looked away. The young warrior would never admit it, but the gods had cursed him with weak ankles.

Harmony plucked a feather from Benu's body. The bird squawked and then nuzzled the pained area with his beak. She brushed Ajax's neck with the long feather for good measure, which caused him to giggle. "Tell us what we want to know!" she whispered.

The sweat dripped off his forehead as he focused on the plume. "The King ordered us to capture all the monsters in Greece and take them to the Labyrinth," he said, panic-stricken.

Cy stepped forward and asked, "Why would he want that?"

"The Minotaur guards the maze. He's a beast so powerful that no human army can defeat it. We know because it has been attempted by countless armies. Any human that enters the creature's lair is never seen again."

"Don't say another word, Ajax," Achilles warned. Harmony walked up to Achilles and put his helm on backward. The young warrior kept complaining, but his words were muffled.

"Continue," urged Harmony.

Ajax resumed. "The King believes that an army of monsters can destroy the Minotaur. If we throw all those beasts into the Labyrinth, something is bound to kill or injure it."

"Why does the King want to slay the Minotaur?" asked Harmony.

"Legends foretell of a weapon at the heart of the maze so powerful that whoever wields it would have the power of a god. Some believe that the weapon turns you into a god. Zeus used the weapon to defeat his father but could not destroy it after he became the King of the Olympians. Rather than let it fall into the hands of someone that could challenge him ..."

"He placed it in the Labyrinth and tasked the most powerful Titan in the universe with guarding it," Harmony interjected. The others turned to stare at her. Solemnly, Harmony continued. "My father told me stories of the Minotaur to force me to behave. I was terrified of the monster." She stepped away, while the others turned back to Ajax.

"Whatever it's guarding, the King wants to use it to conquer all of Greece and possibly the world," said Ajax.

"What's this weapon called?" asked Icarus.

A strong gust of wind blew through the encampment like an eerie forewarning. "Pandora's box," said Ajax. Harmony shuddered in the distance.

"What's Pandora's box?" asked Cy curiously.

"It's god-like power that anyone can wield if you possess it," said Ajax.

"If the King only needed monsters to fight the Minotaur, then why did he take my father?" questioned Icarus.

"Who's your father?" asked Ajax.

"Daedalus, the greatest craftsman in all of

Greece."

"Our last cartographer attempted to chart the maze, but he was lost when the Minotaur attacked. I've heard your father is also a skilled mapmaker."

Icarus knew the dangers of notoriety all too well. His father was a talented cartographer, but he had no cause to go into the Labyrinth, considering the risks. He would only do it if forced with the edge of a sword. If he had not flown away during the Royal Guard's arrival, then he would have been forced into the Labyrinth along with his father.

Harmony put a comforting hand on Icarus' shoulder. "Don't worry, we'll free the prisoners before they're forced into the maze." He looked at her solemnly yet showed the trace of a smile.

Achilles was finally able to shake the helmet off his head. "You'll never stop the convoy. Even if you blocked the road, you'd only be delaying the inevitable. Those monsters are going into the Labyrinth no matter what you do."

Icarus looked at Achilles and pondered for a moment. The mechanisms were turning in his head as he considered a solution. "Perhaps we don't need to stop the transports."

"What do you mean?" asked Cy.

"We enter the Labyrinth ourselves and find Pandora's box. That way, we can trade it to the King in exchange for everyone's freedom. We can free all the captives peacefully." Harmony was surprised and relieved to find that Icarus wanted to save all the creatures, but she was uncertain of his plan.

Achilles laughed. "Armies of skilled warriors have tried to slay the Minotaur and perished. That monster defeated them like it was child's play. What makes you think that you children will fare any better? You'll just get yourselves killed."

"I don't plan to fight the Minotaur. I want to hide, sneak past it, and steal the weapon before it even realizes that we've entered its lair."

"That's a bold scheme," admitted Ajax.

"Silence, fool," barked Achilles. The warrior narrowed his eyes at the boy, but his lips gradually curled up into a sneer. "I don't have to worry about you getting past the beast because you don't even know where the Labyrinth is located."

"Oh, but we do. We found your map," said Harmony, as she waved the folded parchment in front of his upturned face.

"Give that back," he snarled. Harmony and the others stepped away from the two hanging warriors. "Heed my words, you'll never make it out of there alive," admonished Achilles. His words fell on deaf ears as the children packed their equipment and prepared for the long journey ahead.

"You want us to go into the Labyrinth?" asked Cy.

"I think it's the only way to save our fathers from having to battle the Minotaur. We can do it," said Icarus confidently. He stretched out an arm and put his hand between them. Harmony grinned and placed her hand on top of his.

Benu whistled and swayed back and forth atop

Icarus' shoulder. Laelaps stood on his back legs and placed a paw on Harmony's hand. They turned to stare at the cyclops.

Cy's chin slumped to his chest. He looked down at his shuffling feet. "I'm not a giant like my father, nor clever like you, Icarus, and I'm not strong like you are, Harmony." The others stared at the cyclops thoughtfully. "But I have all of you as my friends. As long as we stick together, I know we'll be triumphant." Cy walked up to them and put his hand over everyone else's. They tossed their arms down with enthusiasm.

"You won't last long in the Labyrinth," said Achilles. "The beast will eat you alive." The children made their way to the edge of the clearing.

"Wait, you can't just leave us hanging here," said Ajax anxiously.

"We'll free you on our way home," responded Icarus.

"That means, you should pray to the gods that we succeed," said Harmony with a malevolent smirk. Harmony slung Achilles' leather quiver full of arrows over her shoulder and took his elegant oak bow.

Achilles and Ajax attempted to break their restraints, while the children disappeared into the forest. "Get back here!" Achilles bellowed.

21

JOURNEY TO THE LABYRINTH

The Sun beamed directly overhead when Laelaps and the children exited the forest. They reached a river near the base of a mountain and looked for a way to cross. Icarus refilled his canteen with water and was lost in thought, reflecting on their new plan.

"Are you sure you want to do this?" Harmony asked as she approached the riverbank.

The boy looked over his shoulder and met her gaze. "I don't know how else we can stop an army that size."

She dipped her hands in the water to cleanse them. "Even if the gods protect us, and we somehow get past the Minotaur, taking Pandora's box and handing it to the King is dangerous."

"I've thought about a thousand different ways to free the prisoners, but Minos will never stop capturing mythical creatures. He'll force them into the Labyrinth until he gets what he wants," said Icarus.

"How can you be so certain of this King's determination?" asked Harmony.

"He imprisoned my father and me in a tower for most of my life. All that I know of the world, I learned from my father. If he's capable of imprisoning innocent people, you think he cares about all the creatures he's captured?" asked Icarus solemnly. "My father and I will never be free, nor will Cy and his father be safe, even on their island. We need to bargain."

Harmony didn't want to admit it, but she knew Icarus was right. "You actually think that if we give the most powerful weapon over to a tyrant that he'll just allow us to go home? Forget about the Minotaur, the King would be unstoppable."

"I'll think of something before we get to that point," he said with concern. "You have to trust me."

She sighed heavily. "I pray you do, or the world could be put in peril. Heroes save the world; they do not help destroy it."

The boy turned away to look at the water, and then came back to her. "The story you told us last night, was that you? Are you the child of Aphrodite?"

Caught off guard, Harmony opened her mouth but struggled to find the words. Eventually, she spoke. "My father was a fisherman that prayed to Poseidon to keep him safe during his long voyages. For years, the god of the sea protected him, until one day, a powerful storm appeared out of nowhere. Even after the rainstorm moved beyond the sea, the fishermen that were out on the waters never returned to shore. Days went by until I finally presented Laelaps with my father's scent, but he could not see him. The world's greatest tracker shook his head." A tear rolled down her cheek, which she quickly wiped away.

"I'm truly sorry," said Icarus sincerely.

Harmony took a deep breath and continued, "I've prayed to my mothe..." She held her tongue before continuing, "I mean, I prayed to Aphrodite and the other gods to bring my father home, but they do not answer me. In all the tales my father told, the gods only spoke to heroes. That is why I am on this quest." She regained her composure and stood on the riverbank.

"You hope that the gods can bring your father back from the sea?" asked the boy. Icarus stared at her in stunned silence, truly seeing her for the first time. He knew all too well the heartache of losing a parent.

"I only wish to learn of my father's fate," said Harmony. A sorrowful silence seemed to spread over the land.

Suddenly, Cy sprinted out of the trees and jumped into the river with his knees tucked to his chest. The ensuing splash rained droplets on Icarus and Harmony, breaking the stillness between them. Cy came up for air and laughed as the water shimmered. Icarus and Harmony observed the cyclops curiously, as he swam in the river like a careless child. "I was thirsty," he said, smiling. They grinned, welcoming the much-needed distraction.

Downstream, Laelaps stood over the water like a statue, waiting for a fish to swim between his legs. Plunging his head into the water with his mouth open, he caught several wriggling fish in his jaws and tossed them onto the shore.

Icarus and Cy were amazed by the hound's patience in the river. Harmony knew of Laelaps' fishing talent because he was taught the skill by her father. She kneeled to collect the floundering fishes and added them to their provisions.

The children secured the remaining leather pouches and supply packs. Laelaps swam through the water until he splashed out on the other side of the riverbank. The children used wet rocks jutting out of the stream to cross, but Cy slipped and fell into the stream midway to Icarus' delight. The cyclops was forced to swim the rest of the way.

Once on the other side, Harmony unfurled the map and studied it. Cy and Icarus looked over her shoulder and followed her finger chart a course through the mountains drawn on the parchment. "According to the map, the fastest route to the Labyrinth is also the most treacherous," said Harmony.

"Do you believe we'll reach the maze before the transports?" asked Icarus.

"Their host should be taking the wider road around these hills. Cutting through the highlands will give us at least half a day's lead on the army," answered Harmony. She secured the map in her pouch and led them through the trail between the foothills. Laelaps sniffed the ground up the rugged path, while they followed closely behind.

Achilles and Ajax continued hanging upside down in

their restraints. Achilles grunted as he attempted to tear the ropes with brute strength, but the effort proved futile. Ajax swung his body around to try and break the tree limb, but he only managed to make himself feel nauseous.

"Would you stop that," said Achilles.

Ajax looked up at him. "You think they'll come back for us?"

Achilles' face hardened. "Of course not. They're going to be eaten by the Minotaur. We have to find a way out of this clearing before a pack of wolves ..." As he uttered those words, his line was cut. He fell straight down and landed on the top of his head. Groaning, the young warrior cracked his neck to alleviate the pain. Aside from a few minor scrapes, Achilles recovered quickly. Rolling to a dagger left at the foot of the tree, he managed to grasp a blade in hand and cut his ropes.

"How did you do that?" asked Ajax.

"I didn't do anything."

Achilles looked up as he slashed the last rope around his ankles and saw a fox on top of a tree branch chewing through Ajax's line. Achilles' eyes squeezed shut as the tall brute fell down headfirst. They both looked up and saw the mischievous Teumessian fox climb several tree limbs until it disappeared among the leaves.

"What in the Underworld was that?" asked Ajax as he gingerly rolled onto his back.

Achilles reached his companion and cut him free. "Never mind the fox. I need you to find the King and send word of what's happened," Achilles ordered sternly.

"I'm going after the children."

They collected their supplies and weapons. "Can they actually steal Pandora's box?" asked Ajax.

"I can't take the risk. If the weapon is as powerful as the legends say, then they may not want to trade Pandora's box once they've secured it. We can't let the weapon fall into the hands of children."

Ajax understood the severity of the situation and nodded. They grasped each other's wrist respectfully and shook. "May the gods protect you on your journey," said Achilles.

"And you, Achilles," said Ajax, "The gods are on our side." Once they let go of each other, they dashed away in opposite directions.

*
**

The army trudged up the main road through the mountains. The horses were exhausted, but the men whipped them onward. The path became test of will as the soldiers were forced to push transports up sloping hills.

Brontes cackled at the men forced to shove his massive wagon up a ridge. "Put your backs into it. I'll have died of old age before we get to where we're heading." The cyclops hollered with a gruff cackle. "This would go a lot easier if you unlock my chains and allow me to help." It had been ages since he laughed and enjoyed himself. Every step they took toward the Labyrinth was a step closer to his death, so the giant relished mocking and annoying his would-be executioners.

Daedalus was a lot more subdued after their failed

escape attempt. He sat solemnly at the center of his box, unsure of what his fate would entail. He was convinced that he did not have a lot of time left before he met his demise. *At least I will be reunited with my beloved wife and possibly my son*, he thought. With the countless wars being waged, most men did not live as long as he had. He would have felt comforted in the face of doom if he knew Icarus had survived. All he wanted to know was if his son was still alive. He'd give anything just to set his eyes on his boy one last time.

"Human, take a look at these cretins," said Brontes. Daedalus approached his bared window and looked at the miserable soldiers. The restraints prevented the cyclops from moving his hands too far, but that didn't stop him from jerking his arms up as if he were going attack. The men recoiled in terror and the transport rolled back several paces. The soldiers got a hold of it and dug their heels in the dirt to keep it in place. Several guards ran in to assist until they were finally able to drive it forward.

It took a moment, but Daedalus felt the tug of a smile on the corners of his lips. He welcomed the humorous distraction, as he found Brontes' hooting to be infectious. They both snickered at their wretched jailers.

"Hurry it up, men, we don't have all day," Daedalus said with a titter.

"Good one, human," Brontes howled. "The old man is going to die of sheer boredom." His guffaw was deafening. Their goading echoed throughout the mountains.

The caravan eventually made it over the last tall

hill, and the soldiers rejoiced as they reached a flat surface. Some mocked the giant after they triumphed over the steep slopes and his taunts. Brontes glowered in silence as the guards left his transport and returned to their stations. The cyclops shifted his body uncomfortably on top of the cart. The tedium of the journey settled over the convoy once again.

Daedalus shifted his gaze but noticed there were no sentries in sight. "Why did you save me?" he asked Brontes.

"I could no longer escape. There wasn't much else I could do," replied the cyclops.

"You still didn't have to save me."

"You tried to free me when you could have walked away like the centaur. I owed you a debt for trying to save me."

"For a terrifying giant cyclops, you are honorable."

"For an old smelly human, you are not so terrible."

They both smirked until Daedalus considered the giant's words. "I smell?"

22

THE PROPHECY AND LEGEND

King Minos sat on his bronze throne, irritated with his army for failing to make significant strides over the rocky terrain. Something that conquerors rarely divulged was how tedious it was to build an empire. The dullness of traveling the countryside with a vast host was unbearable to someone that was accustomed to getting anything he wanted. Several days had blended together as they plodded through the windy mountain pass. All he could do was sit and rest his head on the palm of his hand. He fell asleep and had the same dream he had every night for many moons. The one that inspired him to carry out this ambitious campaign.

King Minos wandered through a flowing wheat field in the farmlands outside of his city. The Sun shone brightly, but there was a violent thunderstorm cascading over the distant mountains. He looked over his shoulder, and the harvest began to die. The fields became drought-stricken before his very eyes. A black scourge spread over the wheat, killing everything it touched. Rather than be a victim of this plague, the King sprinted toward a clearing ahead.

The disease was like a dark shadow reaching for Minos. The man wailed and called for help as he stumbled out of the dead field. Looking back, the King noticed that the infection could not enter into the clearing. Breathing heavily, the fresh air caressed his face as he stood on a lush green meadow. "Minos," said a voice in the wind.

"Who's there?" he asked. Searching desperately for the speaker, he noticed a beautiful chest on top of a tree stump. He was drawn to the box, but he dared not reach for it. The voice murmured, "Take the box."

"Show yourself," he responded hastily. Filled with terror, a blinding light shone between the lids and base of the chest. Minos shielded his eyes with his hands. The chest shook the ground violently while the sound of thunder came from within. Anticipating destruction, the King shut his eyes and covered his ears. The noise reached a fever pitch before it began to fade away until there was nothing but silence.

King Minos opened his eyes slowly until he noticed a shadowy hand pressing down on the lid of the chest. The figure was cloaked in black garb. The Sun cast the creature's face in shadow beneath the cowl over its head. The tall figure floated next to the tree stump. Minos looked down and noticed that there was a dark mist where the creature's feet should have been. "Do not be afraid," whispered the being.

The ghostly figure waved its murky hand, and the chest levitated. The box hovered and spun mid-air above the being's ethereal fingertips.

"What is it?" asked the King, his voice cracking.

"It is Pandora's box."

Minos swallowed nervously and asked timidly, "Who are you?"

The spirit removed its hood and revealed his face to his son. King Lycaster's pale face had not changed since the day he was laid to rest. Minos looked into his father's blackened eyes and began to weep. The dark mist below the former King's cloak solidified, and his gray feet appeared. Floating down, he landed and stepped toward his son.

"Father," King Minos whimpered, retreating. "It wasn't my idea to poison you. It was Daedalus' that wanted you dead to take the throne. I told you he was not to be trusted."

"Silence!" said Lycaster. "Stop groveling like a child. I taught you better than that." King Minos sniffled and wiped the tears away.

Suddenly, the ground shifted beneath the King's feet, and they were transported to a double door entrance at the base of a volcano. The smoke billowed from the crest at its peak. The shadowy figure waved its smoky fingers, and the doorway opened ominously. King Minos stepped back, afraid of what was within the dark tunnel.

"Does it lead to the Underworld," asked the King quivering. "Am I dead?"

"No, the gods have plans for you," said Lycaster. He stood in front of the entrance of the underground tunnel with the box floating above his hand. "This is the Labyrinth," he said. He waved his hand, and the chest soared deep into the darkness of the tunnel. "If you wish to rule over gods and men, you must wield Pandora's box. Your divine blood allows you to possess such power."

"Rule over gods and men?" King Minos murmured. A roar from deep within the subterranean passageway frightened Minos. "What was that?"

"It's the only obstacle standing in your way. The Minotaur guards the Labyrinth, and you must kill it before you can achieve your destiny," said Lycaster. He approached his son who shielded his face, anticipating punishment. His father opened his arms and hugged his son. "Make me proud," said King Lycaster as he faded away into black ash.

King Minos' looked at his empty hands. He brushed the dust from his palms in disgust. Lifting his head to stare into the abyss of the Labyrinth, he smirked.

Minos awoke when the Phoenix crash-landed onto the foot of his carriage. The once majestic bird now looked like a plucked fowl as it squawked and tried to catch its breath.

"You failed," the King stated with contempt. The creature put its head down before it tried to explain what terrible misfortune it befell. "Save your breath. We're almost at the Labyrinth. Whatever this wretched cyclops was planning, it's too late."

It felt as though the mountains would never end. The children spent days walking over the uneven path and the occasional muddy snow. When they came upon frozen patches, Cy was afraid to touch it until Icarus fell back on the gray sludge and created an impression of his body.

"Try it," the boy urged. The cyclops fell back, and then sprang up once his skin touched the freezing plot of land. He had never felt anything so cold. Cy shivered the rest of the day as the frigid mountain winds reddened his face. The cyclops wished that he had more than a waistcloth covering his body, but Icarus handed his friend a sheep wool blanket for warmth.

Harmony and Laelaps proved to be a formidable hunting duo and caught several small animals to eat. Cy found and collected berries and mushrooms, and also came across an abandoned beehive with honey. Even with the limited game and plants, they managed to fill their bellies.

Several days passed when Cy finally asked a question that had troubled him. "What is Pandora's box?" he asked as they walked next to a stream.

"It's the power of the gods. At least that's what my father told me," said Harmony.

"But what does that mean?" he pressed. They walked on a log to cross over a river.

"A long time ago, humans were happy with their lives. They were so content that they stopped praying to the gods and preferred to worship wise Kings. When Zeus looked down from Mount Olympus, he was offended by the lack of offerings at his temples.

"What did he do?" asked Cy in a worried tone. Benu squawked and swayed on Cy's shoulder.

"Zeus came up with a plan to unleash a terrible scourge on the world to punish humanity for their hubris." They reached a row of trees, and Laelaps ran off to mark several of them. Harmony continued. "Zeus presented the box to the daughter of the most powerful ruler in all the land. Her name was Pandora. Unwittingly, she opened the chest and unleashed the power of the gods onto the world. This would have destroyed all life on the planet, but Zeus had a change of heart when he realized the amount of suffering he had caused. He reached down from the heavens and shut Pandora's box as only he could. Zeus vowed to prevent anyone from ever opening the weapon again."

"Wow," said Cy. He held the same expression on his face that came from hearing one of his father's tales.

"Zeus decided to punish everyone in the world because humans weren't praying to him enough. He sounds like a spoiled infant," said Icarus. Thunder could be heard in the distance as if warning the boy. Icarus' eyes widened as he looked up at the sky with a sheepish smile.

"My father said that it's impossible to understand the will of the gods. They're completely different from mortals," said Harmony.

"Why can't they just tell us what we should do? Why do they have to be so mysterious?" wondered Icarus.

"It's easier to understand the wind. I fear that we

may provoke the wrath of the gods by stealing Pandora's box. That may be far worse than fighting an army or the Minotaur," warned Harmony.

"What happened to Pandora?" asked Cy.

"I don't know, but her father's kingdom was destroyed," she said. A shiver ran down Cy's spine as his lips quivered.

"It may not be true, Cy. There are hundreds of stories involving the gods, but I've yet to meet one," said Icarus.

They continued their steady progress through the mountains and only stopped to eat, sleep, or relieve themselves. Benu recovered from his injuries and was able to fly high above the clouds. He could see the smoke billowing from the top of the volcano in the distance.

23

THE ENTRANCE

Laelaps led the children out of the mountainous terrain and into a scorched landscape. Icarus and Cy collapsed due to exhaustion several paces away from the base of the massive volcano.

"Can we rest before we enter the underground maze that's guarded by the terrifying Minotaur?" pleaded Cy.

"Rest is for the weak," said Harmony.

"Weak," added Benu, who casually rested on her shoulder.

"Time is not on our side. The army could arrive at any moment," she said with urgency. Harmony followed the base of the volcano in search of the entrance. If she was fatigued from the long journey, she did not show it.

Icarus sighed and slowly got to his feet. "Come on. We can rest once we have Pandora's box." He extended his hand and helped Cy off the floor. They shambled around the mountain in search of Harmony and the entrance to the Labyrinth. After climbing over a few boulders, they came upon ancient statues.

"Who are they?" asked Cy.

"I don't know, but they look like gods," said Icarus.

Carved out of mountain rocks were Zeus, Hera, Poseidon, Hestia, Aphrodite, Ares, Athena, Demeter, Hephaestus, Apollo, Artemis, and Hermes. They were known as the twelve Olympians.

"My papa told me the gods looked like cyclopes," said Cy.

"The gods can take any form they wish. They often transform into animals, at least that's what I was told," replied Icarus. The boy inspected the sculptures closely and wondered how long they had been there. They seemed to be in pristine condition despite the hellish environment. The sculpted Olympians lined the entrance to the Labyrinth. There were dozens of warning signs carved along the mountainside. Over and over again, the writing read:

Keep out or face the wrath of the gods.

Enter those who wish to perish.

Death inside.

Laelaps sat waiting with his tail wagging, while Benu was perched on a rock. Harmony scrutinized the intricate maze carved into the surface of the massive double-doors. She took one of the large ringed handles in hand and pulled. After a few tense moments, she released her grip as the doors shuttered but refused to open. She shook her arms to release the tension in her muscles. "It must be enchanted," she said.

"It could just be locked," said Icarus.

"I've never came across a lock that I couldn't break," countered Harmony. Together, they all grasped onto the ring and tried to pry open the doors, but their attempt proved futile. Icarus took several steps back to examine the maze on the door.

"The two soldiers didn't mention anything about how to enter the Labyrinth," admitted Icarus.

"They withheld that knowledge to prevent us from stealing the weapon," said Harmony angrily. She kicked the door with the ball of her foot.

Icarus moved one piece of the maze, and the entire apparatus changed into a different structure. He studied it closely and thought back to his puzzle-solving days with his father. They would often challenge each other with games like this, but the fate of the world usually didn't hang in the balance.

Harmony grunted as she lifted a boulder over her head. "Move aside. I'm going to smash it. I'll break the doors off their hinges," she grumbled.

Icarus blocked her path. "Wait, let me try to decipher it. I can do it, but I need time," he said anxiously.

"Do it quickly." Harmony set the large rock aside and then sat on it. They watched Icarus and waited.

Cy cocked his head to one side as he scrutinized the intricate doors. "My head hurts just from staring at it," he said, rubbing his eyes.

Deep in thought, Icarus tapped a finger against

his lips unconsciously. "It has a twenty-piece adjustable combination, five riddles to solve, and it may require a goat to sacrifice." The boy cracked his knuckles and began to move pieces.

*
**

Within the King's carriage, Ajax nervously shifted his weight as he told the account of his and Achilles' whereabouts. "They were formidable foes. We barely escaped with our lives," he expressed fervently. He kneeled before King Minos and waited for a response.

"You mean the cyclops and the son of the craftsman have united and are heading to the Labyrinth to steal my weapon?" the King asked anxiously.

"Yes, Your Majesty. But they do not know of the lock. It took the best minds in Thebes weeks to solve the puzzle. They won't be able to complete it before we arrive."

"We can't take that risk. Tell the men to move at twice the pace," demanded the King, "Use the whips if you have to."

Down the line, soldiers became irate once the command reached their ears. The men pushed the caravan harder than they had before. The road was treacherous, yet the soldiers, horses, and steers were pushed to their limit.

Brontes and Daedalus noticed the increased momentum and looked at each other perplexed. They wondered what could have prompted the King to drive his army this hard.

*
**

At the entrance of the Labyrinth, Icarus moved the final

198

adjustable piece into place with a look of self-gratification. "The puzzle looked a lot more complicated than it actually was," he admitted. Still, nothing happened. The boy's eyes widened as a look of confusion stretched over his face. "I don't understand. It should have worked."

"It's time to try my solution," said Harmony. She kneeled to lift the boulder once more, but then a mechanical sound came from the inner workings of the lock. Rusted gears turned, and the miniature maze split at its center. Dust fell as the massive doors shuttered open. The children covered their ears as the screeching iron hinges sounded like the wail of a harpy. A long dark underground passageway was slowly revealed. The air was muggy and reeked of sulfur, as the wind pushed past them as if escaping a dreadful realm.

Icarus removed his flying machine and set it down near the entrance. Cy stared at his friend, confused. "Even if my wings worked, I wouldn't be able to fly in there," said Icarus. "Carrying it would only slow us down."

Harmony whistled to Laelaps. "Get the scent, boy." The hound wagged its tail as he bounded toward the entrance. Laelaps sniffed the air until he acquired the Minotaur's scent. His vision was immediately transported past the doors and into the deepest recesses of the Labyrinth. His foresight stopped in front of a shadowy passageway where he saw a pair of glimmering black eyes staring back at him. The creature sensed something in its presence. It lunged at the dog's vision, and Laelaps recoiled back into his physical body with a whine.

"What's wrong?" asked Harmony in a worrisome tone. Laelaps fell backward with his legs in the air. His eyes were closed while he pretended to be dead.

The children gathered around the dog. Harmony kneeled at his side and rubbed his belly. Laelaps' leg shook, and his tail thumped on the dirt. His tongue rolled out the side of his mouth. "You know that I'll protect you no matter what," she assured him. The hound stood and licked her face. She hugged her companion, and Laelaps became his usual self.

"Can you avoid the Minotaur?" asked Icarus. Laelaps grumbled but eventually nodded. The boy grabbed a torch off the wall and used two pieces of flint rock to ignite the end. He held up the fire and lit the dark passageway as Benu landed on his shoulder. Laelaps took the lead and was followed by Icarus, Benu, and Harmony.

"Do we truly need to go in there?" asked Cy. With a rusted grind, the two bronze doors began to close.

"We have to do this to free all the captives from the army, but I understand if fear has entered your heart," said Icarus.

"You aren't in the least bit afraid?" Cy's voiced cracked, although he tried to mask it as best he could.

"Of course we are," said Harmony, "But I have to protect my friends. I'm more afraid of losing any of you than what's in here." Icarus looked to Harmony, and they exchanged a silent glance.

"You don't have to come, Cy. Secure the entrance, and we'll hopefully return before nightfall," said Icarus. Harmony, Icarus, Benu, and Laelaps walked down the dark path as the doors kept closing. Seeing his friends united with one common goal gave Cy just enough courage to slip through the doorway.

"Wait for me!" the cyclops yelled as he rejoined his companions. Icarus put an arm over his shoulder and squeezed him appreciatively.

Outside the shutting doors, Achilles came sprinting out of the mountains like a charging bull. He ran toward the entrance at a swift pace, as the children disappeared into the dark caverns. He vaulted toward the opening, but the doors slammed shut. Achilles crashed into the gate and then fell flat on his back.

The loud thud startled Cy as he turned around to find the entrance sealed. The sound of the clanging doors reverberated and echoed deep into the Labyrinth, eventually reaching the lair of the Minotaur. The echo sounded like a pin drop by the time it reached the beast's ears, but it was enough to alert the horned behemoth to the presence of intruders. The most powerful monster on the planet let out a terrifying snarl.

24

THE MINOTAUR

The children made their way down a long corridor. "Who built this place?" asked Icarus as he held the torch with a trembling hand.

"Only Hades could have built something so disturbing," retorted Harmony. The massive Labyrinth was built into the enormous volcano by something otherworldly. Ten paces separated the stone walls, which supported the elevated ceilings.

The cavernous tunnels were large enough for Brontes to walk through unaffected, thought Icarus. Magma flow channels were dug deep into the corners of walls, which created an intricate lava stream that illuminated sections of the passageways. Black ash and soot coated most of the rocky floor. Beyond the crumbling underground tunnels were tons of hot earth and molten rocks.

The children came to a divider that split their path into two. After sniffing each passage, Laelaps' body stiffened as he used his snout to point to the corridor to the left.

"Are you certain?" asked Harmony.

The Minotaur's roar reverberated from the opposing tunnel, and the torch's flame wavered. The children covered their mouths as a putrid aroma filled the air. Harmony pulled an arrow from the quiver and nocked it to the string on the bow. She aimed the shot down the dark passageway. Holding their breath, they waited to hear another sound, which never came. They exhaled as one before relaxing. Harmony released the tension from her bowstring.

The dog grumbled at her as he made his way down the tunnel he suggested. Cy fell behind a few paces as he became increasingly agitated. His heart pounded at the mere thought of encountering the beast that resided within these walls.

Icarus stepped on a circular stone and felt it slowly descend beneath his heel. A light rumble followed, and the boy paused to stare down at his foot. The rock sunk under his weight. Perched on the boy's shoulder, Benu said, "Uh-oh."

Harmony grabbed Icarus and pushed him out of the way. *Smash!* The triggered trap dropped a massive barricade from an opening in the ceiling. The slab of stone blocked the path behind them, which prevented any chance of retreat. Benu landed on a rock on the floor and shook the dust from his feathers.

"Is anyone injured?" asked Harmony.

"I'm alive," coughed Icarus as he swatted the dust from his face.

"Where's Cy?" she asked, searching for the cyclops. Laelaps stood and pressed his front paws to the barrier as he barked. Icarus picked up the torch he dropped and shined a light over the solid stone barrier. Harmony got up and tried to find a way around the wall.

"Cy, can you hear us?" called out Icarus.

"Hello," said a muffled voice on the other side of the wall.

"Stay right where you are, Cy. We'll find a way to get you," yelled Harmony.

Cy coughed because of the dust that filled the air. He heard his friends' muffled voices through the wall. A roar came from the path they'd come from, which startled the cyclops. The beast hoof steps could be heard approaching. "He's getting closer. I have to keep moving. Get to the center of the Labyrinth and have Laelaps find me on your way out."

"We can have Laelaps find you now," said Harmony.

"There's no time. Go." Cy felt the ground tremble and ran back the way they came. He noticed a new path in the wall that wasn't there before. *The maze must change like the puzzle on the door*, Cy thought. He slipped through the narrow passageway to the other side as the roars from the beast grew louder. The walls shifted, and the corridor closed behind the cyclops.

Harmony pounded the wall with the bottom of her fists, desperately trying to break through. She only managed to crack the stone when Icarus placed a hand on her shoulder. "We have to continue without him. The sooner we find Pandora's box, the faster we can find

Cy," said Icarus. Laelaps barked in agreement.

Harmony looked at them gloomily and then nodded. Benu landed on her shoulder and squawked. Laelaps followed his nose down the corridor, and they walked directly behind him to avoid any more hidden traps.

*
**

Cy approached a three-way junction when the ground began to tremble. This wasn't the beast but an earthquake. A giant boulder collapsed through the ceiling, narrowly missing the cyclops. The tremors gradually subsided, and Cy let out a deep breath.

The cyclops halted when he saw a giant hoof stomp out of an opposing corridor. Cy's eye slowly moved up as the behemoth's muscular legs came into view. The gigantic monster walked upright on its back legs, and every step he took shuddered the ground. Higher and higher, the beast held a giant battle-ax in hand and wore a long skirt made out of boiled leather. His armor was forged from uniforms of the fallen soldiers that crossed his path. The Minotaur was a gargantuan bull-human hybrid with a muscular body covered in fur.

Cy finally gazed upon the creature's scowling muzzle. The horns on its bullhead sharpened as it scraped the stone ceiling. The cyclops quickly realized that the beast was even taller than his father. The fear proved too great for Cy, who fainted behind the collapsed boulder.

At the center of the crossroad, the creature peered in every direction but did not find the young cyclops.

The Minotaur snorted and continued down the dark tunnel.

Cy was slow to get up when he peeked around the large rock and found the corridor empty. He exhaled, relieved to have survived his first encounter with the beast, but knowing that it would not be his last.

Icarus, Harmony, Laelaps, and Benu arrived at the center of a four-way intersection. They heard scurrying feet, and Icarus flashed the torch toward the noise in the darkness but found nothing. They heard something scamper behind them and turned around.

"It was probably just a rat," Icarus said nervously. A creature screeched to their right, and the boy tensely turned the torchlight in that direction.

Harmony's eyes widened when she saw the floor of the entire path covered with rodents. Some of the vermin were as big as Laelaps. Their eyes glowed red from the glare of the flame. "Run!" she screamed.

They sprinted as the critters shrieked and pursued them. Snaking left and right, Laelaps led them down several curved corridors. Harmony kept the ravenous rodents at bay by smacking the swiftest ones with her staff. "Why did they have to be rats? I hate rats!" she cried out.

They reached the center of an intersection and halted when hundreds of rats descended on them from two of the three corridors. The children ran up the only clear path left. Unfortunately, it led to a dead-end. The skeletal remains of an unfortunate soldier greeted them at the foot of the stone wall. The rodents had herded them into a trap.

They turned around and prepared to make a stand as the army of rats approached them gradually from the far end of the corridor. Harmony tossed her staff at Icarus, who dropped it haphazardly but quickly recovered it. Benu looked on in terror as he hovered above them near the ceiling. Laelaps growled with his teeth bared. Harmony went to one knee as she took out the bow and several arrows. A big rat stepped forward, and she quickly aimed and fired. Her shot struck it between the eyes, and it immediately fell over. Still, the other rats merely crept over its corpse. Harmony unleashed shot after shot and killed dozens, but it didn't discourage the remaining vermin from advancing. Terrified, Icarus tossed the flaming torch at the horde and panicked as they descended upon them.

Suddenly, the rats halted as the ground began to tremble. The vermin turned around and scurried back the way they came. Icarus, Harmony, and Laelaps tried to keep their balance, as the entire structure seemed to shift beneath them. The large wall blocking their path gave way to a magma chamber below. Icarus and Laelaps lost their balance and hurdled to the other side of the corridor as the ground crumbled. Harmony was forced to run back the way she came. They sprinted away from each other to escape the collapsing floor. Benu evaded the rocks that fell from the ceiling at the center of the passageway. The volcano stopped shaking, and they all breathed a sigh of relief.

"Are you injured?" both Harmony and Icarus simultaneously asked each other. Laelaps whined and anxiously paced around next to Icarus. Separated by the pool of magma, Harmony stood alone on the other side of the corridor.

"I'm well," she said. "We each have to try and find the heart of the maze. It will be faster if we part ways."

Benu flew above the magma between Icarus and Harmony, unsure of whom to join. "Benu, go to her," commanded Icarus.

The bird somersaulted and flew over to Harmony's outstretched arm. He landed and hopped over to her shoulder.

"Are you sure you want to do this? Laelaps can find a way around this."

"We don't have a choice. Get to the center of the maze," she urged.

The dog bit down on Icarus' tunic and jerked his head, trying to pull him away. "What's wrong?" Icarus asked.

The Minotaur's roar came from down the long corridor, and Icarus and Laelaps turned to face the beast. The behemoth pawed its hoof into the ground, preparing to charge. The boy's face went pale as he made eye contact with the terrible creature, catching a glimpse of its black eyes.

"Run, you fools!" cried Harmony.

The monster dug into the sides of the stone walls with its fingertips and launched itself. *Thump. Thump. Thump.* Everything slowed down as the Minotaur sprinted toward them with thunderous strides. Laelaps fled, followed closely behind by Icarus. Despite its enormous size, the beast moved swiftly. It knew every twist and turn as it maneuvered its powerful body through the maze.

Icarus and Laelaps tried to lose it down several twisting corridors, but the brute gained ground on them with every step. The dog found a hole in the wall and crawled through it. The boy followed but got stuck midway. He pushed and pulled until he squeezed through to the other end.

The Minotaur used its ax to widen the hole, while Icarus scrambled on the ground to escape. The beast punched his muscular arm through the wall. Reaching blindly on the other side, it came within a hair's length of grabbing the boy. Icarus and Laelaps scuttled away as the Minotaur finally retracted its hand.

From around a corner, Achilles saw the back end of the beast as it let out an angry roar. The monster searched the area when it sensed someone in its presence. Achilles held his breath behind the wall and put a hand over the hilt of his sword. The beast sniffed the air and crept toward the warrior.

Achilles pulled the sword from its sheath and prepared for battle. Noise from a different corridor distracted the beast, and he sprinted up the long tunnel. Relieved, the warrior slid down the side of the wall until he sat on the ground.

25

THE HEART OF THE MAZE

Cy walked down an eerie passage where thousands of small scratches lined every inch of the walls. He felt the grooves of the deep scrapes. *Is this a record of the people the Minotaur's eaten, or how many days he's guarded the Labyrinth?* Cy wondered. The indentations led to a large chamber.

"Whoa," Cy murmured.

He entered the lair of the Minotaur. There was a sizeable makeshift bed in one corner made of mud, sticks, and weeds. A mound of old uniforms, shields, and the rusted weapons of fallen soldiers were tossed in a corner. Finally, crude drawings lined the walls that reminded Cy of his father's cave paintings.

He carefully examined the images on the walls that depicted the Minotaur defending the Labyrinth from both humans and gods. Other drawings showed the creature being isolated within the maze. A strange feeling came over Cy. He felt sorrow for the beast, realizing how lonely it must be in the Labyrinth. The final image portrayed the unleashed power of Pandora's box, destroying the world.

"Oh, no," Cy muttered.

He stepped back and inadvertently tripped into a cluster of armor. *Crash! Smash! Boom!* Helmets spun on the floor, spears tipped over, and several loaded crossbows fired arrows across the room. Cy took cover beneath a large round shield. There was so much noise that he expected the Minotaur to arrive at any moment, but nothing happened. Relieved, Cy wiped the sweat from his brow and crawled out from beneath the heavy shield. He tried to put a few items back the way they were but only succeeded in causing more of a commotion.

As Cy was about to leave, he noticed a scroll within a breastplate of a uniform. He took the sheepskin in hand and unfurled it. His eyes widened, as a detailed map of the Labyrinth was revealed. He scrutinized it and found a clear route to the center of the maze.

The discovery put a smile on Cy's face as he rolled up the map. Looking back to the image of Pandora's box destroying the world, his expression went cold. He made his way to the entrance of the chamber and stuck his head out into the corridor. Finding the tunnels clear, he ran out of the Minotaur's lair as fast as his stubby legs could take him.

Just as Cy scampered down the long corridor and rounded a corner, Achilles arrived at the same scraped passageway from a different route. The warrior cautiously made his way into the Minotaur's lair, and somberly took in the sight of the dozens of soldier uniforms and weapons strewn about within the chamber. He brushed his hands over the Minotaur's trophies.

Most of the uniforms belonged to opposing armies, but he noticed Theban armor among the collection. He extended an arm to touch a breastplate. His arm shivered before his fingers pressed against the corroded steel. The thought of his brothers-in-arms falling to the beast pained him greatly. Achilles wiped the gleam in his eyes and took a moment to kneel before the uniforms to pay his respects. Stepping away, he noticed the terrifying images on the walls that shook him to his core.

Harmony and Benu cautiously journeyed deep into the maze. They peered around every corner and moved swiftly down each corridor. "I hope the others are safe," said Harmony solemnly. On her shoulder, Benu's head hung low, mirroring her sentiment.

The ceiling eventually gave way to a high and wide vent that led to the volcano's opened crest. The sunlight that shined through the crater bathed this section of the Labyrinth in natural light. Benu flew up to get a better look at their surroundings. He hovered above the walls and whistled excitedly at the view.

Harmony swiveled her head in search of a way to reach higher ground. She noticed a crevice on the side of a wall and dashed toward it. Tilting her head up, she followed the crack as it snaked to the top of the wall. Her lips curled into a slight smirk. Sticking her hands and feet into the fissure, she began to climb.

Benu landed on the edge of the steep structure and looked down at Harmony. He swayed back and forth eagerly. The higher she climbed, the more cautious she became, and the slower she went. Once past the midway point, she looked over her shoulder to the ground below and immediately regretted it. Her head spun, so she squeezed her eyes shut and exhaled until the fainting spell passed.

She would not let go of a crevice until her other hand was firmly in place between a higher gap in the barrier. While climbing, a piece of the wall she gripped broke off, causing her to plummet. Her fingertips clawed at the smooth stone until she found another crevice to hold onto. She clung with one hand as she reached with the other. Placing her hands and feet in the twisting crack, she closed her eyes and drew a weary breath.

The Minotaur's roar came barreling down the long corridor. Harmony turned to look and felt the beast's advancing steps through the vibrations in the wall. Looking down at the ground and then up at the remaining distance needed to climb to reach the top, she weighed her terrible options.

Without a second thought, Harmony scrambled up the wall desperately. She had no time for caution and climbed as fast as possible. There would be no escaping the creature's wrath once he turned the corner. If the Minotaur found her, then she would arrive at the gates of the Underworld shortly.

Benu looked down the passageway to where the beast would emerge. He flew down and hovered next to her. In a panic, Benu flapped his wings erratically. Several feathers floated to the ground beneath them. "Faster," he squawked.

"I'm trying," she hissed. The crevice she was climbing ended several feet below the top of the wall. Trapped, she frantically searched for another crack, but the smooth rock was undamaged at this height. They could sense the Minotaur around the corner. She placed her foot firmly between the fractures in the barrier and took a deep breath before she jumped straight up with all her might.

With an outstretched arm, she managed to reach the edge of the wall with only the tips of her fingers gripping the edge. Grimacing from the pain, she swung her other arm up and took hold of the surface. Hastily pulling herself up, she rolled onto her back as the Minotaur stepped into the corridor.

Harmony laid flat on her back, while Benu hid between her arm and torso. They were silent as the horns of the beast rose and fell above the wall with each stride. Fortunately, the behemoth's eyes were below the top of the maze's barriers.

The Minotaur halted next to them when he noticed something peculiar on the ground. He hunkered down and pushed the plums around with a finger. They were Benu's gray feathers that were stuck to his fingertip. The beast gripped the top of the wall and stood on the tips of its hooves. Peering over the barrier, the creature saw nothing but dozens of rows of labyrinth walls.

In the next corridor, Harmony held onto a thin

crack with one hand just below the top of the barrier. Her body dangled dangerously high above the ground, while she held Benu in her other arm. The creature's hands gripped the top of the wall on each side of them as it sniffed the air. The Minotaur snorted and blew out his nose, which caused Harmony to nearly lose her grip. The beast finally stepped back, and she could see the massive horns turn. The Minotaur viewed his surroundings suspiciously but eventually continued onward. It turned down a different path to Harmony's relief.

Harmony and Benu stayed hidden until they lost track of time and felt safe enough to climb back up. She peered over the top of the wall in search of horns but saw nothing. They were out of harm's way for the moment, so she staggered to her feet and placed Benu back on her shoulder. Standing on the ridge, she realized that it could serve as a walkway. She regarded the intricate network of walls that made up the internal section of the maze. It must have been high noon because the Sun shined a bright beam of light down to the center of the Labyrinth from the crater above.

"There's the heart of the maze," she whispered thankfully.

They made their way toward the center by walking on top of the stone parapet. Harmony hopped and skipped over several broken columns. A small chunk of the wall crumbled beneath her weight, and she almost lost her footing. She quickly regained her balance as the rocks hit the floor below. At their current pace, they could reach Pandora's box and escape the Labyrinth before nightfall. Harmony was afraid to admit it, but she was—dare she think it—having fun.

For a brief moment, she allowed herself the faintest smile. She was completely unaware of the giant battle-ax heading right for them. *SMASH!* The weapon came down on the structure with the force of a thousand smiting hammers. The shock pushed her forward and sent Benu flailing off her shoulder. She tumbled over the side of the wall but held on with one hand and shielded her face from falling rock debris with her other. The parrot opened his wings and flew back up to meet her.

Harmony climbed back onto the surface of the wall, while the Minotaur tried to dislodge the ax. Realizing that this was her only chance to escape, she sprinted away on top of the uneven walls. Benu frantically flapped his wings beside her. The Minotaur abandoned his weapon and pursued her from the ground. With his enormous strides, he caught up to her swiftly. He reached up to grab her several times, only to narrowly miss at every attempt.

Frightened, the parrot released his bowels over the bull's head. The white and green substance hit the monster between the eyes, but it had no effect on his intense focus. Benu squawked in terror and flew higher.

From her vantage point, Harmony saw a wall up ahead that would block the Minotaur's path from the ground. She would be able to sprint past the barrier from the top of the wall and escape. Hastening her pace, she ran ahead and looked over her shoulder. The beast broke through the wall horns-first and continued charging after her.

The behemoth reached several other barriers and

smashed through them all. Harmony's breaths came short and fast, as she sprinted ahead of the beast but could not lose him.

Harmony looked ahead and noticed that her walkway would end with a steep plunge to the ground below. She needed to clear a wide gap to reach the top of the wall on the other side of the corridor. A look of determination spread over her face. Instead of reducing her pace, she hastened it toward the precipice. Time slowed when she reached the brink and hurdled through the air for what seemed like an eternity. She flailed her arms and legs mid-air. Unfortunately, she began to plummet well short of the top of the other wall.

Harmony crashed into the barrier and slid down its side. She clawed at the wall, desperately trying to grab hold of anything. Her fingertips clutched a jagged crevice, painfully jerking her body to a halt before she hit the floor. She uttered a guttural cry. It felt as if her arm was nearly separated from her shoulder.

Breathing heavily, she let go of the crack and landed hard on the ground and fell backward. Sprawled on the floor, she whimpered, unable to move. The beast would be upon her shortly, and she no longer cared. She considered pleading with the creature for mercy and surrendering. She'd use her mother's name for protection. *Even the Minotaur would know who Aphrodite was, wouldn't it?* She wondered. *This is what it means to be a hero,* a voice in her head whispered. *Never giving up even when you feel as though you cannot continue.*

Hearing the Minotaur climbing over the last barrier, she staggered to her feet and limped down the nearest corridor. The bull's head peered over the wall as she turned on a sharp corner and kept running. While looking over her shoulder, she inadvertently collided into Cy. They both fell and hit the ground awkwardly. "Ouch," bellowed the cyclops.

Harmony sprang to her feet. "Hurry, the Minotaur is right behind me." Cy barely regained his footing when she yanked his arm forward. They ran down the corridor until they reached a point where it split into two different paths. Harmony hesitated indecisively but then sprinted to her left-hand side.

"No, this way," said Cy. He took her hand and pulled her in the other direction. He examined the map closely, not bothering to take his eye off the sheepskin. As they turned the corner, Harmony's mouth fell open. They halted before three towering walls that blocked their escape. It was a dead-end.

"I thought you knew where you were going?" Harmony said in a panic.

"This is wrong. It shouldn't be here," said Cy, genuinely confused. He turned the map over. "Oh, it should be," he said sheepishly, "We should have gone the other way."

Frustrated, Harmony put a hand over her eyes and raked it down her face. She searched for cracks or dents in the wall that they could use to climb, but there were none. Wide-eyed, she glumly mumbled, "We're going to die."

"I'm sorry," said Cy.

Realizing that the Minotaur hadn't reached them, she pressed a finger to her lips and silenced Cy. She crept back to the corner to steal a glance back down the corridor. Carefully peering around the edge of the wall, she found the passageway clear. They still had a chance to retreat the way they came and escape in the other direction.

Suddenly, the Minotaur's hooves stomped into view. Looking left to right, the behemoth grunted indecisively.

Harmony hid behind the wall and shut her eyes. "Go the other way. Go the other way," she whispered. She felt the vibrations on the floor grow stronger with every ensuing stride and knew the beast had chosen their path.

"Curse the gods," she said with contempt. Realizing they were trapped and probably going to die, Harmony slid down to the floor, defeated. "At least I won't perish alone," she admitted. She turned to look at Cy, but he was nowhere to be found. She quickly vaulted to her feet and searched for him. "Cy, where are you?" she said in a hushed tone.

With the creature plodding toward them, she took the bow and arrow in hand. Harmony went to one knee and settled into a firing stance on the far end of the corner. She was thankful that Cy found a means of escape. She had a better chance of survival if she fought the beast alone.

Harmony would aim for its eyes to try and blind the creature. As the Minotaur approached, a hidden passageway opened behind her. A small section of the wall turned and shifted on its side. Before she knew what was happening, she was pulled back to the other side of the barrier. Cy quickly shut the hidden passageway before the Minotaur reached the dead-end. The behemoth looked down and sniffed the empty space.

Benu landed on top of a wall behind the Minotaur. It squawked and whistled at the creature mockingly. Aggravated, the beast turned and reached for the bird, but the parrot flew up and avoided its savage hands. "Missed," the bird snickered. The creature ignored the pest and lumbered back the way it came. The parrot pursued the beast to keep an eye on it.

On the other side of the barrier, Cy pressed his ear against the wall to hear the creature walk away. Relieved, Harmony finally allowed herself to breathe. After regaining her composure, she approached the cyclops with an infuriated look on her face. She walked up to him with clenched fists at her sides.

Cy anxiously stepped back and tried to explain. "I didn't mean to leave you behind. I fell through the wall after stepping on a loose stone that opened the hidden path. The passageway shut behind me, and I had to find the trigger to reopen the door. I'm sorry!"

Cy closed his eye and prepared to be hit, but she hugged him instead. "You saved me. How did you know there was a passageway?" She held his shoulders at arm's length.

Cy showed her the scroll. "This map shows me where hidden passageways and traps are located."

Harmony kissed his forehead. "You're brilliant," she said with a smile. Cy's cheeks reddened. Noticing his flushed face, Harmony let go of the cyclops and took a step back, placing a hand over her mouth to hold in a giggle.

"You're welcome," he said in a low mumble, staring at his feet.

"Can we arrive at the heart of the maze with that map?"

Cy smiled and nodded. "Where's Icarus and Laelaps?" he wondered.

"We were separated after we lost you."

"We must reach Pandora's box before Icarus. The chamber is a deathtrap. Hurry!" Cy grabbed her hand and led her down the corridor.

26

PANDORA'S BOX

Laelaps and Icarus reached the center of the maze. The dog pointed its snout toward the large chamber with a swirling magma reservoir. The lava guarded a small golden chest, which sat on top of a round black island in the middle.

"That must be Pandora's box," said Icarus. *Not much to look at*, he thought. He edged closer to the spinning pit of death and noticed dozens of stepping-stones that led to the landmass. "I could have used my wings right about now."

Laelaps envisioned the boy successfully jumping off the solid ground with his flying machine, but then gliding past the chest and straight into the fire. The dog snapped out of his daydream and shook his head with a grimace.

"Wait here, I'll get the weapon." Laelaps grumbled disapprovingly yet laid down on the floor.

Icarus used Harmony's staff and lightly tapped a stone jutting out of the magma. It sank almost immediately. "I hate to admit it, but this is more of a task for Harmony."

The boy placed the staff aside and took a few steps back. He drew in a deep breath before running toward the room but halted at the entrance at the last moment. Stepping back, he jumped around to ready himself once more. Sprinting toward the room, he stopped again at the edge of the stone floor. He continued this practice several times, while Laelaps yawned with boredom. "I'm preparing myself," he told the dog. He sighed heavily and mumbled, "Be as swift as a lightning bolt. Be as swift as a lightning bolt."

Finally, gathering enough courage, he sprinted into the room and hopped from stone to stone as they descended into the lava underneath his weight. A heavier person would have stumbled to their demise, but Icarus had a fleetness of foot that allowed him to scarcely touch the rocks. He reached the small island and staggered to a halt.

The boy hunched forward and rested his hands on his knees to catch his breath. He sniffed the air and smelled burnt leather. Noticing smoke wafting from beneath his heels, he shrieked in pain. He stomped the floor and then lifted his legs to pat the bottom of his sandals with his hands. The embers were smothered, only leaving charred remains on the soles. Fortunately, the footwear still offered enough protection from the intense heat.

Laelaps barked and stood on his hind legs encouragingly from the entrance. The hound settled down and panted due to the sweltering heat coming from the chamber. Looking back at the dog, Icarus noticed there were fewer stones to traverse for his escape. That did not matter for the moment as Pandora's box engrossed him. The blue and gold-encrusted chest had an intricate weather pattern design that lined the exterior. The boy brushed beads of sweat from his brow with the back of his hand.

Icarus shut his eyes before cautiously reaching for the chest. The boy's trembling hand neared the box. Laelaps whined and paced around, sensing something amiss. The boy closed his eyes and laid a hand on the weapon. As if expecting to be struck by lightning, he opened one eye and then the other. He became emboldened and casually picked up the item. Wondering if the simple chest was even Pandora's box, he made his way to the edge of the island. "That wasn't so hard," he said.

Suddenly, the entire structure of the maze began to shake violently. The island he was standing on began to sink, while the magma reservoir grew volatile. Laelaps barked when Cy and Harmony met him at the chamber's entrance.

"Icarus, do not touch the—oh, you already did," said Cy disappointingly.

"Now you tell me!" responded the boy.

Harmony looked up and saw large chunks of the volcano's inner crust break off and come crashing down. "Get out of there!"

"What do you think I'm trying to do?" Icarus said, panicking. "Here, catch." He tossed the chest, and it floated toward the entrance. Cy opened his arms and prepared to catch it, but it struck him in the face. It bounced up and into Harmony's grasp, while Cy collapsed to the floor, stunned.

Icarus jumped off the isle as it was consumed by the magma. He hopped from stepping-stone to stone on his way out of the chamber. The molten rock spewed up as if reaching for the boy. The last few rocks needed to escape sank before Icarus could use them. With no time to think, he used his momentum to scale the side of the chamber wall until he reached the exit. Cy had staggered to his feet when his friend hurdled out of the room and landed on top of him. They both grunted when they smacked the solid ground.

"We have to get out of here," urged Harmony. Cy and Icarus were slow to their feet when they noticed the lake of fire surging out of the chamber. They sprang up and sprinted away swiftly, as the entire room was engulfed in flames.

The Minotaur used the sides of walls to keep his balance as he lurched down corridors. Hidden on top of a pillar, Achilles waited for the beast to lumber past. As soon as the behemoth was within striking distance, the warrior jumped onto the creature's back and cried out, "For Thebes!" With blade in hand, he plunged his sword into the beast's shoulder, and the monster howled.

Unable to reach the warrior with its hands, the Minotaur bucked and spun, trying to toss the human off its back. Achilles let go of his short sword and slid down to the ground before the creature slammed his back into a barrier. The warrior landed on the ground and rolled forward to his feet. He removed the long sword from the leather holster on his belt in one smooth motion and got into an offensive stance.

With one hand, the Minotaur reached to its back and pulled out the bloody blade. He held the weapon between thumb and forefinger, and then snapped it in two. The beast looked down at the warrior, who struggled to keep his balance during the quake. The ground ripped between their legs, which distracted Achilles long enough for the Minotaur to seize him. The beast grabbed him with both hands and put intense pressure on his body. The young warrior held his tongue, refusing to give the monster any gratification by masking the excruciating amount of pain he felt.

The floor continued to rumble under the creature's hooves. Realizing that this wasn't an ordinary earthquake, the Minotaur roared in alarm. He flung the warrior down the long corridor like a rag doll. Achilles bounced off the wall before he hit the ground and slid into unconsciousness.

Icarus, Cy, and Harmony followed Laelaps through several corridors. They reached an intersection when Cy held up the map and said, "No, this way." Laelaps responded with a bark and a growl as he tried to lead them in the opposite direction.

Harmony kept a keen eye on the molten rock, rushing toward them from behind. "Will you two just make up your minds!" she shouted, exasperated. They turned around and gawked at the approaching river of fire.

"Let's go your way," said Cy, dashing past Laelaps. They rushed around a bend and skidded to a halt when they saw the Minotaur lumbering toward them from the far end of the passageway. They tried to retreat, but the flowing magma blocked their path. Trapped with only a few precious moments left to live, the only option they had was how they chose to perish, by fire or at the hands of an enraged monster.

Panic set in, leaving the children petrified. That's when Icarus remembered that Harmony was holding Pandora's box. He snatched the chest from her grasp. Before she could protest, he handed the staff back to her and tried to open the box.

Cy jumped on the case. "No!" he cried, "You'll kill us all!" They each grabbed onto the chest with both hands and tried to wrestle control of it from the other.

"Kill us? I can't even open it," pleaded Icarus desperately. Harmony wrenched Cy away and held him back. Benu flew in and landed on Cy's shoulder to calm him down. The Minotaur's roar boomed down the corridor. They all turned and gawked at the hulking beast that would soon be upon them. The boy used his limited strength to try and open the container. "You useless box! Do something!" he yelled.

"Let me try," said Harmony, as she took back the case. With a hand on the lid and the other at the base of the chest, she used all her might to pry it open, but only managed to redden her face. She finally relented and drew in several breaths. They grew increasingly agitated with each succeeding hoof-fall from the beast. The creature's thumps soon became all they could hear.

Icarus retook the box and observed it carefully. Everyone else's attention shifted between the boy and at the approaching Minotaur plodding down the corridor. "It must have a locking mechanism," said Icarus. "I-I c-can solve it. Give me a moment."

"We don't have a moment to spare," retorted Harmony. She took the bow and arrows out of her quiver and took aim at the Minotaur. Nocking and releasing several shots in quick succession, the arrows flew through the air until they struck the beast across his torso. Unfazed, the behemoth casually brushed off the arrow shafts with one hand. What little confidence Harmony had in their odds of survival dwindled as the beast continued to grow with every advancing stride.

Without any more arrows, Harmony tossed the bow aside and took her staff in hand. She stood boldly, determined to fight until the bitter end. Laelaps growled and barked at the approaching monster.

Icarus desperately turned the box every which way searching for an answer. He finally felt the grooves on the sides of the chest. The boy pressed down on a golden lightning bolt design, and the container clicked. A bright light shone through the narrow opening between the cover and the base of the chest. Even the Minotaur was bewildered by the glowing radiance and thunderous sound emanating from the box. The children bowed out of the way as Icarus pointed the weapon in the behemoth's direction. The beast roared and lunged at the boy with its oversized hand.

The cover divided down its center, revealing two

interlocked lids that sprang open on opposite ends. A powerful bolt of lightning shot out of the box and struck the monster squarely in the chest. In an instant, the Minotaur soared through several stone walls until it crashed through the side of the mountain. He created a direct route out of the Labyrinth. Icarus's eyes were shut as he clutched the container nervously. The lids reconnected as the electricity dissipated. His hair stood on end electrified as his breaths came short and fast. They were awestruck by the unnatural force he wielded in his hands. This was the true power of the gods.

They stood in stunned silence as the lava continued to flow in their direction. Finally, Harmony yelled, "We have to flee!" There was no more time to linger, so they ran for their lives. They used the path created by the Minotaur's expelled body to escape from the Labyrinth. Working together, they climbed over the remnants of the walls. They maneuvered around the scattered rubble with the flowing lava reaching for them at every turn.

Magma pooled at the final section of the maze, preventing their escape. "What do we do now?" asked Harmony.

Icarus inspected the chest once again and found an engraving in the shape of a snowflake. "I'm going to try something," responded the boy. He pressed the symbol and opened the chest, releasing an icy vortex. Quickly realizing he could freeze the magma in place, he turned and aimed the polar winds at the flowing lava all around them. Once he extinguished the fires, Icarus shut the box and exhaled a cold breath.

Harmony tapped the hardened rock with the end of her staff. "I think it's safe," she said. They walked across the black frost-covered surface as lava flowed toward them from their flanks. With the molten rock hot on their heels, they fled out the opening. Once outside the volcano, they noticed the Minotaur's motionless body buried beneath a mound of rubble. Only a single massive hand was visible underneath the piles of rock, dirt, and obsidian.

The children looked up and saw the magma spewing out of the crest of the volcano. The black ash expelled from the summit sparked and lit up the darkened clouds with lightning. Icarus noticed the front entrance a short distance away and sprinted toward it.

"Where are you going?" called out Harmony. He reached the melting doors and picked up his broken flying machine. Once he put on the backpack, the lava burst through gates and rushed toward him. He dashed out of the entryway as the molten rock reached for him.

"We should flee," said Icarus, sprinting past the others. They rushed down the road to get as far away from the Labyrinth as possible. The dirt covering the Minotaur shuttered.

The children made their way down the road when they came across Achilles blocking their path. The bruised and bloodied young warrior limped toward them grimacing.

"Stay back," warned Harmony.

"I don't want to hurt you," said Icarus sincerely, as he placed a hand over the top of the weapon.

Achilles collapsed to one knee and pleaded, "I

don't want to take the weapon."

"Then what do you want?" asked Cy.

"I saw what you did to the beast. You vanquished the Minotaur like it was an insignificant fly."

"We're stronger than you think," Harmony countered.

"That may be true, but it doesn't change the power of that weapon. Pandora's box makes armies futile. Whoever wields that chest will essentially be a god, and that is terrifying to me. You cannot bestow King Minos with such power. It's too dangerous to fall into the wrong hands or anyone's hands."

"What would you have us do?" questioned Icarus.

"We need to help each other," said Achilles.

"You expect us to trust you? After what you've done," said Harmony.

"The King will either lock you in a dungeon or kill you once you hand him that weapon. I know how ruthless he can be. I'm the only chance you have to save the people you care about."

The children exchanged uncertain glances. Icarus asked, "We do not agree to your offer, but what is your plan?"

27

THE POWER OF THE GODS

Cy and Laelaps ran past a cluster of trees to reach a wide-open field. The cyclops clutched Pandora's box in his arms as he came to a sliding stop. The army halted its march to the Labyrinth when the volcano erupted and set up its defenses. The King sat on his throne behind several infantry lines and Royal Guards.

"This? This is the rogue cyclops that caused us so much grief?" asked the King with a scowl. His lips curled back, revealing his crooked teeth. He covered his mouth, trying to contain a giggle but soon roared with laughter. A few soldiers let out a nervous titter, but the King stared scornfully at those that did not find this amusing. The entire front line began to laugh uncontrollably, and the laughter soon spread throughout the rest of the army. The King put a hand up, and the men were immediately silenced. The Phoenix watched the field on the edge of its perch, expecting some kind of ploy.

Cy and Laelaps saw the sheer size of the military and tried to retreat, but several soldiers walked out of the trees preventing their escape. Faceless helmed soldiers surrounded them on both sides. A jagged mountain range thwarted any possibility of escape to their left, while several rows of archers lined the shore of the lake to their right flank. Even if they got past the arrows, it meant swimming to the far side of the vast lake. Cy and Laelaps were trapped at the center of a beautiful green meadow.

"I should thank you, cyclops. You've gifted me what no one else could," said the King.

Cy noticed the man on the throne moving his mouth but could not hear his words. "What are you saying?" cried out the cyclops.

Minos leaned down to a guard at his side. "What did it call me?"

The soldier stiffened nervously. "I think he's challenging you, Sire."

The King felt disrespected. "That little beast will pay for his insolence."

Cy narrowed his brow at the man on the throne, "Are you the King?"

"Now he's questioning the legitimacy of your rule, Sire," said the soldier. "And I believe he just insulted your mother."

Minos' faced reddened. "Bring me Pandora's box and the head of that little beast," demanded the King. He turned to a general and said, "Let's hear those drums. We came all this way, might as well make a show of it."

The general ran from the King's side to the nearest infantry lines and yelled, "Drums!"

The men at the rear raised large mallets over war drums and brought them down powerfully. The instruments were cylinders carved out of hardwood with deer hides stretched over the top. The methodical beating created a dreadful sound: *thump ... thump ... thump ... thump ... thump ... thump ... thump ... thump!*

The soldiers began hitting their shields with the staff of their spears to the tune of the drummers. The general paced fiercely at the head of the frontline and shouted, "Sacred Band of Thebes!" The small unit grunted boisterously in acknowledgment. "Seize that chest for your King and kill those cretins!" the general ordered.

The Sacred Band of Thebes separated their small unit from the rest of the host and gave a guttural cry, "Oooraaah! Oooraaah!" These warriors were considered to be the most skilled fighters in the entire Theban army; King Minos' answer to the highly trained Spartan soldiers. They held up a shield in one arm and advanced with a spear in the opposing hand. Cy desperately searched for an escape route, while the dog growled with his fangs bared.

The King slouched on his seat, bored and disinterested. The first wave of soldiers readied their weapons as they came within striking distance. Laelaps barked at the armed men. Cy raised the chest over his head and pressed down on the lightning symbol. Pandora's box glowed until the lids flipped back, and a bolt of electricity was unleashed. A few paces from the cyclops, the hoplite soldiers halted as they balked at the energy slashing the sky. They turned and retreated swiftly back into their ranks. The drums fell silent and were replaced by wails from the terrified men. Every human and monster within the convoy looked up at the darkened sky as lightning spread in every direction.

Achilles, Harmony, and Icarus lay on their bellies on a grassy hilltop overlooking the convoy. They saw the impressive display of power that Cy unleashed in the meadow.

"That's the signal," said Icarus. They stood up and made their way to the encampment below. Achilles led the two children by ropes tethered to their bound wrists. The electricity finally retreated, and the blue sky returned.

"I hope this isn't a trap," muttered Harmony to Icarus.

"We have to trust him," responded the boy in a hushed tone. Benu flew in and landed on Icarus' shoulder. "Find father," said the boy. The parrot whistled and dove toward the road. Spreading his wings, he swooped down into the campsite and searched for Daedalus.

A cloud of smoke wafted around the sealed chest. Cy's arms trembled as he continued holding Pandora's box above his head. The cyclops opened his eye slowly and glanced at the spectators around him. Soldiers gawked at the cyclops in sheer terror. A few men threw down their weapons and kneeled before the cyclops as if he were a god.

King Minos snapped out his stupor and frowned

at the kneelers. "Get up, you fools. He's not a god. It's the chest that gives him power." The men on the floor grabbed their weapons and got back in line.

Cy tried to keep his composure as he breathed heavily and sweated profusely. The cyclops brought the chest down carefully until he secured it in his arms. He advanced on the King's position with Laelaps by his side. Minos turned to his men, nervously. "What's he doing?" The front lines were unsure of what to do as the cyclops approached the King.

Cy halted once he was within shouting distance of the King and stood boldly before the army. "I can destroy you all with this weapon," he yelled. Several men griped nervously. "All I want is the other cyclops to be released from captivity, and for us to receive safe passage back to our island. If you honor my proposition, then you will never see or hear from us again."

The King took a moment to compose himself before he responded calmly, "You're a brave one, cyclops. I will grant your request if your words are true, but I want the weapon first."

Cy sighed and said, "I accept."

The King turned to the captain of his Royal Guards. "Get me that weapon and kill the little beast once you take it," he commanded under his breath.

"But you have to collect Pandora's box yourself," added Cy.

The King was caught off guard and looked at the cyclops with disdain. "What did you say?"

"The weapon is too powerful to fall into the hands of mere mortals. Only a King with divine blood should wield something this powerful." Cy went to one knee and held out the chest.

The King tensely considered this for several moments as he looked at his soldiers. Distrustful of the cyclops, the Phoenix squawked and shook its head in protest, but the King ignored the creature.

"What is your decision?" asked Cy. Laelaps barked impatiently.

Fearing the loss of respect from his soldiers, the King exclaimed, "Very well!" Reluctantly lifting his massive body off the seat, he strode down the steps of his carriage to the dirt below.

Benu flew from cage to cage, searching for Daedalus. He landed on a barred windowsill of a wooden carriage. "Master?" asked Benu. The silhouetted man turned toward the parrot. The shadow transformed into a tall birdlike creature when it sprung into the daylight. Squawking, Benu jumped back as the overgrown hawk reached for him.

The parrot continued down the center aisle until he finally came across a familiar face. Daedalus heard the distinct bird whistle and turned around to find Benu clung to a bronze bar. "Hello, old friend," greeted Daedalus.

Achilles stepped onto the road with Icarus and Harmony as his prisoners. They infiltrated the army's camp and walked between the transports. The warrior yanked them forward to their displeasure.

"Not so hard," whispered Harmony through

clenched teeth. She was worried that Achilles had played them false.

"Hurry it up, or I'll feed you to one these beasts," retorted Achilles.

The only sentry on watch was surprised to see his commander. "Achilles, you've returned," said Magus. Icarus' eyes widened as he hid behind Harmony. He looked down to shield his face in hopes that his former guard would not recognize him.

"I came to lock these two up. Are you the only soldier on watch?" he asked.

"Yes, sir." Magus eyed the boy and was stunned. "Icarus, is that you?" The boy looked up and smiled sheepishly.

"Hello, Magus, how's the eye?" asked Icarus.

Magus lunged at the boy and grabbed him by the tunic. "What are you doing here?"

"Stand down, soldier. This is my prisoner," stated Achilles firmly.

"Sir, this boy escaped imprisonment at the Tower of the Winds."

Achilles cleared his throat and said, "Which is why he's in my custody."

"Of course," said Magus, releasing the boy. He looked Achilles in the eyes and stiffened. "The King needs every soldier at the front, sir. He probably requires his best warrior at his side. I wouldn't wait. You shouldn't concern yourself with these children. Let me take them."

"They're dangerous traitors," said Achilles. "I want to personally lock them up. These creatures aren't going anywhere. Head to the frontlines, I'll be right behind you. That's an order."

Magus nodded and stepped back. "As you wish," said Magus. He turned and made his way up the center aisle but halted after a few paces. "Wait," said Magus, suspiciously. Achilles grimaced and put his free hand over the hilt of his sword. "You're going to need the keys to lock them in a cell," said Magus. He took out the keys hanging from his belt and tossed them to Achilles.

The young warrior caught them and nodded. The naïve soldier continued up the road.

Once Magus was out of earshot, Harmony said, "Your soldiers are fools. Who trained them?"

"I did," admitted Achilles as he unsheathed a dagger from his scabbard. Icarus and Harmony stepped back as the warrior walked toward them. He grabbed the boy's wrist and cut him loose, and then did the same to the girl. "Let's release some beasts."

Achilles handed them a set of keys, and they parted ways to cover more ground. They sprinted to different cages and cautiously began to release the imprisoned creatures.

Harmony removed the shackles restraining the giant tortoise. "Go on, you're free," she said enthusiastically. The tortoise gazed at her indifferently, and then slowly retracted its head into its shell. Baffled, she moved on to the cell holding a massive boar.

The large Nemean lion roared and lunged at Achilles within its cage. As the ferocious predator paced back and forth, the warrior fearlessly unlocked the cell door holding the enraged beast. The creature growled before it crept out of the cage and past Achilles.

"I put you in there, I can put you back," said the warrior firmly. The lion snarled and then strode up the road. Achilles stood courageously until the beast was out of sight. He exhaled nervously, placing his hands on his knees. "I hate cats."

Icarus stood terrified in front of the holding cell of an enormous hairy spider. Its countless eyes were fixated on the boy as drool oozed out its mouth and slid down its mandibles. "Let me out," whispered the chilling monster. Icarus shook his head frantically and shambled away wearily.

The lad moved on to a pen holding a large buck with majestic golden antlers. He released the stunning animal, and it took its first steps of freedom up the road. It frolicked and then halted to gaze back at the boy appreciatively. Icarus waved goodbye to the stag as it dashed ahead. Suddenly, the Nemean lion jumped out from behind a carriage and tackled the deer to the ground.

Icarus looked on helplessly as the carnivore mauled the beautiful creature. "Why do the gods mock me?" whimpered Icarus. He covered his eyes as the lion roared.

The archers on the range had their arrows fixed on the cyclops but relaxed the tension of their bowstrings. Battling boredom, the hoplite soldiers stood idle or leaned on the staff of their spears. Laelaps yawned and stretched his body on the ground. He then sat up, and his head bobbed up and down with his eyelids drooping. Cy wearily sat on top of Pandora's box with his elbows on his knees so his hands could support his head.

Meanwhile, the Royal Guards struggled to fasten the King's breastplate to his stout midsection. "I don't think it fits, My Liege," said one of the men.

"It's the same one I wore at the palace. How could it not fit?" he questioned.

"Perhaps you've gained weight, My Liege." King Minos walloped the insubordinate guard's helmet.

"Make it fit, or you'll meet the same fate as those cretins in the field." The guard nodded nervously and pulled on the straps with all his might.

Icarus released a group of satyrs from their cage. The top half of these creatures resembled a little person, but their bottom half was that of a two-legged goat. They baaed excitedly as they hopped out of the cell. Although they were short and stout, the rounded ram horns which sprouted from their tussled hair made them appear formidable.

"Thank you for freeing us," said the leader of the tribe. With a gray and white goat's beard hanging from his chin, the elder satyr approached the boy with an oak walking stick. "We are in your debt."

"I'm going to need your aid shortly," said the boy.

The clan stood behind the elder, awaiting his command. "We will do everything within our power. What is needed, child?"

Icarus turned around when he heard a familiar parrot's whistle. Benu bobbed his head excitedly from the windowsill of a carriage. "Will you grant me a moment?" Icarus said to the elder. The satyrs bowed respectfully, and the boy walked off to meet the bird.

Icarus stopped when he saw his father through the barred windows. The creatures were silent, and the air was still, as they gazed at each other for a moment. It felt as though they hadn't seen each other in years.

"Icarus, what are you doing here?"

"I came to rescue you," he said. He made his way to the door and unlocked it. The door swung open, and they hugged each other like never before.

"I thought I lost you, son."

"You aren't that fortunate," said Icarus with a smile. For once, Benu looked on in silence, genuinely pleased. They would have held each other forever, but the boy remembered that they still had a task to complete. "We have to help my friends." Icarus removed his backpack and handed it to his father. "Can you fix my flying machine?"

Daedalus took one long look at the broken contraption. "What happened to it?"

"I collided with a Phoenix – mid-air," the boy muttered.

"You did what?"

"It's a long tale. Can you do it?"

"I don't know if I can fix it without my workshop."

"You're the world's greatest craftsman. Of course, you can." They grinned at each other. Together, they felt that nothing could stop them.

Achilles walked to Brontes' carriage with the keys at his

side. The giant cyclops watched him intensely. "The warrior, I was starting to believe that the crab ate you."

"I came to release you, but I need your word that you will not harm me once I do."

"I cannot give you my word."

"Then I can't free you."

"Very well, but if I ever get unleashed, I will hunt you down to the end of the world."

Achilles swallowed nervously. "Well, now I truly cannot release you."

Harmony approached them. "We don't have time for this, Achilles."

"Did you not hear what he just said?" he gripped nervously.

Harmony unlocked the shackles on the giant's wrist. Brontes sat up gingerly and stretched his torso. As he twisted his back, it sounded like a tree being split in two. "That's better," the cyclops grunted.

"I journeyed all this way with your son to rescue you," said Harmony.

Brontes' eye widened as confusion stretched over his face. "Cy came here to save me. Where is he?"

They removed the shackles from his ankles. "He's alive, but we don't have a moment to spare," said Achilles.

"Was he injured?" Brontes growled.

"No. We needed to distract the army to set you free. Your brave son volunteered," said Harmony.

Once his ankles were unchained, Brontes stood up, which reminded Achilles of the giant's intimidating stature. "I'll deal with you last, warrior," spat Brontes.

Achilles stared up at the cyclops with a sense of dread. Icarus and Daedalus joined the group.

Brontes looked down at Icarus. "You," hissed the giant.

"This is my son," said Daedalus.

"He's the one that brought the soldiers to my island."

"It wasn't me," exclaimed Icarus as he pointed to Achilles behind his back.

"We were given strict orders from the King to capture you," interjected Achilles.

Brontes leaned in toward the boy. "Did you endanger my son?"

A chill ran down the boy's spine. "He wanted to save you."

"You better pray that no harm comes to him, or I will eat the two of you," said the cyclops, as his gaze darted between Achilles and Icarus.

Icarus forced a nervous smile. "It was his scheme," said Icarus through clenched teeth, pointing once again to Achilles.

The cyclops turned and lumbered toward the frontlines. Harmony had to sprint to remain alongside the giant. "Wait, we have a plan, but it requires your help," she said.

Brontes continued striding ahead. "I have my own method for saving my son."

"What is it?"

"Destroy the human army and rescue my son."

"That might work, but it will be safer for you and Cy if you work with us. It's unwise to fight the army alone."

The cyclops halted and sighed. With a somber expression, he looked down at the girl. "What is your plan?"

⁎⁎⁎

Achilles, Icarus, and Harmony sprinted toward the frontlines when Ajax stepped into view. With the guilty expression of a thief, they slid to a halt. Fully armored but with his helm at his side, the large brute blocked their path. "Achilles, you've returned," said Ajax suspiciously. His focus shifted to the unbound children. "What are you doing with them?"

Achilles was caught off guard. "I'm – I'm taking them to a cell."

"The cells are back down that way." Ajax pointed to the back of the caravan.

Achilles thought quickly, desperately searching for a convincing explanation. "I plan to take them once I've ensured the King's protection."

"Would you like me to imprison them?"

"No, I wish to personally see to it myself."

Growing increasingly agitated, Harmony finally interrupted, "We don't have time for this, Achilles. He's your second-in-command, just tell him the truth."

"Tell me what?" asked Ajax, confused.

Achilles sighed and then met his companion's confused gaze. "Ajax, we must stop the King from getting his hands on Pandora's box."

"But that is the purpose of this entire campaign."

"It's too powerful for him or anyone to control."

Ajax's eyes narrowed as he put a hand on the hilt

of his sword. "I don't know what they did to you, but disobeying a direct order from the King is punishable by death. You taught me that."

"Keep moving. I'll hold him off here," Achilles whispered to the children. Icarus and Harmony vigilantly paced around Ajax. The brute's head was rigid with his chin held high toward Achilles, but his eyes tracked the children until they were out of sight. "I can't serve the King anymore. You and I both know that he's a coward."

"He may be a coward," said Ajax.

Achilles listened intently for more, but that seemed to be the end of his response. Ajax put on his helm and then unsheathed his sword.

"We do not have to do this, friend," pleaded Achilles.

"Draw your sword, oath breaker."

"I refuse."

"Very well, but I will show you no mercy," said Ajax as he prepared to attack. Achilles stood boldly as he was accustomed. There was a steady silence in the air that went on longer than they realized. A breeze blew dead leaves between them ominously.

Finally, the tall warrior lunged at his former commander, sword first. Achilles stepped aside and dodged the attack. In a single motion, the young warrior drew his blade and settled into a defensive position.

Normally, defeating an opponent as big as Ajax would be a simple training exercise for Achilles, but he was not his usual spry self. After suffering a punishing defeat at the hands of the Minotaur, any opponent would prove formidable. Achilles grimaced while lifting his sword, the pain radiating up to his shoulders. A twisted ankle made shifting his weight a dreadful task, which limited his nimbleness. Ever since his head struck the Labyrinth wall after being flung by the beast, it was challenging to keep his balance.

"I don't want to hurt you, Ajax," said Achilles as he tried to mask the stiffness he felt over every inch of his body.

"Good. That will ensure my victory," responded Ajax wryly. He noticed the beads of sweat gathering on his former commander's forehead. The brute licked his dry lips like a hungry predator stalking its prey. "You aren't looking like yourself, Achilles. Are you sure that you don't want to surrender?" teased Ajax with a grin. His confidence was growing with every passing moment. He did not know why Achilles was weary but understood the longer the fight progressed, the greater his chances of triumph.

Knowing that each step could lead to an attack, they circled each other guardedly. "The gods appear to be on my side," said Ajax, as he lifted his sword. He brought it down in a slicing motion, but Achilles caught the edge of the striking blade with a vertical block before he parried to one side.

Achilles may have been weak, but his mind was as sharp as a knife's edge. The young warrior never felt more alive than in battle. His reflexes slowed time to a crawl. He could even distinguish the sparks flying when steel met steel.

"This is your last chance to yield, Achilles," said a

poised Ajax.

"Never," stated Achilles valiantly. "Rather death than dishonor," he said, echoing the sentiment of all great warriors. Achilles braced himself for the next series of assaults.

Ajax lurched forward and rained down steel on his former companion. Slashes and lunges came from every angle, giving Achilles only an instant to block or evade. Ajax was unusually swift for a man his size and would seldom leave himself exposed to a counterattack. Achilles had to wait for the right opportunity to strike, but time was not on his side in his weakened state.

Achilles found himself on the defensive more than he was accustomed. He was forced to run around cages and stoop under carts, which irritated his opponent. "Stand your ground!" cried out Ajax impatiently, as their weapons clashed once more. Achilles wasn't proud of this tactic, but he needed to catch his breath from the endless onslaught.

The tall soldier was anxious for victory. He knew that defeating a warrior of Achilles' caliber would make him a legend. In one fell swoop, he'd be the most feared and revered soldier in all of Greece. Ajax wanted this victory more than anything. Achilles could see the fire in his opponent's eyes and came to the harsh realization that this fight was lost.

28

THE REVOLT

King Minos' armor was finally fastened to his massive frame. He nodded to the captain of his Royal Guards, who proceeded to raise his spear. "Ooooraaah," grunted the commander. The remaining guards echoed the call until they encircled their ruler. Once in place, they raised their bronze shields above and around the King to create an impenetrable phalanx.

The soldiers marched forward with the tips of their spears extended beyond the protective shields. The King strolled comfortably at the center of the phalanx as they plodded toward the cyclops. They resembled an overgrown porcupine trudging across the field.

"I only asked for the King. No weapons, shields, or guards!" yelled Cy exasperatedly. Laelaps barked in agreement.

The soldiers halted, and the King spoke. "You expect me to meet you in the field without protection?"

"I am a lone cyclops with a dog, and you have an army at your back. Yet you cannot stand before me," Cy stated scornfully.

"How do I know if your words are true?" countered King Minos. As they continued bickering, the soldiers' eyes darted back and forth between the cyclops and the phalanx.

"You're the one with all the soldiers. Why should I have faith in you?"

"You're the one with Pandora's box. Why should I trust you?"

"Are you afraid?" Cy asked.

King Minos peered between the shields and noticed the soldiers on the front lines whispering to each other. The archers pointed their arrows toward the ground, while the generals rolled their eyes in annoyance. Some of the men began to yawn out of boredom. The King sweated profusely within the sweltering phalanx, while the cyclops stood in the open, a light breeze at his back. "Leave me," King Minos told his men.

"But sir..."

"I said leave me," snarled the King. The Royal Guards grunted as they removed their linked shields from around the King, and then marched back to their unit. Minos cautiously approached the cyclops as the canine growled. He reached Cy and held out his hand, keeping a keen eye on the dog as he lowered his body into an attack position. "Hand over Pandora's box," said the King.

Cy took a step back and secured the chest at his

side. "I must warn you that this chest contains all the destructive power of the gods."

The King took a deep breath, and through gritted teeth said, "I am aware of the legends."

The cyclops looked for any sign of his friends. "You give me your word that you will allow us to leave this land unharmed?" Cy asked. He spotted Benu soaring overhead. Relief flowed over the cyclops' body like a cascading waterfall.

Exasperated, the King's jaw clenched. "You have my word." The King reached for the chest and tried to pry it away by force, but Cy proved mightier than he appeared. "Hand it over you one-eyed cretin." They fell to the ground and wrestled for control of the weapon. Laelaps bit the King's leather skirt and tried to pull him off his friend.

Benu squawked as he landed on the King's head and pecked at his face. The King wailed in agony as he swatted at the pesky bird. His wig fell off his head, revealing his balding scalp. The soldiers were aghast as their Majesty reached for his hairpiece. Benu clutched the horsehair and flew away.

"I'll kill you," he told the bird, seething. He reached for the box again and continued fighting for possession.

The army was fixated on the pitiful wrestling match before them. "What should we do?" asked one soldier, confused.

A general cried out to his King, "Your orders, sir?" Minos was too distracted by the brawl to give an order.

Benu hovered above the fight when an arrow sailed past him. Before he could react, another shot caught the hairpiece and ripped it out of his talons. Several archers nocked arrows to their bowstrings and took aim at the parrot. They fired, forcing the bird to evade the volley of arrows. Benu flew up beyond their range, but there was little he could now do to help his friends. From his vantage point, he noticed reinforcements approaching and whistled in excitement.

At the rear, a short soldier tried to get a better look over the taller warriors. "What's happening? I can't see anything. Can some of you kneel?"

"Let me help you," said a gruff voice. The giant cyclops picked up the short man and carried him high above the crowd.

The man's face contorted silently. Too terrified to squeak, the soldier faced the scowling creature and gazed into its eye. He was the same soldier that Brontes tossed into the sea back on the island. "Not again," croaked the man.

Brontes tossed the soldier into the nearby lake. The man screamed as he soared into the water. The remaining soldiers turned around and found all the nightmarish beasts they had captured standing before them. No one moved as the once brave warriors held their collective breath. A man's sneeze broke the silence and triggered the attack. The monsters broke through the army's unsuspecting lines. Brave men tried to hold their ground, but it was complete pandemonium. Dozens of angry mythical beings overwhelmed the units.

Icarus rode into battle on the back of the giant

Erymanthian boar. He yelled in excitement as the hog charged headfirst into a shielded phalanx and sent the hoplites flying in all directions.

Harmony used her staff and superior strength to fight multiple opponents at once. She flipped, kicked, punched, and battled her way deep into the army's ranks. The soldiers were befuddled by the prowess and might of the little girl. She disarmed and defeated several foes singlehandedly.

The Nemean lion hurdled over Harmony and pounced on several Royal Guards. It slashed at the bronze shields with its enormous claws while avoiding spear thrusts from the terrified men.

Brontes roared at the stunned humans, as they retreated to avoid his assault. He grabbed men like wooden figurines and tossed them into the lake one by one. Several soldiers schemed to trip the cyclops like they accomplished back on the island. The army believed that if they could defeat the giant, then the other creatures would eventually fall.

The freed satyrs joined the fray by running beneath Brontes to prevent his capture. Using their rounded horns, they rammed any man attempting to topple the cyclops. The giant looked down at his new allies and nodded appreciatively.

Panic-stricken, the Phoenix stirred on its perch atop the King's carriage and swiveled its head around frantically. He gawked as the army was overwhelmed on multiple fronts. The bird closed its eyes and concentrated on igniting its body, but only managed to create a few sparks and a sputter of black smoke. Several woodland nymphs climbed onto the carriage with sharpened sticks. They looked like children with wooden features that allowed them to conceal themselves among the trees. The Phoenix struggled to fly as the stunted beings approached his position. One grabbed onto his talon, but the bird managed to take to the sky and shake off the creature. The other nymphs pelted the Phoenix with rocks, forcing him to fly higher.

Through sheer will, the Phoenix ignited its body mid-air. It grew in size and terrified several mythical creatures on the ground. The soldiers cheered at their powerful ally. The firebird let out a deafening screech, but then shrieked in horror when it spotted a meaty fist heading in its direction. Brontes swung and struck the Phoenix with a powerful punch that snuffed out its flames instantly. The cyclops laughed heartedly as the soaring creature disappeared in the distance.

Magus escaped the chaos of the battlefield by fleeing into the mountains. He planned to reach higher ground and hide until the hostility ceased. Following a trail, Magus ran into the base of a cliff within the canyon. In a panic, he tried to climb up but slid down the dirt surface several times.

Realizing that it was impossible to scale the cliff, he rushed back the way he came. Magus halted when he heard a creature approaching and retreated to the dead-end. A terrifying beast brought down several trees as it plodded around the bend. Magus gawked and screamed when he witnessed the frightening creature slowly approaching. "Help me!" cried Magus.

On its stumpy feet, the giant tortoise trudged forward at a snail's pace. Magus attempted to dart around the beast, but the creature snapped its mouth at him at every attempt. The creature's massive shell trapped the one-eyed soldier in place, so he dropped to his knees and begged for mercy. The tortoise blinked at the pleading man before it bellowed dreadfully. No one heard Magus' horrid scream.

The King was finally able to pry the chest away from the young cyclops. "I have it!" he cried triumphantly. Minos held the box above his head and out of Cy's reach. His excitement was short-lived, however, when he gazed at the freed monsters devastating his army. The panic slowly crept into the King's heart as he turned in every direction to witness the scope of the destruction. Cy and Laelaps were equally amazed yet excited about their prospects of victory.

Despite having their defenses penetrated, several divisions regrouped and recovered ground. The soldiers pushed the creatures back and hollered in unison, "Oooraaah! Oooraaah!"

As severe as the surprise attack had been, this Theban military force was skilled enough to withstand an assault from a horde of monsters. The men had defeated these creatures out in the field before and believed that they could do it again.

"Hold the line!" called out several generals. In quick succession, the soldiers let out a series of boisterous grunts and wails. They pressed forward with their heavy shields and forced the wild creatures back. The beasts were fierce and powerful, but they were also disorganized and undisciplined.

The generals believed that they could quell the upheaval. Suddenly, the soldiers felt the ground shaking beneath their sandals and noticed pebbles vibrating on top of the soil. The warriors holding the line looked over their shoulders when they heard yips and hoots coming from a hill. Suddenly, several tribes of centaur fighters charged over the peak and descended into the meadow. They howled and carried out a loud battle cry. Rhath led the charge swinging a club over his head.

Gray-coated centaurs flanked the unsuspecting archers near the lake. The bowmen dropped their weapons and fled as the gray tribe fell upon them.

"Sacred Band of Thebes, to me!" cried out a general. Half of the hoplite soldiers were rerouted to face the oncoming horde of fierce horsemen. They planted their large shields in the dirt and readied their spears. Several centaurs shot arrows at the defensive line as they galloped toward them. The four-legged archers proved to be accurate shots even as they raced forward. Shields protected most of the warriors, but some of the men fell back after being wounded. A soldier securing the rear would take up the shield and replace the injured man, but they were taking heavy losses.

The mythical beasts on the opposing end reengaged the thinned line of warriors. The regiments were pressed onto each other's back and were forced to fight on two opposing fronts. Beast roared on one side, while centaurs stampeded toward them from the other. The army was pinned down and had to make their final stand.

The general paced down the centerline. "This is it, the moment of truth where boys become warriors. We either rise to the challenge or flee in crushing defeat. What's it going to be, men?" Terrified, the soldiers peered through their shields at the oncoming assault.

The centaurs leading the charge formed a tight triangle like the tip of a spear. They smashed through the soldiers' shields and pierced the front line. Once the tribe breached one side of the defenses, they galloped down the center and attacked the men from behind. The soldiers had no choice but to flee the battlefield in all directions. The centaurs crushed the army's morale, and everything fell apart.

Rhath bucked his back legs at a soldier as he trotted to Brontes' side. "I thought you ran away," said the cyclops.

"I did, but my honor prevented me from staying away," said Rhath as he punched a man in the face.

"Look out!" yelled Brontes as he kicked a soldier that was preparing to attack the centaur from behind.

Rhath looked back at the fallen man and then back up Brontes. "Thank you. I would have been here sooner, but it took time to gather the tribes," said Rhath, as he kicked a soldier's helmet. "Please forgive my betrayal."

"All will be forgiven if you help us win the battle," Brontes said sternly.

"Consider it done." They continued fighting the remnants of the army together.

_*
_{**}

As their swords collided, sparks flew around Achilles and Ajax. The fighters parried, blocked, punched, and kicked each other but failed to gain an advantage on the other. Every subsequent offensive and defensive motion exerted more energy than Achilles could bare. He gasped for air after every mighty blow from Ajax. Their swords met in between them as they leaned and pressed into each other.

"I respect you, Achilles, but I have wondered who would win in a fair fight. I guess the answer was right in front of me all along." Ajax shoved the young warrior to the ground with ease. He was toying with his opponent.

"You're the mightier one, Ajax. There's no denying it. I knew you would best me in a fair fight." The big brute's shadow loomed over his former companion.

Achilles got to one knee and let out a ragged breath. Beads of sweat trickled down his protruding veins like rivers through a hillside. The young warrior had one final tactic to end the fight, but it would be risky. If it failed, he would leave himself vulnerable to a fatal blow, but with his body exhausted, he saw no other option.

"Are you ready to yield, commander?"

Achilles staggered to his feet and stood defiantly. "Never." Lunging forward, they met with steel on steel, for the final time. They each tried to overpower the other, digging their heels into the dirt. Back and forth they went, their muscles swelled, and tendons bulged out of their bodies.

Ajax noticed Achilles close his eyes as if in

prayer. *Achilles must be desperate*, thought Ajax. "Praying to the gods for mercy, Achilles? Only a vanquished warrior would do so," Ajax said with a grin. Achilles smirked curiously before he slanted his blade. He raked his sword down, creating metal sparks. The angle of the sword forced heated shards into Ajax's eyes. The brute staggered back and winced in pain. Dropping his sword to remove his helmet, he rubbed his eyes.

"I told you not to underestimate an opponent," said Achilles, as he stuck his sword in the dirt. He grabbed Ajax by his breastplate. "You still have much to learn." He head-butted the brute and knocked him senseless. The tall warrior wobbled before crashing down onto his back.

Achilles staggered on his feet but stood victorious. That's when he noticed scores of soldiers and mythical beast flee past him. He picked up his sword and trudged toward the battle.

Minos hyperventilated as he witnessed the continued devastation of his army. The fleeing soldiers left him to fend for himself even as he called them back. His nerves calmed when he realized that he clutched Pandora's box in hand. *Those beasts and cowards will pay for their insolence*, he thought. He would use the power of the gods to defeat them all singlehandedly.

"You'll pay for this, cyclops," said Minos as he turned to Cy. He grabbed the top of the chest and pulled, but could not open it. "What is this?" He put the box on the ground and used both hands to grip the lid, but it was locked.

"Only a worthy person can wield Pandora's box. I suppose you aren't worthy," said Cy with a snicker.

The befuddled King was irate. "Stop laughing at me, you little beast."

A deafening roar silenced every fleeing soldier and mythical creature. Everyone halted to survey the area as the ground shook. Horns were spotted from over the hilltop as the Minotaur pushed through the trees and stomped into view. The behemoth towered over every mythical creature in the meadow. The King gawked at the sheer size of the beast.

The Minotaur searched the area until it found Pandora's box. It snorted and narrowed its eyes on the man holding the chest. The King handed the weapon back to the young cyclops and paced backward, only for Cy to toss it back to him. They both retreated from the advancing horned behemoth.

Realizing that his only hope for survival was using the weapon against the terrible monster, Minos examined the chest for answers. Accidentally pressing an engraving on the side of the container, the chest glowed from within. It generated a thunderous sound waiting to be unleashed. Having discovered its secret, he pressed every symbol on the sides of the container in a panic. "I have you now," said the King. He opened the lid, and the ultimate weapon was unleashed.

29

CLASH OF THE TITANS

A torrent of weather patterns surged out of the container. The King was dragged around violently as he tried to control Pandora's box. The chest wrenched free from his grasp and fell to the ground at his feet. A bolt of lightning escaped from within the chest and struck the King. Energy flowed throughout his body until the thunderbolt sent Minos soaring up into the sky until he disappeared into the clouds.

The skies turned gray as the weapon cracked the earth beneath it. Benu took flight, while Cy and Laelaps sprinted away, narrowly avoiding the expanding sinkhole created by Pandora's box. The chest unleashed a torrent of rain, snow, lightning, hail, and strong winds from its depths. The powerful storm created a protective cyclone barrier around the container.

The volatile weather conditions terrified every

man, animal, and mythical creature in the area. The fighting ceased, and the remnants of the forces fled alongside their enemies. The Minotaur was alarmed as his worst nightmare came to fruition. He charged at the polar vortex in an attempt to contain Pandora's box.

The Minotaur reached the edge of the spinning winds and stuck his arm into the powerful barrier shielding the chest. Frost began to cover his burly torso as he reached down to the base of the crater to close the lid.

A white fog rolled out of the pit and covered the area, obstructing the Minotaur's vision with the white haze. The behemoth raked the ground with his overgrown hand in search of the container. His fingers grazed the side of the box when a tornado burst out of the chest and threw him back. The horned beast was swatted away and crashed onto a cluster of large trees in the distance. Chunks of wood flew far and wide as the creature rolled to a stop. The weapon had easily vanquished the planet's mightiest creature for the second time that day.

The behemoth was slow to get off the dirt. Pushing his body up, the Minotaur winced and collapsed to one knee. Gloomily gazing at the powerful storm, there was nothing more he could do to prevent Pandora's box from destroying the world. If he couldn't stop it, then no other mortal could.

The Minotaur noticed Cy looking at the vortex with dread. The beast faulted the young cyclops and his friends for bringing about the apocalypse. If all life on the planet were to be forfeit, then he would at least punish those responsible. The bull saw red and staggered to his feet with a surge of energy. The beast charged at the one-eyed boy headfirst.

Cy closed his eye and shielded himself as the enraged bull descended upon him at full force. Suddenly, Brontes stepped in front of his son and grabbed the Minotaur's horns. "Papa!" called out the surprised child. The elder cyclops held the beast at arm's length as he was pushed back.

"I'll hold him off, son." The Minotaur raised both arms and brought his fist down on the cyclops' forearms, freeing his horns. They stood upright grappling with each other as they each tried to gain an advantage. They got a hand free and simultaneously punched the other in the jaw with such force that they staggered back several paces. The giants briefly halted the fight to regain their composure.

Despite their impressive heights, the Minotaur towered over the cyclops, and their bodies were complete opposites. The Minotaur had the ultimate muscular physique that could put fear in the heart of a god. Meanwhile, Brontes was a chubby cyclops with bad eyesight. Regardless of his deficiencies, the one-eyed giant still stood boldly before his fierce opponent. He would do anything to protect his son. Pounding their chest with their fist, the giants roared at each other as they prepared for the ultimate clash of the Titans.

Charging at each other, they collided mightily in the middle of the field. Brontes put his arms around the Minotaur's midsection and lifted the brute off his hooves. The bull thrashed and wailed as the cyclops turned and slammed his body to the ground. They both went down with a thunderous *boom* that sent shockwaves across the field, rivaling the destructive power of Pandora's box. The Minotaur grimaced and cried out when he hit the floor. The bull bucked its hooves and kicked the cyclops off his body. Brontes went soaring and landed on his massive rear end, but then rolled back onto his feet.

The behemoths staggered up and met each other's gaze with intense rage. Colliding into each other once more, they punched one another bloody as they each tried to give the final blow. Not since Atlas fought Zeus, had a battle been worthy of the gods to behold.

Icarus, Cy, Harmony, Achilles, Benu, and Laelaps gathered beyond the whirlwinds of the growing storm. "How do we stop it?" asked Achilles desperately.

"It's all coming from Pandora's box," responded Cy. "If we close the lid, then it should stop the storm." Achilles sprinted toward the wind-guarded barrier.

"Wait, we need a plan of attack," said Icarus.

The young warrior took out a dagger from his scabbard and tossed it at the storm. The blade was sucked into the dark mist and was then flung back at him. Achilles dodged the spinning weapon and continued onward undeterred. The ground shook violently until enormous ice shards burst through the soil. The warrior evaded each jagged spike attempting to impale him but was forced to retreat. "I can't reach it," yelled Achilles as he reunited with the group.

"We cannot attack it from the ground," said

Icarus. A deafening howl emanated from the base of the crater as if the chest was warning any mortal brave enough to attempt to contain it. Pandora's box was defending itself. Daedalus approached with the flying machine. "Did you fix the wings, father?" asked the boy.

"I won't know for certain until it's tested," said Daedalus. Icarus grasped the pack in hand, but his father did not release it. "Let me go, son. It's too dangerous."

"You're too heavy, father. Besides, I'm the only one with experience."

"I don't want to lose you again, Icarus," said Daedalus.

"You're going to lose me and everyone else in the world if I don't go," pleaded Icarus. With eyes widened, Daedalus finally relented and released the flying machine. The boy hastily strapped on the pack. Daedalus looked at his only son solemnly but nodded in agreement. Icarus hugged his father, and Daedalus hugged his son. "It's our only hope. I have to go," said Icarus as he stepped away from his father's embrace.

Harmony stepped forward. "Are you certain that you want to do this?" she asked.

"I'm open to suggestions if you have a better plan." Icarus adjusted his headgear and placed the goggles over his forehead.

"The gods will protect you. You're a hero whether you close the chest or not," said Harmony.

"But do not fail, or we're all going to end up in the Underworld," added Achilles. Harmony punched the young warrior in the shoulder. Reminded of her might, he grimaced and clutched his aching arm.

"What if you don't make it back?" asked Cy solemnly.

Icarus put a hand on his friend's shoulder. "Ensure that my father gets as far away from here as possible," said the boy. The cyclops' eye widened with distress, but he eventually nodded.

Icarus turned to the vortex and sprinted toward the storm. He outmaneuvered the massive ice shards springing out of the soil. Finding a small opening, he darted toward several frozen spikes.

The Minotaur pummeled Brontes as the fight progressed. He sent the outmatched giant stumbling down to the dirt. The swelling around the cyclops' bruised face made it difficult for him to see. He tried to keep track of the horned beast, but his swollen eye would soon shut, and he'd be forced to fight blind. Cy sprinted to his father's side.

"Papa, you can defeat him. You're still the same cyclops from the stories that you told me every night."

"He's too big and strong. I've never fought anything like him before."

"Size has nothing to do with it, Papa. It's what's in here that matters," said Cy as he pointed to his father's heart. Brontes nodded and mustered all the strength he had left in his weary body.

The cyclops felt a steely resolve from deep within himself. Brontes slowly got up and stumbled to his feet. Cy was forced to shield his head from the clumps of dirt that rained down from his father's bruised and battered body. He stepped over his son with a look of determination in his bloodshot eye. "Don't worry, son. This ends now." He walked to meet the Minotaur one last time. The clash would end one way or another.

The oversized bull kicked up dirt with one hoof and shook his head, preparing to charge. The cyclops stood his ground and brought his fists up near his chin. The aggressive Minotaur put its head down and hunched his shoulders as it charged with the intent to gore his adversary into oblivion. Brontes closed his eye and stirred, yet he kept his fighting stance and waited patiently. The remaining spectators looked on in horror as the elder cyclops seemingly refused to evade the bull's incoming horns. "Papa, get out of the way!" Cy cried out desperately.

Brontes breathed calmly and heard the approaching hoof falls. The cyclops opened his eye and put everything he had behind one powerful punch. His fist shot between the horns and struck the bull's snout with full force. He hit the beast with such raw power that it created a thunderclap that pushed the wind back toward the storm. The massive bull staggered backward, stunned. With blood dripping down its snout, the beast collapsed to the dirt and into unconsciousness. The earth shook briefly and then fell silent.

Brontes put his arms up toward the heavens and proclaimed, "I defeated the Minotaur!" He grimaced after uttering those words and clutched his ribs.

"I knew you could do it, Papa," said Cy. Brontes picked up his son in one hand and embraced him. Their tender moment was short-lived as the vortex expanded violently. Lightning continued to discharge from its core, the dirt continued to crack, and hail fell from the sky. The elder cyclops shielded his son from the hailstones and considered fleeing, but he knew there was no safe place to go.

*
**

Crawling out from under the jagged frozen barrier, Icarus reached the flat dirt surface. The boy gawked at the sheer size of the revolving storm, which stood idle a few paces ahead of him. He tilted his head up toward the sky, and the whirling winds stretched far beyond the dark clouds above.

"May the gods of Mount Olympus protect me," Icarus muttered nervously, as he placed the goggles over his eyes. The boy sprinted and jumped into the swirling storm. He released his wings and was caught in the powerful updraft. The impenetrable cyclone barrier carried him up in a rotating course. It felt like his body was going to be pulled apart by the sheer force of the storm. He was violently jerked every which way as he screamed in terror.

"I see him," called out Harmony as she pointed up. The wings of the flying machine were visible in the distance. They all cheered briefly, but the celebration turned sour as the boy soon vanished from view.

30

THE BOY THAT COULD FLY

Icarus flew higher than any bird had ever flown before. It was freezing, and the boy struggled to breathe, but the strong winds continued to force him upwards. He did not know how much more punishment his body could withstand. He then noticed the Teumessian fox revolving around the twister on the opposite side. The critter appeared to be swimming mid-air as he spun around the whirlwind. The trickster was just as surprised to see the boy at this altitude. Suddenly, a dark mist engulfed the small creature, and the boy lost sight of him.

A bright light from above caught Icarus' attention. Sunrays penetrated through small openings in the dark clouds, giving him hope. The boy broke through the thunderstorm and glided above the dark vortex. A gorgeous view of the heavens greeted Icarus as he soared beyond the destructive power of Pandora's box. The sunshine kissed his cold wet skin, and for a fleeting moment, he felt at peace with the world. He sighed somberly when he felt the ominous feeling that he would never see something this beautiful again.

Icarus retracted his wings and was violently sucked into the dark void. He plunged wildly back down to earth through the eye of the storm. The boy dodged lightning, hail, dirt, and rocks. Caught in an intense spinning descent, Icarus lost consciousness. The darkness swallowed him entirely, and he allowed it to take him.

Icarus' eyes were closed as he floated down peacefully. The boy didn't know where he was and did not care to find out. He somehow sensed that this place was eternal. Unsure of how he arrived or where it would lead, he kept his eyes closed and relaxed his mind for once. That's when he heard a familiar voice and a touch that he hadn't felt in ages. The back of a woman's hand caressed his cheek as she spoke softly. "Icarus, you have to get up now."

"I don't want to," he responded. He kept his eyes squeezed shut, defiantly.

The woman laughed as she tussled his unkempt hair. "Stop it. Stop trying to wake me," he said scornfully.

"Very well, you can stay, but all life on the planet will be disappointed if you continue sleeping. Think of your father and all your friends that are hoping you succeed. The world is praying for a savior," she responded in a soft and gentle voice.

Icarus exhaled wearily. "I'll get up, but can I come back here once I'm finished?"

"Of course, but you have to get up now, Icarus!"

The boy immediately opened his eyes and saw the ground fast approaching. Icarus instinctively pulled on the cord and released his wings as he braced for impact. He landed on the loose gravel that lined the crater and slid down its edges until he reached the hardened surface below. It took him a moment to remember where he was and what he was doing. His breaths came quickly and heavily, as he witnessed the intense weather flooding out of the opened chest.

Icarus lied down on his belly, beneath the reach of the powerful storm. He wasn't as affected by the violent weather patterns as those outside the barrier. Sensing a threatening presence, Pandora's box began to defend itself. Rain and hail were released in Icarus' direction. Fearing that the winds would expel him from the eye of the storm, the boy retracted his wings.

Slowly edging toward the box by the tips of his fingers, he crawled on the ground to avoid the icy blast aimed at him. The chest refused to be contained. It roared at the intruder and unleashed lightning from its depths in all directions. Icarus hastened his pace.

Once he neared Pandora's box, Icarus extended his arm to close the lids. As if conscious of its impending doom, the weapon furiously wailed and unleashed a deafening blast of power. The boy yelled as he pushed the lids closed with every fiber of his being.

From the exterior, the others heard a thunderous

explosion come from within the barrier. Lights flashed, followed by a blast from within its core that sent shockwaves across the meadow. The weapon gave out a final gasp as the violent storm began to dissolve. The sky cleared, and the sunbeams shone through the dark clouds.

Benu took flight in search of the boy from above. Brontes limped toward the nearest abandoned carriage and grabbed it. The cyclops lifted the cart and used it to smash through the massive ice shards. A path was cleared for the children to run through. Cy, Harmony, and Laelaps rushed in to find their friend.

Icarus awoke on a lush green meadow and sat up. Confused by his surroundings, he rubbed his eyes in disbelief. It was an unfamiliar land with golden wheat fields, a crystal-clear lake, and a shining marble castle atop a green hill. The Sun's warmth hugged his face, while the wind caressed his skin. He felt his shoulders for the flying machine's harnesses and realized that he wasn't wearing it anymore. Looking at his body, he noticed that he was now wearing a clean white tunic and gold-encrusted sandals.

The boy staggered to his feet. "Hello, is anyone out there?" he asked timidly. He saw a human figure standing in the shadow of a pomegranate tree. The woman stepped into the light. "Mom," the boy said, confused. His mother approached him, but she looked younger, healthier, and happier than he remembered.

"Hello, Icarus," she said with a smile. The boy ran into her arms, and they held each other for what seemed like an eternity.

"I missed you," said Icarus, his eyes glistening.

"I missed you more," she said, as tears sparkled in her eyes. "Let me get a good look at you." She held him at arm's length. "You've gotten so big, sweetie."

"Where are we?" asked Icarus as he looked around.

"We're in a land known as the Elysian Fields. Where the souls of the virtuous and heroic go when their time in the mortal realm ends."

"Am I dead? Did I perish?" He glanced at her sorrowfully.

"No, don't worry. You came close, but it's not your time yet. I couldn't pass up the chance to say hello to my little boy," she said sweetly.

His face stiffened. "What if I don't want to go back?"

"Your father would be heartbroken, your friends would mourn, and the world still needs you."

His lips thinned bitterly. "Will I ever see you again?"

"Of course, one day you'll be back here, but not for a long time." His head dropped forward loosely, but she lifted his chin with her hand. "Until then, I am all around you. When you see a star flicker at night, that's me smiling at my special little boy. I am so proud of you, Icarus." She kissed her son on the forehead, and he closed his eyes.

"I love you."

"I love you more. Take care of your father for me."

Icarus kept his eyes shut as she let him go. He felt

as if he was floating away.

**

Benu was the first to see Icarus suspended over a small puddle of water with his mechanical wings extended. He looked like an angel that had fallen from the heavens. The parrot landed softly on Icarus' chest and nestled the boy under his chin. Laelaps, Cy, and Harmony reached them and jumped into the pond. They shook their friend. "Icarus, are you still alive?" asked Cy.

"Wake up. Please wake up," pleaded Harmony. Icarus' eyes began to flutter as he regained consciousness.

Groggily, he muttered, "Did you see me fly?"

"We saw you fall," responded Harmony, tears streaming down her face.

"I think I flew a little too close to the Sun," said Icarus with his lips curled. The others let out a much-needed sigh. Together, they splashed out of the pond, and gradually climbed out of the crater. Icarus lumbered gingerly and was helped out by Harmony and Cy.

Achilles stood just beyond the broken ice shards as they approached. "Thank you for showing me what a true hero is supposed to be," said the young warrior. Achilles extended his hand to Icarus.

"I'm no hero, just the son of a craftsman," said Icarus as he took Achilles' hand and shook it.

"I hope you can forgive me for the errors of my way," said Achilles.

"We all make mistakes," added Icarus.

Achilles released the boy's hand, and Icarus proceeded to shake off the sting from the young warrior's firm grip. "Hopefully, when this story becomes legend, people won't even know that I had a part of it," Achilles said with a chuckle.

The warrior turned and bumped into the side of Brontes' leg. The giant hunkered down to get a better look at his foe. "Would you like to shake my hand?" asked the cyclops with a wicked grin on his face.

Achilles swallowed nervously as he extended his arm, and the giant gripped the forearm in his meaty palm. He shook the young warrior up and down violently. Brontes released his arm and had one of his big belly laughs, while Achilles clutched his tender right arm to his chest but did not wince.

"I won't eat you today since you helped release me. But if I ever see you again, I'll make sure to be hungry," Brontes said with a hearty laugh.

"I'll stick to human conflicts from now on," said Achilles as he scurried away.

Icarus hugged his father. "I knew you could do it, son," said Daedalus. They separated, but Daedalus kept his son at arm's length. "You flew. How was it?"

"Terrifying. I think we should keep our feet on the ground for a while."

"We're free, we can create whatever we wish."

"While I was lying on the water, I got an idea for a craft that will allow us to explore the depths of Poseidon's oceans," said Icarus excitedly.

Daedalus put a finger to his lips and started to imagine the design of the device. "Interesting," he muttered.

"Can we go home first, father?"

"Of course, we have a long journey ahead."

Harmony stood next to Laelaps, who sat on his hindquarters. "No more running off with strangers unless I say so, understood?" she said with authority. The dog grumbled. "I got to be a hero, but that's no excuse. You could have gotten yourself killed." Laelaps whined and barked. "I don't want to hear it!" The dog snapped his teeth in protest, and they continued arguing.

Daedalus observed the dynamic of the girl and hound with interest. Benu landed on his master's shoulder. "Can she talk to that animal?" asked Daedalus. Benu nodded and squawked. "Fascinating," said the craftsman.

Icarus approached Harmony and asked, "Would you like to stay with my father and me? You can bring Laelaps as well."

Harmony looked from Icarus to Laelaps, and then from Laelaps back to Icarus. "Maybe for a time, until we find another adventure," she said. Laelaps barked in agreement as Icarus kneeled down to pet him. Harmony smiled at them and allowed herself to breathe a sigh of relief.

The Minotaur awoke and sat up slowly. He looked around to observe the calm environment. Birds were chirping, and a light breeze ruffled leaves in the distance. Everything appeared serene and peaceful once again. A butterfly landed on his fingertip, and he knew that the world had been spared from the wrath of Pandora's box. The apocalyptic weather had vanished, and all that remained were a few remnants of its destructive power.

The heroes gathered before the Minotaur

cautiously. Achilles approached the terrifying creature with the chest in his hands and kneeled. Several chains and locks were wrapped around the weapon to seal it. The beast took Pandora's box in his large hands suspiciously. Achilles stood respectfully. "I understand why you were defending it now," he said somberly. The Minotaur nodded and exhaled. His face expressed remorse for his past actions.

The defender of the maze struggled to stand, so Brontes stepped forward and gave him a hand. The Minotaur looked up at the giant doubtfully but eventually accepted the assistance. It took a moment for the bull to regain his balance, but he got back up on his hooves.

"Good fight," said the bloodied cyclops. "The gods were on my side today." A smirk stretched over Brontes' face.

The Minotaur snorted and let out a bitter sneer. He turned and limped back to his mountain with Pandora's box in hand. The beast was unsure of how he would guard the chest now that the Labyrinth was destroyed, but he knew that it was his duty to protect all life on the planet.

"I guess that means that your father is the new King of the Monsters," Brontes told Cy. He rubbed his son's head, but then recoiled when he felt a sharp pain in his tender hand.

"I always knew you were, Papa," responded Cy with a smirk.

"You're the hero, son. Did you really come all this way just to save me?"

"I couldn't have done it without my friends."

"What's a friend?" said Brontes.

Cy laughed and said, "I'll tell you about it on the way home."

Ajax awoke abruptly to find Achilles' hand extended to him. He glared at it suspiciously, but eventually took it and was helped off of the ground. "What happened?" asked Ajax woozily.

"The King is gone, and the world was saved."

Ajax paused to ponder this information. "Glad, I didn't miss anything important."

"Nothing that they will ever write songs about," said Achilles with a snort. They began to walk up the road.

"What are we going to do now that we don't have a ruler?"

"I'm going home to visit my family for the first time in years," said Achilles.

"Can I accompany you – commander?"

Achilles grinned. "My father could always use an extra farmhand. You'll have to get up bright and early every morning for some intense training. The Great Peleus is demanding."

"If you want to be the greatest, you have to train with the best," said Ajax excitedly.

"That's the spirit," said Achilles.

"I almost beat you, didn't I?" asked Ajax.

Achilles scoffed. "You weren't even close, my friend." They strolled into the sunset.

31

THE PASSAGE HOME

The route home took longer to traverse than the one taken to reach the Labyrinth. For several days, the heroes navigated through woods and hills of the countryside. Most of the group had injuries to contend with, so they bypassed the main roads to avoid further conflict with humans. Fortunately, Daedalus was experienced at mending wounds and provided everyone with remedies for their ailments. Icarus learned many healing techniques from his father during this time and began to apply them to the others. Brontes referred to their methods as sorcery and refused treatment until Cy assured his father that his friends were trustworthy.

During their travels, Brontes learned more about his son's new friends. The cyclops asked them hundreds of questions regarding humans that he had always wondered about. "Why do humans smell so terribly? Do you create clever tools because you are so weak? Why are you so ugly?" Those were just a few of the questions he'd relentlessly ask. Daedalus and children were at a loss of how to answer.

In turn, the humans had a few questions regarding cyclops habits and culture, which Brontes was thrilled to talk about. Daedalus and Icarus found the stories of his forest clan particularly fascinating. Tears were shed when they learned about the assault on the cyclops clan's cave from a human army. They understood why the elder cyclops distrusted people after hearing that tale. There were also many laughs as they bonded during the long trek home.

During the campfire nights, the children told Daedalus and Brontes about the challenges they faced during their quest. The children took turns retelling their version of the adventures; how they tried to free them while they were in transit but were continuously thwarted by unexpected obstacles.

Harmony, Laelaps, Benu, and Cy reenacted the action behind Icarus as he told the harrowing tale. They chronicled the angry mob of Thebans, the battle with the fiery Phoenix, and their encounter with the Minotaur. For once, Brontes sat upright and wide-eyed near the campfire. The giant held onto his son's every word when he recounted their terrifying escape from the Labyrinth.

"Then what happened?" Brontes asked eagerly.

Cy paused for effect and said, "I turned the hidden door on its side and pulled Harmony through it before the Minotaur found her."

Brontes put a hand to his head and let out a deep sigh. "Oh, that was a close one." That was his favorite part of the story.

For some reason, Brontes did not care to hear about the children's battle with the Karkino in the woods. Despite the young heroes urging that it was an exciting moment, the cyclops requested a different story. Noticing the giant's reddened face, Daedalus agreed with his friend. The children groaned but moved on. The giant smiled sheepishly and thanked the craftsman for keeping his secret.

On one clear night, Icarus lay down on the green grass to look up at the sky. "What are you gazing at?" asked Daedalus, approaching from behind. He took a seat next to his son to stare up at the starlight.

"Oh, just the stars," said Icarus.

"I believe that the stars are similar balls of fire like our Sun, except further away."

"Do you believe our loved ones are watching us from up there?"

"I don't know. It's possible."

"Do you think my mother is watching over us?"

Daedalus looked down at the ground solemnly. He sighed before looking up at the night's sky once more. "I'd like to think so, son," he said. "You know she loved you, right?"

"I know, father. And she loved you too," Icarus said somberly. They looked up at the cosmic flickering candles until they drifted into a peaceful slumber.

When the group finally arrived back at the Tower of the Wind, they all rested for the next few days. Without a corrupt King or guards to imprison them, Daedalus viewed the estate as a safe refuge. Icarus, Harmony, and Cy each chose a room in the servants' quarters, while Daedalus lodged in Magus' former chamber. With the walls protecting them, Brontes slept peacefully in the courtyard with Laelaps.

On sunny days, villagers from the nearby coastal town would see the giant cyclops relaxing near the rocky shores. Travelers began to kindly wave at Brontes. It took some encouragement from the others, but the elder cyclops eventually returned the friendly gesture. Once the locals realized that the giant wasn't a threat, they would visit the tower with a food offering.

It appeared that humans and mythical creatures could accept one another if they demonstrated that they posed no threat. The villagers that visited were eventually treated to a few of Brontes' tales and his raucous laughter.

In the courtyard, Icarus presented the scrolls for the traps that he planned to build to capture the Teumessian fox. Harmony and Cy inspected the parchments alongside Laelaps, who sniffed them. "With these traps, you won't even need to chase that fox, Laelaps," said Icarus confidently. The dog wagged his tail and licked the boy's face in approval. They were unaware, however, that the mischievous fox was sitting on the windowsill next to Benu.

"I wish I could see you capture the fox," said Cy.

"You can return at any time. You're only a short voyage away," said Icarus.

"After everything we survived, I want to rest for

a while, but we will see each other again."

"It's time to depart!" called Brontes from the outside. They all sprinted out of the courtyard and toward the beach.

*
**

Brontes loaded the last of the provisions onto a raft, while Daedalus stood nearby with parchment noting the inventory. "What are you doing, human? Sorry, I meant, 'Dada-les.'"

"I'm taking stock of the provisions. I wouldn't want us to sail all the way back here because I forgot something."

"You don't have to do anything more for us. You already built this raft and gave us food from your stores. You've done more than enough."

"Nonsense, we were travel companions for a time. It's the least I can do."

"I'll try not to bother you again. I miss my island, but you have opened my eye to the truth."

"What truth is that?" asked Daedalus.

"That not all humans are terrible."

"It's good to know that cyclopes do not eat humans."

Brontes stuck out his tongue and gagged. "Not enough meat on your bones, I'm afraid." The giant had a big belly laugh. Cy ran down the hill, followed by Harmony, Icarus, and Laelaps. They all loaded onto the raft. "Is everyone coming to the island?" asked Brontes, confused.

"We want to ensure that you arrived home safely," said Icarus. The giant shrugged his shoulders and accepted the kind gesture. Daedalus stepped onto the raft with a map of the land and sea in his hands. Brontes removed the ropes tethered to the shore and pushed the raft out to sea before stepping aboard. They were off to the final destination of their long journey.

The seas were calm, which allowed them to arrive at Cyclops Island late in the day. The sky was a gloriously pink, as the Sun was close to setting on the ocean's western horizon. Laelaps ran off the raft to explore as soon as they landed on the beach. Harmony called after him, but he disappeared into the forest to mark some unfamiliar trees. Brontes stepped onto his island and breathed a sigh of relief. The giant looked down and noticed a few weapons the soldiers left behind in the sand. He remembered thinking that he would never see this land or his son again. A feeling of serene calm came over him as he looked around and felt eternally grateful to be home.

Cy walked up to his father's side. "Papa, can I show my friends our cave before they leave?"

Brontes smiled and said, "Let's show them together."

Benu flew into the cave and landed on Cy's makeshift bed. The two cyclopes led their guest through the entrance. "It's not as impressive as your tower, but it's home," said Brontes.

Cy rushed to a corner and grabbed his wooden toys to show his friends. He laid them out before Icarus and Harmony. The figurines were in the shape of cyclopes warriors.

Holding up one of the figures, Harmony asked,

"Did you make these Cy?"

"No, they were my Papa's from when he was little," responded Cy.

Daedalus looked at the cave paintings closely and was impressed with the artistry. "Did you draw these?" he asked Brontes.

The giant nodded. "I tried my best to recreate the ones from my clan's cavern."

"They're amazing. You have a talented eye," said Daedalus.

Laelaps found them and rushed inside toward the children. He approached the figurines Cy held and sniffed them. Catching a scent, the hound's eyes went milky white.

Through oceans, beaches, forests, cities, and mountains, his foresight took him further than he had ever seen before. His vision finally circled a massive snowy mountain where he observed a giant wearing several layers of sheep's wool while standing on the edge of a cave. The creature was trying to stay warm as it approached a wood fire within the cavern. There were drawings all over the walls. She turned around, revealing her single amber-colored eye.

Laelaps snapped out of his vision and barked excitedly. Everyone gathered around the dog. Harmony spoke. "He saw another cyclops in a snow-covered mountain."

Brontes was stunned by this revelation and hunkered down near the others.

"Laelaps, can you lead us to this cyclops?" asked Icarus. The hound circled excitedly and barked in acknowledgment.

"Can we try to find them?" Cy asked his father.

Brontes was in a state of shock but eventually nodded. "We aren't the last of our kind," he whispered.

"We can find more cyclopes," said Harmony excitedly.

"You could rebuild your clan," added Daedalus in astonishment.

"Well, we can't let you go on this adventure alone," said Icarus as he put an arm around Cy's shoulder.

"You can't take my dog without me," mentioned Harmony. Laelaps barked in agreement. Benu squawked and swayed back and forth enthusiastically.

"This will give me a chance to test out some of my latest inventions," stated Daedalus as he tussled his son's hair.

They all gathered around Cy and Brontes, who smiled at each other and then nodded.

THE END

CAST OF CHARACTERS

Mortals

Achilles

The hero of the Trojan War as described in the Illiad is a much younger version of himself in this tale. If the Illiad was his greatest adventure, then this was his origin story. His exploits in this legend are what teaches him to become the greatest warrior in all of Ancient Greece.

Icarus

A twelve-year-old living in ancient Greece, he dreams of becoming a world-renowned craftsman like his father, Daedalus. Unfortunately, he has spent most of his young life imprisoned in a tower. After building a flying machine, he escapes captivity by flying off the tower. With no control of his direction, he's pushed out to sea by the winds. After crash landing on an island with mythical creatures, he must return to the mainland and rescue his father from a mad King that plans to use the brilliant craftsman to conquer the world. Before Hercules found his strength, before Odysseus was lost at sea, and even before Achilles went to the Trojan War, there was Icarus, the hero that time forgot.

Daedalus

The gifted craftsman of Ancient Greece, Daedalus has built numerous devices that have helped humanity beyond the gods' wildest dreams. His unique talents make him a target for powerful and ambitious rulers that wish to harness his brilliance for their nefarious schemes.

Benu

Icarus' pet is an African gray parrot. Even with his limited vocabulary, he speaks the right words to assists his human companions.

Ajax

The tallest and strongest warrior in all of Greece, Ajax puts fear in the hearts of any man. The other soldiers often refer to him as the Greek Freak to describe his exceptional size and might. Like other great heroes, he will one day fight for the Greeks in the Trojan War, but he learns how to be a warrior in this tale under the tutelage of Achilles. He meets and befriends Achilles during their quest and becomes the trusted confidant of the young warrior.

Harmony

Harmony appears to be your average maiden, yet she possesses unique divine abilities. She's mighty, intelligent, a gifted combatant, and can understand her dog Laelaps.

King Minos

The son of the great King Lycaster, this vile man inherited the throne and threw the City of Thebes into disarray. He plans to rid the world of mythical beasts by trapping them in the Labyrinth to fight the Minotaur. Once they've destroyed each other, he will be able to acquire Pandora's box, which sits at the center of the maze.

King Lycaster

The most exceptional leader Thebes had ever known, King Lycaster, took the small village and turned it to a sprawling city. The jewel of Greece had its best years during his reign and progressed far beyond the other city-states. Unfortunately, he did not realize that his offspring would become such a terrible leader after his untimely demise.

Mythical Creatures

The Minotaur

The most terrifying Titan that ever walked the earth is an enormous bull-human hybrid. This fearsome creature was tasked with guarding the Labyrinth, and the ultimate weapon concealed at its core from gods or mortals alike. Pandora's box can grant humans or mythical creatures god-like power.

Cy

The young cyclops is small in stature, even when compared to most human children his age. He's a sweet and innocent boy that has been raised on a secluded island under the protection of his giant father, Brontes. He's the complete opposite of his father, who attempts to teach him to be fierce and distrustful of all humans. He lacks a ferocious personality necessary to guard their island against invaders or survive in the harsh human world that is Ancient Greece.

Brontes

Local sailors describe the gigantic cyclops that lives on a remote island in the Ionian Sea as a horrific monster that eats humans and picks his teeth with their bones. The truth about this large one-eyed creature is far more complicated than anyone ever realized. His exterior may be frightening, but it's what is on the inside that makes this giant uniquely sympathetic.

Laelaps

As a divine hunting dog, Laelaps can track anyone on the

planet when presented with the faintest scent of the individual. The only creature that continues to evade his capture is the Teumessian fox.

The Teumessian Fox
A cunning trickster with a supernatural ability to never be captured, the Teumessian fox is the perfect foible to Laelaps. Their gifts create a paradox that would give Zeus a headache. Like all foxes and hounds, they would be rivals even if they had no unique abilities.

Rhath the Centaur
Part of a fierce clan of centaur fighters known as the Ixion tribe, Rhath is a warrior that resides in the Foloi woods with his people. They live off the land and often clash with humans that trespass into their territory. They defend lesser mythical creatures that cannot fend for themselves and are purely a hunter-gatherer group.

The Karkino
An enormous crab-like monster that lives near Greek shores yet attacks from the sea with its powerful pincers and mandibles. This mindless beast terrorizes humans and other mythical creatures alike. Its tough crustacean shell makes it nearly impervious to man-made weapons.

The Phoenix
A mystical creature that was found in the woods and gifted to King Minos, the Phoenix can ignite its scrawny body and transform into a flaming bird of death.

Pandora's Box

The chest was presented to the daughter of a King, who was worshipped like a god. To punish the beloved King, Zeus gifted the mystical box to his daughter named Pandora. After she opened the box and released unimaginable nightmares onto the world, Zeus observed the suffering and relinquished his penalty on the innocent maiden and the rest of humanity. The item was named after her following this event.

The Nemean Lion

A large and powerful beast, the Nemean lion ravages the land of Nemea by hunting the locals.

Erymanthian Boar

A giant and fierce animal, the boar torments the people in the primitive highlands of Arcadia.

Satyrs

The top half of these creatures resemble a little person, but their bottom half is that of a two-legged goat. They bleat excitedly as they frolic in the Foloi forest. Although short in stature with their small and stout bodies, the rounded ram horns on their heads make them a formidable foe.

Woodland Nymphs

They look like children with wooden features that allow them to conceal themselves within trees. They are stunted creatures yet fierce in battle when they utilize wooden weapons.

The Gods

Zeus

The King of the Gods, Zeus harnesses the power of lightning to threaten his enemies and put fear in the hearts of men. He is a benevolent deity that watches over humanity and mythical creatures.

Poseidon

The god of the sea and earthquakes, Poseidon preferred to have dominion of the oceans and leave the lands to the other gods, including his brother Zeus. There are far more secrets in its depths of the oceans than on the surface for Poseidon to explore. Many of the terrifying sea creatures are his loyal subjects.

Aphrodite

The goddess of love, Aphrodite, is the most stunning goddess of them all. She brings care and affection into people's hearts but struggles to find her own happiness.

Ares

The god of war, Ares is a ruthless and powerful god that enjoys pitting tribes of men against each other. He values the art of war above all else. Watching battles waged from high atop Mount Olympus is his favorite pastime.

Hades

As the god of the Underworld, Hades torments the souls of cruel men in his subterranean domain. The afterlife can be a rewarding or cruel place depending on how you lived your life, but Hades will punish your eternal soul as he sees fit if you end up in his realm.

Athena
Although a goddess, Athena's real power lies in her wisdom. She is capable of outsmarting even the cleverest god or human without any real effort.

Prometheus
In the beginning, when gods walked the lands with humans and mythical creatures, Prometheus defied Zeus by stealing fire from a chest within his palace. As punishment, he was to be tormented for all eternity.

ABOUT THE AUTHOR

Oscar K. Reyes is a Los Angeles native with a passion for music, art, culture, and the stories of others. As a writer, his primary focus has been on crafting screenplays. Recently, he completed his debut novel titled Children of the Lost Gods with several subsequent entries planned for the series. Following the completion of his first novel, he will be adding more titles to his repertoire over the next few years.

Oscar graduated from the University of Cal State Long Beach with a degree in Film and Electronic Arts. He continued his writing education by honing his craft through various writing jobs in multiple industries.

Growing up in an impoverished neighborhood, Oscar developed a unique imagination. "I was a daydreamer as a child because my household was too poor to travel. Transforming my imagination into written words was an invaluable habit that I continue to develop." His hopes bleed into the types of stories he wants to tell. "I want to inspire as well as challenge readers when they pick up my books."

Children of the Lost Gods, his debut novel, was six years in the making. It took a Herculean effort to complete the story, but he is ecstatic with the final outcome.

Thank you for reading.

AUTHOR'S NOTE

Thank you for taking the time to read the first entry in Children of the Lost Gods. It was a daunting task several years in the making. I had always wanted to write my own version of a Greek Mythological legend, but I struggled to come up with a viable idea that would fit into the world. I grew up being fascinated by Greek legends when I was a child. I read all the great myths like The Trojan War, The Odyssey, and The Twelve Labors of Hercules. They inspired me to write my own mythological tale, but I knew that I needed to create my unique version of a legend. By creating my own characters and blending them with some of the heroes of those myths, I knew that I could write the story.

I was inspired to use Icarus since there had been no modern take on his tale. That's when I had the epiphany of teaming him up with a little cyclops named Cy. There had never been a sympathetic cyclops that you could identify with in the ancient myths. They were always viewed as these giant terrifying creatures, but I figured that they had to be innocent kids at some point. Even the scariest animals look adorable in their formative years.

I came up with the Cy character while I was bored at work one morning. My imagination has always been my escape from the mundane reality of the workweek. My co-workers hate this lousy habit of mine. From a young age, I had always been a daydreamer, and it's what got me through some of my most boring classes.

My first attempt to write this story, originally titled Icarus, came five years ago and ended miserably. In that version, Icarus was a mortal human living on Mount Olympus. He grew up believing he was a demi-god when Athena adopted him after an evil king had imprisoned his father (I'm sure that you're already bored by this explanation, but wait there's more). The boy runs away from the protective world of the gods to save his father, who was locked away in the Labyrinth. The story was a mess that I could never crack the story because it had too many issues that didn't make sense. *"Why didn't the gods realize that a human was living on Mount Olympus?"* That was the question I was asked continuously. It proved to be a puzzle that I could never solve.

I shelved this story and worked on several other projects for the next few years. During that time, I continued to hone my craft by polishing my writing skills. My mind would always come back to this tale, however, and I would try to figure out a new way to make it work. I knew these characters were special and would be loved by countless others if I could just figure out the quest that they needed to go on. I thought of a new journey that made a lot more sense, and I wrote it in record time.

It does feel like this story is the culmination of my life's work. I've known these characters for a long time, and they've grown with me. These characters will continue to live on in my next book, which I have already started outlining. I hope you are as eager to read it, as I am to write the next adventure of Icarus, Cy, Harmony, Laelaps, and Benu. Thank you.

ACKNOWLEDGMENTS

Thank you, Stephen King, for writing every single book you've ever written, but also for releasing <u>On Writing: A Memoir of the Craft</u>. It inspired me to attempt to write my first book and to finish it. Your advice in that book was invaluable to me.

R.S. Gray, thanks for showing me what it takes to be an author through your social media accounts, and for responding to me when I had questions about writing. Thank you, Ali Hyder, for the outstanding painted book cover. I gave you little guidance, so your imagination created a fantastic illustration.

I couldn't have written this book without the help of Jairo Ochoa. You drew all the early sketches on some of the chapter pages. I've known you since high school, and you always had a talent for drawing. I'm glad we're still friends and that you continue to draw my crazy ideas. Thanks to Leena Hoang, for helping me add the title and making the colors of the image pop a bit more. You're a talented digital editor who taught me a lot in a short amount of time.

A special thanks to Sara Aquino and Hector Azpitarte, who read so much of my terrible early writing and helped me elevate myself to a level where I believed writing a novel was possible. Sorry for putting you through so much torture during those early drafts. Thanks for toughing it out.

I can't express how much gratitude I feel for my nephews, Brian and Joel. From an early age, they have been my inspiration for some of my characters. They were happy children playing games on the front lawn, but our combined imagination created the world you just read.

I want to thank my entire DS Team, for believing in me while I took on this monumental task. I can't stress the importance of having a hobby that allows you to exercise and get your mind off writing for a few hours a week, and dancing is my special activity and therapy. The people that are in my dance team are also my support group: Rebekah One, Erik Salazar, Erika Mejia, Jenelle Cherek, Roxy Arteaga, Bernard Martinez, and Sonyo Martinez.

A special thank you to Nancy Villalta for always supporting my foolish endeavors. When I said that I wanted to write a book, you were the first person that believed I could do it.

I absolutely need to thank my editor, Stacey Kucharik, at Polished Print for her tireless effort. Also my copy editor, Jenny Davis, who helped my manuscript reach the highest level possible. I will need your help again in the next book.

Thank you to everyone that sent me encouraging messages through social media when I posted an update regarding my first novel. There were a lot of hard days and tough nights, but your kind words fueled me. I will need more of it if you don't mind, as I try to tackle my next novel. Thank you.

Made in the USA
Coppell, TX
10 September 2021

62137911R00184